STEVE HIGGS
LYME REGIS LAYOVER

BOOKS

Vinci Books

vinci-books.com

Published by Vinci Books Ltd in 2026

1

Copyright © Steve Higgs 2023

The author has asserted their moral right to be identified as the author of this work in accordance with the Copyright, Designs and Patents Act 1988. This work is a work of fiction. Names, characters, places and incidents are the product of the author's imagination or are used fictitiously. Any resemblance to actual persons, living or dead, places and incidents is entirely coincidental.
All rights reserved. No part of this publication may be copied, reproduced, distributed, stored in any retrieval system, or transmitted in any form or by any means, including photocopying, recording, or other electronic or mechanical methods, nor used as a source for any form of machine learning including AI datasets, without the prior written permission of the publisher.
The publisher and the author have made every effort to obtain permissions for any third party material used in this book and to comply with copyright law. Any queries in this respect should be brought to the attention of the publisher and any omissions will be corrected in future editions.
A CIP catalogue record for this book is available from the British Library.
Paperback ISBN: 9781036708887

The EU GPSR authorised representative is Logos Europe, 9 rue Nicolas Poussion, 17000 La Rochelle, France contact@logoseurope.eu

The title for this final book in the series came from a competition I ran on my Facebook group.
Gillian Duffy, Anthony Simpson and Carol Anderson Kerker devised the elements of the name. They each have their names forever enshrined here in the book's dedication and all got a signed copy delivered to their homes.
I hope they are all happy with the story itself.

By Steve Higgs

Albert Smith's Culinary Capers

Pork Pie Pandemonium
Bakewell Tart Bludgeoning
Stilton Slaughter
Bedfordshire Clanger Calamity
Death of a Yorkshire Pudding
Cumberland Sausage Shocker
Arbroath Smokie Slaying
Dundee Cake Deception
Lancashire Hotpot Peril
Blackpool Rock Bloodshed
Kent Coast Oyster Obliteration
Eton Mess Massacre
Cornish Pasty Conspiracy
The Gastrothief
Lyme Regis Layover
Majestic Mystery

Blue Moon Investigations

Paranormal Nonsense
The Phantom of Barker Mill

Amanda Harper Paranormal Detective
The Klowns of Kent
Dead Pirates of Cawsand
In the Doodoo with Voodoo
The Witches of East Malling
Crop Circles, Cows and Crazy Aliens
Whispers in the Rigging
Paws of the Yeti
Under a Blue Moon
Night Work
Lord Hale's Monster
Herne Bay Howlers
Undead Incorporated
The Ghoul of Christmas Past
The Sandman
Jailhouse Golem
Sparks in the Darkness
Shadow in the Mine
Ghost Writer
Monsters Everywhere
Modern Fairy Tale
No Such Thing as Magic

Prologue

LANDSLIDE

The storm carried a deluge of rain as it swept in off the sea. Rising to get over the high cliffs, the clouds began to leak, bombing the land below the same way they had for millions of years.

The town of Lyme Regis on the Dorset coast paid little attention to the rain. The land had seen it all before and was largely indifferent. For the town's inhabitants, their lack of attention was mostly due to being asleep in their beds. All except for one man who had ill-intent on his mind.

Despite the wet and cold, he set out to commit his crime. He'd waited hours to be sure the inhabitants of Lyme Regis would be asleep, and when the clock ticked around to three in the morning, he knew it was time. Not because it was the dead of night and the likelihood of being seen was as close to nil as he could hope to get, but due to the position of the moon.

High tide would occur in the next thirty minutes.

It was too windy out to employ an umbrella and the raindrops were too fat and too constant for his best raincoat to keep him dry for more than a minute. His legs were soaked before he made it to the end of the street and by the time he got to the caravan his feet were squelching in his boots, the right one especially where he now knew there to be a small hole.

High above his head the rain continued to fall. The man let himself into the caravan, careful to make no noise and worried the water dripping from his clothes would be enough to wake the person snoring soundly in the caravan's tiny double bed, he closed the door and took out the heavy rock he'd carefully carried all the way here.

Unaware and uncaring, the rain lashed against the landscape.

A short while later, when the terrible deed was done and the lone figure was on his way home, the water-logged land chose to shift. It was an event neither the rain nor the land itself thought worthy of note, yet for the last two centuries, the people of Lyme Regis had watched and waited for such an occurrence.

It barely moved at all at first, just a few tons of porous sedimentary rock slipping into the crashing waves - hardly worth mentioning. However, that was just a precursor to the main event, a warmup if you will.

Less than a mile from the site of the caravan on the side of a hill sweeping up toward the rocky headland, a rift appeared. It was thirty yards back from the drop off where the world seemingly ended to plunge two hundred feet down into the maelstrom below.

The rift opened, a line snaking its way along the land when a huge chunk of the cliff moved as one. It slid a yard then stopped, much akin to a weightlifter gripping a heavy bar to then pause and focus before performing the difficult exercise.

Lyme Regis Layover

Lightning forked across the sky, bringing blinding light and casting deep shadows. Had anyone been awake to look, they would have seen a lone figure hurrying through the puddles, keen to get home so they could breathe a sigh of relief and crawl back into bed. There the figure could pretend they had never left. They might be tired tomorrow, but no one would question the hand covering their mouth when they yawned.

The rain continued to fall, and though no one could say which one of the billions of rain drops it was that finally tipped the balance and brought a million tons of ancient sedimentary rock crashing to the shore below, one of them had to be to blame.

Blood in the Air

"You know, Rex," Albert gazed along the beach. "It feels strange to not be looking over my shoulder."

Rex sniffed the air. His human was talking, but he couldn't figure out what the old man was trying to tell him. They were at the coast again, the air loaded with the tang of salt. Rex turned his head a little to the left where a half-eaten sandwich lay forgotten under a bench. Tethered to his human, he couldn't get to it and if he were to try, Rex knew the old man would haul him back before he could snaffle it up.

It was cheese and ham. Not that Rex cared all that much. It was food.

Albert's backpack and the small, blue suitcase were in his room at a small bed and breakfast called Beach View Guesthouse. He hadn't booked in advance because he had no plans to visit Lyme Regis until the previous day. However, deep into autumn and thus out of season for the Dorset town of Lyme Regis, Albert arrived convinced he would see 'room vacant' signs everywhere he looked.

Peering through the train window as it slowed to stop at the station, he'd smiled to himself when he spotted the first such offer before his feet could even hit the platform.

Beach View wasn't just a clever name; Albert's room dominated the first floor at the front of the house looking out to sea.

With a click of his tongue to get Rex moving, Albert set off toward a set of steps that led down to the beach.

Rex twisted his head to eye the sandwich forlornly.

"Come along, Rex," Albert frowned when the dog hung back. Seeing why, he tutted. "You've not long had lunch, dog." Albert had bought a sausage baguette to share in Exeter when they changed trains.

Rex huffed, a sound that carried multiple responses. It wasn't a case of being hungry; it was defensive eating. When food is available, dog will eat. The simple equation held true for almost every dog Rex had ever met. Quite why humans struggled to comprehend it he had no idea.

However, with his human adding more leverage by leaning toward the direction he wanted to go, Rex accepted he wasn't getting the unloved sandwich. Moving away, his eyes now turned toward the beach, a squawk and kerfuffle made him look back in time to see two seagulls fighting over the bread-based snack.

One took off, the lion's share of the prize trapped in its beak.

The sand on the beach was mostly flat where the receding tide left it looking pristine. Here and there, black rocks jutted from it like the spinal ridge of a whale breaching the surface of the ocean. Albert aimed his feet west, walking ten yards inshore from the rolling waves where they crashed relentlessly into the sand. To his right, high cliffs of sedimentary rock rose toward the sky. They were so famous for bearing fossils, the whole region was known as the Jurassic Coast.

Off the lead, Rex padded happily through the rockpools he found, sniffing here and there and leaving his mark. Abruptly, he stopped moving. There was blood in the air, its coppery note impossible to mistake for anything else.

Albert saw his dog angle away to the right, heading for the rocks at the base of the cliffs but let him go. A few hundred yards ahead were several dozen hopeful fossil hunters. Unbeknownst to Albert, he arrived amid a rush of fossil prospectors, all racing to Lyme Regis from across the country and beyond.

A section of the cliff had fallen the previous night during a storm that buffeted the coast for hours. It had blown inland by daybreak and the skies were a dull grey with no sign of rain by the time Albert arrived a little after noon.

He was in Lyme Regis, a final stop on his tour around the British Isles, to sample a local delicacy rather awkwardly named Dorset Knobs. They were a savoury biscuit made only in this area and were reported to go rather well with another local dish, Blue Vinny cheese.

Albert liked blue cheese. Not that he really needed an excuse to visit the town; he could do what he wanted. Well, sort of. Widowed more than a year ago, he'd taken the trip, setting out on the anniversary of his wife's death, to escape the terrible and constant reminders in his house. It was just him now. Plus Rex, of course. His children were all grown, so too some of his grandchildren, though his daughter had one late surprise pregnancy in her mid-forties so at nearly eighty, Albert had a sweet, if somewhat precocious, granddaughter to adore.

At seventy-eight, he had much to be thankful for,

including a long life. Not that he was done yet, not by a long way. He was what many would call sprightly for a man nearing his eightieth birthday. A retired senior police detective, his keen nose and enquiring mind habitually made him ask questions he all too soon regretted for the Pandora's box they tended to open. Since the summer, with Rex at his side, the duo had travelled Great Britain, stopping off in towns made famous by dishes everyone in the country could name.

The idea was to take cooking lessons at each destination, yet somehow his plan had a tendency to be scuppered. Most often by a murder.

His dog, Rex, was a former police dog, but not one that got too old and had to retire. Rex completed only six months in the field before he was deemed unsuitable for the role. His handlers wanted rid of him, and Albert was beginning to suspect why that might have been the case: Rex was too bright. Too bright by half.

The dog had a knack for finding clues that helped Albert solve the crimes he stumbled across. Weeks and weeks of close observation left Albert questioning if his dog was doing it deliberately. That was silly, of course, but though Albert smiled and dismissed the idea each time it rose, he could not shift the feeling that Rex was trying to solve the cases too.

The walk along the beach was to ensure Rex was well exercised, but also so Albert could say he had seen more of the town and region than just the inside of public houses and eateries.

Karl Fielding, a man he'd met only yesterday, had convinced Albert to visit his shop where he produced Dorset Knobs daily. They met in Wales when Albert freed him from captivity. That's a whole other story there's no time for here. Suffice to say Mr Fielding was thoroughly grateful and hoped he might be able to give Albert a free meal or three plus some of his finest, freshly baked goods to take home.

There wasn't a good reason for Albert to resist, so he didn't.

Rex let his nose lead him, not that it took a lot of effort to track the source of the blood. It wasn't fresh, he knew that the moment he detected the first whiff, nor was it old. If tasked with pinning down a time since the blood was spilt, Rex would argue that it couldn't be much more than a day old, two at the absolute most.

His former training as a police dog exposed him to human blood more times in a few months than most dogs get in a whole lifetime. He was taught to track it and to find the person leaving it behind. He was repeating that now, but unlike then when the victim was quite often running away with their wound, on this occasion Rex knew the person at the source was going nowhere.

He could smell that too.

Albert continued onward, aiming for the amateur palaeontologists, if that was the right term for them. As he understood it, the collapsing cliff face would have exposed rock not seen for millions of years and that could mean untold fossil riches.

His boys had been big on dinosaurs when they were little, but lost interest as they grew older. Once or twice, he'd considered bringing them to the Jurassic Coast – there were lots of nice resorts where one could spend a week in the summer – yet for one reason or another the trip was never planned or executed.

Albert's interest in what the people ahead were doing was minimal; the beach was just a good place to walk his dog. However, he was going to walk all the way to where they were before turning around.

"Do you think they'll find a big dinosaur bone, Rex?" Albert asked, turning his head to see where his German Shepherd might be. To his surprise, Rex was more than fifty yards behind him and standing on a boulder at the base of the cliff. They were yet to reach the part that had collapsed, that began where the fossil hunters were digging around, otherwise Albert would have called his dog back for fear another section might fall to bury him forever.

Nevertheless, he called Rex to catch up.

Rex heard his human calling and huffed out a breath.

The source of the blood was a body. He'd known that before he saw it, of course. Just as he could tell it was a man. Though the victim had been in the sea and much of his natural aroma was washed away, sweat, cologne and other products remained in sufficient quantities for his nose to identify.

"Rex!"

This time when the old man called, Rex turned to face him and barked in reply.

"You might want to take a look at this. There's a body here."

"Rex! Come on! Don't dally or we'll never get to Karl's place to taste the Dorset Knobs. I promise I'll buy a few extras for you."

Rex puffed out a weary breath and parked his backside on the rock. Humans were wonderful, his especially. He had deep affection for the old man, but they were tiresome too. They never listened, they were always rushing about trying to achieve far more than was possible or necessary. Well he wasn't moving, so his human would have to come to him.

Albert checked his watch. He'd told Karl to expect him

at three o'clock and when he gave someone a time, he liked to be prompt. It was already two thirty three and he would need to get a wiggle on if he was to avoid being late.

"Rex!" He called again adding an urgent get-a-move-on gesture with his right arm. The dog refused to move, voting instead to turn around so he was facing away from Albert. About to employ some harsher language and set off to collect his dog, Albert stopped and watched.

Rex was looking at something. It was out of sight behind the boulder on which the German Shepherd stood but the dog would look down, twist around to look at Albert whereupon he would bark, and then go back to staring at whatever it was he could see.

Another pet owner might have continued to grumble, but Albert had learned to trust his dog. And to listen.

Rex was about to bark again when he saw that his human was finally heading his way. He wagged his tail, but not fast to show he was excited. He was standing over a dead body and while it thrilled him to have found it since he knew humans didn't like to have their dead littering the place, he also knew his human would be upset by the find – it was someone they knew.

Tide and Time

Albert reached the end of the sand and made sure to keep at least one hand in touch with the rocks as he clambered over them. Most were solid, but not all, and the chance to slip when one moved was great enough to make him move with caution.

Rex bounded across the rocks like they were stepping-stones in a lake. Wagging his tail and spinning, he barked, "Come on, old man. I know you're not going to like it, and I'm sorry about that, but you need to see it anyway." Setting off again, he bounded back to the same boulder he'd been standing on and looked down once more.

Thirty seconds later, Albert caught up with his dog.

"Right then, fella, what is it that's got you so excited?" Albert pushed with one hand to haul himself up and onto the same boulder and looked over the far side to see what had caught his dog's attention. The next word from his mouth was unprintable.

Rex sat back down to watch what his human would do next.

Albert's lips were pressed tight shut. The body didn't smell the way they so often do, but it was clear it had been in the water and the sodden clothes were masking the smell. The right arm was bent at an impossible angle; broken and dislocated, Albert surmised. It wasn't the only limb to have suffered trauma.

The man's skull was intact, and he lay on his back with his left foot propped on a rock. Left behind by the receding tide, the body was tucked out of sight in a gap between the rocks. Dozens, possibly hundreds of people must have walked by it today since the tide went out. It was coming back in now and that made it a race against time to gather any evidence that might be scattered on the beach.

Tipping back his head, Albert looked at the cliff face. Directly above the body, the land reached up to the sky, seemingly touching it so high above Albert's head it was hard to see where it ended.

Had he fallen? Had the tide cut him off and washed him out to sea? Was the damage to his ruined body post-mortem?

Questions filled Albert's head, but the biggest one of all was not who the victim might be. There was no need to check his pockets for a wallet, for Albert already knew the man's name. They met just twenty-four hours earlier.

Sad and angry, Albert looked down at Karl Fielding's broken remains and wondered how such an end could come to pass so soon after returning home. He was Earl Bacon's most recent captive, taken just a week before Albert arrived to set them all free. Less than a day after being released, he had died.

The pathology team would determine how long he'd spent in the water, whether Karl drowned or might have died from other injuries first. They would figure out if his death was a murder or misadventure, but while they were doing that, Albert would be conducting his own investigation.

It was possible the man he followed to Lyme Regis died as a result of an accident, but Albert was already willing to wager that was not the case. Karl Fielding had been excited to return home. He had a girlfriend waiting for him and a thriving business. He was one of the first of the Earl's captives to leave. The moment the paramedics were done with him, he'd caught a lift home – there was no end of offers to help the captives get back to whatever corner of the nation they hailed from. His parting words to Albert were to reinforce his desire to gift Albert with free food from his Lyme Regis bakery.

The man Albert met had everything to live for and was excited to get home. Now he was dead, and Albert Smith was going to find out why.

Slumping onto the boulder with his back to the body, Albert lifted his right arm. When Rex tucked himself under it, Albert hugged his dog into his body and with his spare arm he took out his phone, fumbled it a little as he fought to operate it with one hand, and pressed the nine button three times.

The call lasted almost eight minutes, far longer than was needed for the dispatcher to deploy a car to the beach. That was taken care of in the first sixty seconds. The rest of the time was eaten up by the dispatcher when he asked Albert his name and then made a joke about it being the same as the man who was all over the news.

You can imagine how he responded when Albert admitted he *was* the person on the news. Albert didn't like his quasi-famous status. Not one bit. He understood that he had done something special, that he had put his personal needs and desires ... his life on the line to achieve that which he believed was necessary, but there had never been any hope for personal gain or for infamy. He would have happily returned home and walked back through his front door without anyone knowing what he had done. Contentment and satisfaction would have come from knowing the job had been done.

There was no avoiding the fame though. Jessica Fletcher, an investigative journalist he met in Eton, came away from Wales with hours of footage. Reports from the persons held captive, shocking scenes filmed inside the Gastrothief's lair, and one-to-one candid interviews with the people who travelled to Wales to help Albert in his hour of need. It was all some news channels were playing.

For more than a week prior to the drama in Wales, Albert had chosen to avoid the news because they were accusing him of criminal activities and calling him a wanted man. Now they were praising him as a hero, and he genuinely couldn't decide which he preferred.

With his arm around Rex and the waves continuing to break against the shore, he nodded congenially at some of the fossil hunters as they called it a day and headed home. They didn't need to know he had a body lying a few feet behind him. They could go back to their homes and their lives without the burden of knowledge he possessed.

Rex began to think about food. The remains of the sandwich under the bench would have gone a long way to staving off his growing hunger. Still, he was content just sitting with his human. Neither had spoken in minutes, there being no need for words. The sun was close to the horizon, the light of the day fading already as the tide clawed its way back up the beach.

When the cops arrived, they did so in numbers. Albert

was watching for them so saw the first two uniforms when they arrived at the seafront. He lifted an arm, removing any doubt they might have about where they needed to go. When they started in his direction, he pushed up and off the rock, relieving a slight ache in his back and the numbing cold that had penetrated through his clothing and into his backside.

"Over here," Albert used his right hand to draw them closer and stepped away so they could see the body without his long shadow covering it.

"You're Albert Smith," said the first cop, pausing when she drew level with him. They were both women in their mid-twenties, young and vibrant as all people that age are.

Albert nodded. What else could he do? "I am," he admitted.

She held back to talk to him while her colleague ventured forward to check the victim. "I'm Constable Massie." She indicated her companion. "This is Constable Pearson. What brings you to Lyme Regis, Mr Smith?" she asked. The tone she employed was completely neutral, yet the question sounded like an accusation, nevertheless.

Albert knew she was only doing her job, a job he himself had performed a thousand times. He gave an honest answer.

"Knobs."

"Excuse me?" A cautious expression of warning appeared on Constable Massie's face.

"Knobs, my dear. I came to Lyme Regis to sample Dorset Knobs."

Massie relaxed, a smile creeping onto her lips. "I see." Switching subjects she turned her head toward the victim. "Dispatch said you identified the body already."

With a nod and a tight grimace, Albert said, "Yes, it's

Karl Fielding. He was one of the people being held by Earl Bacon. I met him yesterday and I guess you could say I followed him here. He makes Dorset Knobs you see. That's why Earl Bacon had him." Albert figured he didn't need to embellish his explanation. If she knew who he was then she knew about Earl Bacon and all the mad fool had done.

Constable Pearson chattered into her radio, relaying her findings to dispatch. She couldn't confirm who the victim was – there was nothing on the body to identify him that she could immediately find and wasn't going to start moving it.

With the dying rays of the sun, more fossil hunters were drifting back along the beach. A few stopped to see what might be occurring and were politely asked to move along. Most looked like kids to Albert – university age. They chattered excitedly, their day rather more fulfilling than Albert might have guessed. One stopped to observe for a moment, a man this time, not a teenager. He wore a hat and rugged clothing spattered with mud. His shaggy blonde hair fell over his ears and piercing blue eyes met Albert's with an unspoken question.

He didn't pause for long, but wandering along the beach with the younger people all around him, Albert thought he heard someone address the man as 'Professor'. He did not look like a professor. More like an adventurer. He had to be six feet four inches tall, and his shoulders were wider by half than an average man.

There was no reason for Albert's interest; it was just something for his eyes to do while he passed the time and let the police do their thing.

The tide continued to make its way up the sand, twenty yards became fifteen and there was no doubt it was going to reach their position. The only question was how long they had before it did.

More police arrived along with a pair of men from the crime scene lab. They approached in full body suits, following their standard protocols though the chance of finding trace evidence around the body was next to zero.

A man wearing a drab suit introduced himself as Detective Sergeant Gavin Rogers. He was in his late forties and completely bald though it was clear he shaved the side and back of his head to match the top rather than let the fuzzy stubble grow where it still existed.

He lit a cigarette and blew the thick blue smoke into the air where the breeze whipped it away.

"You knew the victim?" DS Rogers wanted to confirm what he was being told.

Albert made sure to provide an accurate picture. "I met him yesterday, which is to say that I know who he is and could recognise his face. I know nothing about him though."

DS Rogers took another puff of putrid smoke and nodded thoughtfully, his eyes on the body now bathed in temporary lights.

Addressing the crime scene guys, he asked, "Suicide, right?"

Neither of the crime scene men looked his way, but the elder of the two, a man in his fifties called Jenkins, said, "There's no obvious sign of foul play. I'll need to get him back to the lab ..."

"Suicide," DS Rogers concluded, sounding bored already. "The tide is coming, boys. You've got less than half an hour. Better pack it up now."

Albert tried to hold his tongue. Tried, but ultimately failed.

"You're seriously going to label this as a suicide and let that be that?" he demanded of the detective, his voice every bit as harsh and critical as he meant it to be. When DS Rogers reacted with surprise, Albert pressed on. "When I last spoke to this man yesterday, he was full of joy and excited to get home. He has a girlfriend and a thriving business. He did not commit suicide." Statement made, Albert closed his mouth to see what Rogers might have to say in reply.

"That's what you know, is it? Well done, Sherlock. I guess the rest of us can go home and let you crack the case." DS Rogers was unimpressed by the old man. He'd seen the news: Albert Smith, a retired former senior detective was at the epicentre of a story being touted on every channel around the world. A madman with fantasies of a global cataclysm made an underground bunker and had a team of henchmen kidnap chefs and steal food to stock it. Albert Smith busted the whole thing wide open, freeing the people being held and exposing a crime spree no one else had even noticed.

So what?

That gave the old man exactly zero credit in Lyme Regis.

Looking away from Albert, DS Rogers stared up at the cliff again. "We get a couple of jumpers most years. Sometimes there's a good reason behind it, often as not their woes could be sorted if they just stopped drinking or gambling or took better care of their wives. Karl Fielding's death will be investigated, Mr Smith, but only because protocol directs that we must. I'll wager he had a falling out with his girlfriend or came home to find her with someone else. Or perhaps he exaggerated the success of his business and in reality he's in financial deep water. There will be a reason for his suicide. Maybe not a good one, but a reason all the same." Dismissing Albert Smith, he aimed a question at Jenkins. "You got a time of death? I suppose we know it has to be in the last twenty-four hours."

Jenkins rolled back onto his haunches and levered himself to sit on a rock. Searching his hand to find a digit not covered in sand or muck, he scratched at an itch below his left eye.

"Well, that's a little tricky. The body cools much faster in the water than it otherwise would and affects the rigor ..." He would have continued to give reason why he could not be exact at this time had it not been for his junior assistant, an annoyingly pedantic and unfairly talented individual called Kevin.

Kevin twisted to show Karl Fielding's left wrist. "His watch stopped at three minutes after eleven. The face is smashed." He leaned his body out of the way so people could see. "That will be your time of death."

Albert rolled his eyes. "That's hardly scientific proof, gents."

DS Rogers had listened to enough from the old man. He had a job to do and a hot dinner to get home to. He would do his job, but it was going to take a lot to convince him Karl Fielding was a victim of anything other than his own poor choices.

"Thank you, sir. I know we're just local cops in a sleepy seaside town, but we are capable of conducting a thorough investigation. The victim's body will be transferred to the morgue where a full autopsy will be able to give an accurate time of death. I'll be needing a statement from you later, Mr Smith. Constable Pearson will escort you back to the promenade now, thank you. Please give her the address of the place you are staying and watch your step on the way back," he warned, the amusement in his tone telling Albert he was about to say something he thought to be clever, "we wouldn't want you to trip and fall on your celebrity status."

Albert sucked a slow breath in through his nose, held it for a second while his eyes were locked with the detective's, then let it go as he made peace with the planet. Twenty years ago, he would have torn the man's head off. Now though, he saw things differently.

"Very well, Detective Sergeant. Please treat Mr Fielding with dignity. I fear you may be wrong about the nature of his demise." Parting words spoken, Albert looked away to where Constable Pearson waited.

Half expecting DS Rogers to fling a snarky retort his way, Albert was almost disappointed when he didn't.

Escorted wordlessly to the edge of the beach where the stone steps led back to the promenade, Albert's stomach rumbled. His watch told him it was quarter to five which meant the afternoon had already been lost. His hope to visit Karl Fielding's bakery and sample his tasty delights could still be achieved, but did he still care to do so now that the man himself wouldn't be there?

Rex nudged his human's leg with a wet nose. He was bored and getting hungry. Taking a walk on the beach had been a great idea, right up until he found a body. The humans had been arguing about whether the man was murdered or not which confused him no end - the concept of killing oneself was not a thing he could grasp.

A dog would never commit suicide. The thought would never even enter a dog's head. So it was murder, plain and simple. The victim had a distinct scent that was locked in Rex's head. Cinnamon, nutmeg, and allspice among other easily identifiable and pungent spices permeated the man's hair and clothing. The water had almost completely removed them. Almost, but not quite. Annoyingly, any scent the killer might have left behind had been washed away by the sea. Not even a trace remained. That left Rex with good, old-fashioned detective work if he was going to figure out what happened.

When his human reached down to scratch his ears, Rex sought confirmation, "We are going to investigate, aren't we? I mean, we have everywhere else we've been. I cannot imagine why this time would be any different."

Albert stopped his own thoughts to look down at his dog. "What are you trying to tell me, boy?"

Rex lifted his back end, excited that his human was listening. "We should start with where he worked and then maybe explore where he lived. There's bound to be some clues in one of those places. You humans are always killing each other. It makes no sense to me, but there are patterns if one cares to look. I bet the killer was someone close to him."

"Is it food, Rex? Are you asking me about food?"

Rex stopped his paws from their agitated dance. "No. I never once said anything about food. Why would you think that?"

Interpreting Rex's stillness as a 'no', Albert tried again. "You're thirsty?"

Rex tilted his head to one side, cocking an eyebrow in an expression Albert took to mean 'Are you stupid?'.

Albert crouched to bring his face closer to Rex's. "Were you trying to tell me something about the body?"

Rex wagged his tail and tried to lick Albert's chin. Albert knew well enough to expect the dog's party blower of a tongue to come at his face and was ready to duck out of range.

Albert puffed out one cheek, thinking aloud when he

shared his thoughts with his dog. "I think Karl Fielding was murdered. I don't think there's any chance he took his own life and I have to tell you, that really makes me angry. Maybe DS Rogers' boss will have other thoughts about how the investigation ought to be conducted. In the meantime, how about you and I snoop around a little?"

Rex barked and twirled. Okay, so his human hadn't exactly understood what he was trying to say, but they got there in the end.

Albert levered himself upright and was thinking about what he ought to do next when Constable Massie jogged up the stairs from the beach to find her colleague at their squad car.

"Come on, Rogers wants us to deliver the notice of death."

Pearson was using her phone to message her boyfriend. She finished and hit send before looking up. "To whom?"

"His brother, Daniel. They run the bakery together. Karl Fielding has a daughter too. She's nineteen. I want to see if the brother will come with us to see her."

Pearson tried the passenger door of the car, looking at Massie when it failed to open.

"We can walk," said Massie. "It's just around the corner."

Hearing their conversation, Albert clicked his tongue, winked at Rex, and began to follow the duo of uniformed cops.

Selfie

The bakery really was just around the corner. Checking the road was clear before he crossed to the other side, Albert continued to follow the cops on their terrible errand.

It was dark in Lyme Regis now, the sun was long gone, and businesses were already shutting up for the day. Streetlights shone overhead to beat the darkness back into the alleyways and spaces between the buildings where it lurked, quiet and foreboding.

One business with its lights still on, but clearly in the process of shutting up shop, was Fielding's Bakery. Large windows set either side of a recessed entrance sat below a backlit sign declaring the name of the business. It was next to a chip shop, the alluring aromas of salt and vinegar spilling out through the open door to compete with those coming from the bread and cakes. Albert noted the roaring trade and queue of people waiting to get their fish dinner with a mental note to return if he fancied some proper chips during his stay.

Ordinarily, since he was hungry, a bag of chips to share

with Rex would suit the bill. In the wake of discovering Karl Fielding, food was the last thing on his mind.

Inside the bakery, a man with his back to the street stacked a chair upon a table and reached out to grab the next. At a counter to the right as one entered, a young man served goods from a glass cabinet.

Constable Pearson let Constable Massie lead the way, though Albert imagined they had already performed rock, paper, scissors, or some other such game to determine who got the task of breaking the terrible news.

He knew they would want to take Karl's brother somewhere private. Already wondering if the man stacking chairs might be their target, it was confirmed in the next second when they reached the door and he looked around. The man's features, while different from his brother, were too similar for there to be any doubt Albert was looking at Daniel Fielding.

Albert quickened his pace, covering the last yards at a jog to get inside before the constables could start talking. He arrived just in time to hear Massie ask, "Mr Fielding?" It was obvious she knew she was addressing the right person; her decision to confirm it a formality.

Unfortunately for her, Daniel Fielding had just looked up to see who else was coming in.

"Hey! You're Albert Smith!" he exclaimed loudly. The people at the counter and the lad serving behind it all stopped what they were doing and turned to look Albert's way.

Both constables spun around to aim their eyes at Albert and did nothing to hide their displeasure at his presence. They didn't say anything, but Albert had to avoid their combined glare lest it sear his face.

Unsure how to respond since he knew why the cops

were there, Albert froze. The victim's brother was going around Massie and Pearson, putting the reason for their visit on hold so he could greet the man coming through his door.

"I have you to thank for my brother's return!" Daniel Fielding all but cheered, making Albert feel terrible inside. "He said you might drop by today, but I never thought you would. He was always one for tall tales, my little brother. You're probably wondering where he is. I am too, as it happens. I think he probably went on a bender last night and had a few too many. Granted, he deserved to let his hair down after being held captive for more than a week. Terrible business …"

Daniel Fielding had a bad case of verbal diarrhoea, but the urgent messages Albert sent with his eyes got through in the end.

When finally Daniel stopped talking, a question forming on his lips, Albert said, "I believe these police officers have a rather urgent matter to … discuss with you, Mr Fielding." Albert aimed his eyes at Massie and Pearson.

Acting as though it was an inconvenience and making no attempt to hide it, he waved a hand for someone to speak.

"Come on then. Spit it out. Is it that Connor Entwistle moaning about the loading van taking too long to deliver my goods again? I can't help it if I have to block the street twice a week, can I?"

His attitude wasn't helping matters and to make things worse, the family at the counter stopped to talk to Albert on their way out.

"Can we get a selfie?" asked the mother, spokesperson for her husband and two teenage kids.

Taken aback and unsure what a correct response might

be, Albert missed what Constable Massie said next. Whatever it was did the trick. When Albert next looked their way, Karl Fielding's older brother was leading her and Pearson across the bakery to a backdoor labelled 'Staff Only'.

"Quickly, kids," the mum hustled her family into position in front of Albert, the lot of them facing her phone as she held it in the air. Four big beaming smiles stood in stark contrast to Albert's awkward expression.

They thanked him anyway and were jabbering with exhilaration as they left through the front door.

Their departure left just Albert and the young man behind the counter. The young man looked his way, saying nothing.

Sitting next to his human's feet, Rex was thinking about the smells in the bakery. He was also thinking about how he could convince the humans to leave so he could raid the baked goods inside the display cabinet, but that was just the standard, background noise of his brain ticking over.

The bakery smelled of cinnamon. There was nutmeg and allspice, sage, rosemary, and other flavours. They filled the air, the frequency of their use such that they had seeped into the wood of the floorboards and the fabric of the curtains. It was the exact same scent that clung to Karl Fielding, the same combination at the same relative strengths.

"Got any Knobs left?" asked Albert so he had something to say. He wasn't in the mood for them anymore which was a shame because until he found Karl Fielding's body, he'd been thoroughly excited to try the unusual savoury biscuit.

The young man pushed his lips to one side to make an apologetic face.

"Sorry. That family took the last of them. We're about

to close, but I can still serve you if there is anything else you might like." He looked down at the meagre display of baked goods remaining.

Albert didn't care to look. His appetite would return when it was ready, and he would seek dinner in a public house somewhere later in the evening. He was about to say something along those lines when a wail of disbelief and denial filled the silence in the bakery.

Daniel Fielding had not taken the news well which was to be expected. His younger brother, returned to home and safety less than a day ago, was dead. Had the constables expressed the opinion that it might be suicide? Probably, Albert decided, but would do so by asking if there might be any reason why Karl would take his life. They would have said that his death appeared to be suicide. They would not have said it as a statement, but to lead the victim's relative to reveal what he knew about Karl's mental and emotional state.

Albert took a step towards the door. Convinced Karl Fielding had not chosen to take his own life, unconvinced the police were going to do anything about it, and feeling like his belly was filled with the hot lava of justice, he nodded a farewell to the young man behind the counter and returned to the street outside. The best person to speak to was the victim's older brother, but Daniel Fielding deserved to be left alone.

Rex lifted his nose to test the air. There were dog smells around, but that was to be expected. The enticing aroma of a lady dog receptive to advances caught his nose and was gone, the scent drifting on the breeze and possibly carried many hundreds of yards before it reached his nose. There were seagulls, of course, plus cats and rats, both of which Rex filed under the same category: vermin.

His stomach rumbled, reminding him, yet again, that he hadn't eaten since lunch. When he heard his human's stomach rumble the next second, he turned his head upward to catch his attention.

"Hungry are you? Maybe that sandwich sounds a little tastier now, huh? I would have split it with you, you know." Truthfully, Rex knew he would have scoffed it in one bite, but had the old man picked it up and split it, he would have accepted that partners share and forced himself to be satisfied with his portion.

Albert misinterpreted Rex's grumpy face. He was thinking about what he ought to do next. Touching a hand to his belly when it gurgled its emptiness – he was supposed to have filled it with cheese and biscuits two hours ago – his thoughts were not on food, but on where he could obtain information.

Standing outside Fielding's Bakery, with the option of going left or right, Albert chose neither. Reversing course like a soldier performing an 'about turn' he found the young man just about to turn the 'open' sign so it would display 'closed' and had one hand reaching for the lock.

Albert nudged the door open an inch and pushed his face to the gap to say, "Sorry. I know you're trying to close. Can I ask you a couple of questions?"

The young man, taken slightly aback, turned the sign anyway, but stepped back from the door to let Albert open it.

"You are the man on TV, aren't you?" he asked, making it sound like he knew it was true yet struggled to believe it.

Albert showed him a wry smile and stuck out his right hand. "I'm Albert. This is Rex."

Rex wagged his tail. They were back in the bakery and that meant food. The smells of delicious baked goods still filled the air. He didn't care what he was given though something with a meat filling would go down well.

"Troy Macclesfield," the young man shook Albert's hand, his grip pleasingly solid. "What is it that you want to know?"

Albert was on tricky ground now. He was under no obligation to keep Karl Fielding's death a secret, yet believed it would be wrong to go around blurting the news like a town crier. He started with a simple question.

"Are you related to Karl Fielding?"

Troy's eyebrows jumped. "No. Why would you think that?"

Albert waved a dismissive hand. "I was just checking. You'll hear some news about him soon, news I'm not at liberty to share. What I need to know from you is where I might find Karl's girlfriend. Do you know her name? Do you know where Karl lived … err, lives, sorry," Albert corrected himself quickly and fired in another question to cover up his error. "Does he have any family nearby other than his brother?"

A touch of pink came to the kid's cheeks. Albert wondered what that might be about, but didn't pursue it yet.

"Well, I do know he has a daughter." Troy's cheeks went a shade darker. "She … um. She lives in Brookes Lane." His cheeks were burning, and Albert felt forced to ask why.

"You appear to be heating up there, Troy. Is there something you need to tell me about Karl Fielding's daughter? For instance, how it is that you know where she lives?"

Troy was beginning to sweat, and Albert found himself questioning if his skull might start to billow steam like a kettle.

"Well, I know because I dated her a few years ago. It's

how I got to know Mr Fielding. That was when we were still in school though. I doubt she would remember my name now."

Interested, Albert asked, "Why is that?"

"Because she's the hottest girl in town now. She works in El Mango."

"El Mango?" Albert made a mental note of the name.

"It's a gentlemen's club," Troy's cheeks went another shade darker as he revealed the news, and now looked like he might faint.

Albert said, "Ah." He didn't pass judgement on people in general. Not until they were doing something that negatively impacted other people or made profit from their suffering. Then he had all kinds of judgement for them. Ladies who chose to show their ... goods, had been around since Biblical times; fighting it and calling it wrong was like trying to convince the moon to stop shining. It wasn't his cup of tea, but any negative thoughts in his head were aimed at the men who chose to attend such an establishment, not the ladies working there. "Well perhaps she might be more receptive to your advances than you think," Albert replied in a tone he hoped would impart some confidence.

"Ha! Not likely. She's dating a total tool. He just got released from his latest stint in jail. He'd break one of my arms if I so much as looked at her. Mr Fielding, Karl that is, even he doesn't have anything to do with Daisy these days."

Albert pursed his lips. The information about Karl's daughter was all very interesting but it wasn't getting him anywhere.

Rex nudged Albert's leg. "Are we going to eat anything? There's food right over there. Surely you can smell it, even with your nose?"

Albert ruffled the fur around Rex's neck. "How about his girlfriend?" he pressed.

Troy just shrugged. "I've seen her come in here a few times, I think. Short woman, a bit dumpy. I don't know her name though."

"How about where she lives?"

Finally Troy had something worthwhile to reveal.

Armed with an address, Albert thanked the young man and ducked back out the door just as Constables Massie and Pearson were exiting the bakery's back room. He missed the longing look Rex gave the display of baked goods and it was probably a good thing he couldn't understand what his dog said when he escorted Rex back outside.

Sic 'em!

Karl Fielding had lived on Anning Road for as long as Troy could remember. Having gone to school with his daughter, Daisy, Troy's original relationship was that of classmate, though according to Troy the young girl had been a knockout even when her age could be measured in single digits.

Unsure what he might find, Albert wasn't going to break the law in pursuit of the truth, but hoped one of Karl's neighbours might be able to tell him something.

Albert knew enough about the region and England's history to recognise the 'Anning' connection. Mary Anning, a famous palaeontologist at a time when women were not allowed to be a famous anything, had found and identified more prehistoric creatures than almost anyone alive. She became so famous they made up a poem about her.

The street was easy enough to find but not because he was following Troy's directions. Following the debacle with his phone in Wales where he unintentionally messaged more than half the people in his contacts list with a cry for help, Albert forced himself to learn how to do more than just turn it on and off. His instructors were Donna Agnew and Toby Simmons, two teenagers from Melton Mowbray. Not just experts on the subject of all things pork pie, they operated a mobile phone as if it had been part of their education.

So now, and feeling rather proud of himself, Albert Smith navigated the streets of an unfamiliar town using a map on his phone. He could zoom in and out, alter the perspective from 2D to 3D and even have it talk to him so he didn't have to keep looking at the screen.

He felt like Stephen Hawking.

Number 12 Anning Road was a semidetached house connected to number 13. A newish model silver BMW 5 series sat idle on the driveway, the number plate B4KER, denoting it had to belong to Karl. Otherwise the property appeared to be in good order. The small front garden had roses growing up a trellis either side of the front door to a height of more than ten feet and the paint on the front façade was bright and new.

Much to Albert's surprise, for he had assumed Karl Fielding lived alone, there were lights on inside and a television playing; its flickering light shining out from behind the curtains.

He chose to knock.

Rex sniffed at the door, confirming to himself they were at the home of the man he found on the beach.

"Rex, sit," Albert nudged his dog's backend until Rex lowered it to the ground. Rex was a friendly and gentle dog but also enormous and imposing. Plus, not everyone likes dogs.

Someone was coming, a woman if Albert was judging

the approaching outline correctly. Ten seconds after knocking, the front door opened to reveal a short, dumpy woman.

He didn't know her name, but he was well-practiced at knocking on doors.

"Good evening," he smiled generously. "My name is Albert Smith …"

"Good Lord," the woman gasped. "Here, Milo!" she turned her head and shouted into the house without taking her eyes away from the man on her doorstep.

A man's voice echoed back. "What?"

"Get out here!"

"Why?"

"Just do it!"

Albert was looking at the number on the wall next to the door. Was he at the wrong house? Clearly a man and woman lived here, so it could not be Karl Fielding's place. However, he would swear it was the address Troy gave him. How had he managed to get it wrong?

Returning her attention to Albert, the woman said, "I was just watching you on the news. Did all that stuff really happen? Is that really where Karl has been for the last week?" Her voice was quiet and to Albert's mind she sounded a little upset perhaps.

Albert said, "Um, yes. Karl was held captive in Wales. They kidnapped him when he got to work one morning just a little more than a week ago."

The woman said, "Oh."

Albert wanted to ask if he was standing outside Karl Fielding's house, but Milo arrived before he could.

"What is it, woman?" he demanded, showing his class. "Who's the old codger?"

Milo had earrings in both ears, a fat belly, a scar on his

neck and a tattoo on his face. It contained a misplaced apostrophe.

Rex leaned his head toward the door. Food smells were emanating from inside. Pizza, he believed, the underlying aroma of oregano playing a tune his nose knew only too well.

The woman, who was yet to introduce herself or give Albert a chance to ask her name, swung a hand to slap Milo on his chest.

"This is Albert Smith," she berated him. "He's all over the television!"

Milo, unhappy at being struck, ducked back a pace, "Oi, watch out! This is brand new." The article of clothing at the centre of his complaint was a West Ham United football shirt. Checking to be sure she hadn't somehow ruined the material, he looked up at Albert with an unimpressed expression. "Yeah? So what's he doing on my doorstep?"

"It's not your doorstep. It's ... it's my doorstep."

Albert's patience reached its limit. "Is this the home of Karl Fielding?"

Milo sniggered, raising his left arm to lean nonchalantly against the wall.

"It used to be."

The woman's face flushed a little.

Albert focused on her. "I'm sorry, I didn't catch your name."

Sounding less sure of herself now, she said, "Heather. I'm Heather Banks. Are you here to help Karl get his house back?" She sounded meek and apologetic.

Milo threw in his thoughts on the subject, "He's not getting it back. He absconded and you moved on. End of."

Getting the picture without having to ask any real questions, Albert filled in some blanks and checked to see if he was right.

"This is Karl's house. You lived here with him, but when he went missing, you ... what? You thought he had run away with another woman?" He could tell by her face that he'd hit the nail on the head.

"He didn't return any of my calls or texts."

Albert quipped, "Yes, being held captive tends to reduce one's communication options. You went out and found someone new. How long did that take?" He was being judgemental now and didn't care one bit how it made her feel. The man had been missing for a week and came home to find someone else living in his house.

Again, it was Milo who jumped in with both feet. "She didn't find someone new, all right? I was already on the scene. Karl just didn't know it."

Heather looked yet more ashamed, and her eyes wouldn't rise to meet Albert's anymore.

"He didn't deserve her," Milo continued, unable to read the warning signs from his girlfriend. "He got what was coming to him."

Albert's muscles froze. *Got what was coming to him?*

Speaking calmly and slowly as he filed his thoughts into order, Albert asked, "What happened when Karl returned home yesterday?"

"That tattooed moron wouldn't let him in," said a new voice.

Albert jerked around to find a lady roughly his age leaning out from the front door of number thirteen. It was the other side of the garden fence and about four yards away. The woman had white hair tucked into curlers and a mint green dressing gown that reached mid-shin and came all the way up to her neck. It hung from her frame as if a soup chicken had borrowed it from a pig.

"That's right, Heather, I saw and heard it all," the neighbour continued. "You ought to be ashamed of yourself."

"Please, Mrs Brown, go back inside. This doesn't concern you."

The voice of a man, presumably Mrs Brown's husband, echoed Heather's sentiments but the old gal wasn't about to slow her vitriol.

"Carrying on with a new fella and in Karl's home. He's a lovely man, that Karl. You need to get out and let him come home."

Turning his attention to Mrs Brown since she wanted to talk, Albert encouraged her to tell all.

"They got into a fight in the street," Mrs Brown replied with a gasp to accentuate how awful she found it. "That one," she jabbed a bony finger at Milo, "was using all kinds of language."

Milo chose that moment to relive a few highlights of his, ahem, conversation with Karl Fielding by telling Mrs Brown what he thought she should do with her evening. Albert might have slapped the man's face if he'd been a few years younger.

Instead, he chose a better option. "Rex! Sic him!"

Rex sprang from the ground to snap his teeth at Milo's groin. It was right there facing him. There was little Milo could have done to defend himself and Rex moved so fast Milo hadn't even registered what was happening when the dog's jaws closed on a rather sensitive part of his trousers.

"Rex. Hold."

Rex twitched his eyes without moving his skull, checking

to make sure he understood the command. His human looked pleased, his arms folded across his chest.

Heather screamed and cried, her hands holding her face. Milo yelped and tried to grab Rex's head.

"Oh, I wouldn't do that," Albert coached. "He's likely to bite down if you mess with him."

Heather cried, "Don't mess with him! Don't mess with him!"

Milo, his voice coming in painful gasps asked, "What the heck do you expect me to do? He's got my wotsits in his mouth!"

Rex decided it was time to growl and twitch his jaw, giving an unnecessary, yet entertaining nip.

"Waaaaaaah! He's going to bite them off."

Enjoying the show, Albert said, "I should probably apologise if I were you."

Eyes the size of flying saucers, Milo moaned and wheezed, but gabbled, "Sorry, Mr Dog. Sorry for whatever ..."

"No," Albert cut him off. "Apologise to Mrs Brown."

Milo made it clear he possessed no wish to do anything of the sort, yet when Albert snapped out, "Rex!" in a tone that suggested the next word of command might be, 'Castrate!' Milo got to talking real quick.

It wasn't much of an apology, truth be told. Hardly heartfelt, but the point had been made.

Satisfied a lesson had been taught, Albert said, "Rex, heel."

Rex checked again, this time turning his head to look at Albert. Milo danced and yelped as he followed the dog's mouth through the arc it prescribed. When Rex opened his mouth, Milo ran into the house, vanishing from sight with a trail of obscenities turning the air blue in his wake.

Mrs Brown called him a word she would not normally admit to knowing.

Left on the doorstep, Heather Banks, Karl Fielding's estranged girlfriend, shot Albert another look of ashamed apology. Without a word, she stepped backward and closed the door.

Rex had a piece of cloth stuck to a tooth and was using his tongue to work it free.

"That was fun," Rex chuckled, giving up on the wedged piece of cloth. "Can we do it again?"

Albert ruffled the fur on his dog's head, happy as always to have someone so reliable by his side. Turning to Mrs Brown, he had just one question.

"I don't suppose you might know where Karl would have gone?"

Caravan of Clues

It was clearly quite a hike to get to the caravan park where Mrs Brown felt certain her former neighbour would have gone. Consulting the map on his phone with Mrs Brown cooing at how clever he was, she pointed out its location.

It looked to be a hundred yards from the cliff.

Albert felt a little bad for not telling Mrs Brown that her neighbour was already dead and had to find neutral responses when she expressed how much she looked forward to watching Karl kick Heather and that awful Milo out.

Thanking her for her time, Albert bade her goodnight and set off back the way he'd come.

His watch showed quarter after six, and his stomach insisted he stop for dinner before getting into any more adventures. Rex, of course, needed to be fed, so Albert aimed his feet in the opposite direction to the one he wanted to go. A five-minute walk later, he was letting himself into the bed and breakfast place.

Beach View Guesthouse was a Georgian building

arranged over four floors, one of which was a basement. Albert viewed the basement as a poor choice given the building faced the ocean and had to be susceptible to flooding every once in a while, but a small flight of steps led down to it just as another led up to the front door. That the basement possessed its own entrance suggested it might have once been a separate residence, perhaps intended for servants of the house; very much an 'upstairs, downstairs' arrangement.

Brain too full of other subjects to give it any further thought, Albert closed the door behind him and took another set of stairs, these made from wood and covered in carpet, to the first floor. Or was that the second floor, he mused, unsure what counted for what when the basement sat half above and half below the level of the street outside.

Rex knew where they were going and pulled at his lead to get them there faster.

"Hungry, hungry, hungry, hungry," he wheezed, his lead digging into his throat as the old man fought to keep up.

Believing he was the only resident, Albert let Rex go. "Go on then, dog," he paused to catch his breath on the stairs and got to watch the dog's athleticism.

Rex bounded joyfully up the rest of the stairs, planting his feet on the landing at the top to spin around and bark at his human.

"Come on then! It's dinner time! Rex is hungry!"

"Yeah, yeah," Albert trudged the remaining steps, pausing again at the top for another breather. His hips, legs, lower back, and ankles were yet to forgive him for his time in Wales. Rex had vanished - Albert still didn't know how he did it, but the dog had found his way inside an underground bunker. The same underground bunker that belonged to Earl Bacon, the criminal mastermind Albert tracked all the way to Wales and subsequently exposed. The vast underground lair was being explored by the police still and there would be a documentary about it at some point. The footage Jessica Fletcher and her crew took on the day when they filmed the events outside and then became the first film crew ever to set foot inside, was going to make the stockholders at their paper very happy indeed.

In their room, Albert sorted Rex's dinner first and took a drink of water from the tap in his bathroom using a glass provided. By the time he'd slaked his own thirst, Rex's dinner was long gone. With nothing left in his bowl but a smear of saliva, the German Shepherd was lapping noisily from his own supply of H_2O.

Albert allowed himself a minute to rub his knees. Sitting on the edge of the bed, he felt that he could just flop backward and be asleep in seconds. He'd slept well last night, the moderate amount of alcohol he imbibed ensuring he started to snore less than a minute after getting into bed. One night, however, was not going to make up for all the lost sleep that came in the days and weeks beforehand.

Sleep, while attractive, could wait he decided. He needed to eat first and provided he only had one drink with his meal ... well, maybe two, it would recharge his energy levels for the next few hours.

One thing he knew for certain: the first few hours of a murder investigation were the most critical. You had a limited window to capture evidence before weather, the person or persons responsible, or other unanticipated elements eroded or removed it.

The caravan park was all the way back along the seafront and then up the hill. It looked like a steep climb, and he was going to have to work himself up to it. A hearty meal was called for.

At The Boat House, a venue he chose because it was one of the only restaurants with people in it, Albert chose a steak and kidney pie. It came served with wholegrain mustard mashed potatoes, peas, carrots, and a jug of gravy for pouring. No shop bought or pre-made pie, the chef had committed to making pastry that would rise to a height of two inches above the meaty filling contained within.

Attacking it with keen anticipation, Albert found delicate yet plentiful morsels of beef along with an abundance of kidney. Mushrooms and grape-sized onions complemented the meat wonderfully.

Rex watched the plate arriving with great interest. He knew his human's appetite and that the old man generally had eyes bigger than his belly. Instructed to 'lie down' Rex did so, but with his ears and nose attuned to the scraping sounds coming from Albert's plate – there was no chance he was going to finish it all.

The dog's patience was rewarded some ten minutes later when Albert sneakily lowered his leftovers for Rex to clear.

Albert washed it all down with a pint of local ale, electing to be sensible and maybe get another drink on his way back to his lodgings in an hour or so. Quite how long it might take him to get up to the caravan park and find the one belonging to Karl Fielding he could not guess. His only hope was that the journey might be worthwhile.

During his meal and even now as he gave himself a minute to let his meal settle, Albert thought about Milo. The man was an idiot for sure, but was prone to violence if Mrs Brown's account could be taken at face value.

Did that make him a killer? Wherever he had come from, wherever Milo lived before, clearly wasn't as cushy as Karl's house. Karl's girlfriend wasted no time in writing him off, moving a new (albeit supposedly current) lover into Karl's house before his side of the bed was even cold.

Karl arrived home to be turned away by his girlfriend with the addition of threats from her new man. Milo stood to lose a lot with Karl's return.

In some ways this played into the concept that he might have committed suicide. Angry and feeling betrayed, undoubtedly traumatised by the kidnap and captivity, and with no one to whom he felt he could turn, he'd adjourned to his grandfather's caravan, Karl's one remaining place of refuge. It begged Albert to question why he hadn't sought out his brother? They worked together, so even if they weren't close, they had to have a semi-healthy relationship.

Karl didn't go to Daniel though. Or he did and was turned away. Had he then drunk himself into a stupor and chosen to kill himself? Was it an unfortunate accident?

Albert was never going to know, but the concept of Milo killing the man that stood between him and harmonious cohabitation with Heather was easy to believe. For that matter, it wasn't much of a stretch to imagine Heather suggesting it.

They acted as though neither had any idea Karl was dead, but Albert had seen plenty of great actors during his time in the police. Some would live their lies so convincingly they would continue to protest their innocence even if caught on camera committing the crime.

Belly full, Albert paid his bill, finished his drink, and with Rex at his side, set off to find Sunny Days Caravan and Motorhome Park. According to Mrs Brown, who seemed to know far more about the subject than was reasonable to expect, Karl's father, Henry, had bought the caravan in the seventies before his eldest, Daniel, was born. It was an investment, supposedly, that never really paid off as the ground rent, upkeep fees and the tax the government took from his profit, eroded almost everything he made from renting it out in the summer.

The man who owned the ground and placed the caravans on it was something of a salesman and a local bigwig who went on to run for mayor before a tax fraud scandal robbed him of the chance to win. The caravans were all factory rejects he'd bought for pennies, but that didn't come out until years after he'd sold them all, been exposed as a cheat, and had chosen to leave town.

The fraudster still owned the land, or his children did perhaps, Mrs Brown couldn't say if he was still alive or not. Either way, Henry Fielding found himself stuck with a caravan that no one wanted to buy, but for which he could just about cover the annual costs through a few summer rentals which was all he ever got.

Now Daniel and Karl co-owned it and if he was in the area, that was where Karl would be found.

Albert knew Karl was to be found in the local morgue, but leaning on the fence at the entrance to Sunny Days Caravan and Motorhome Park while he gathered himself for the final push, he stared at the lines of tired caravans and wondered how he might determine which one he wanted.

"By heck, dog, I hope it's easier going back down." The route would have been less taxing had it taken a winding route. It didn't. Instead it followed the line of the coast and went straight up from the beach to reach the cliffs however many hundred feet above they were. The incline at times felt like that which a fighter plane might take as it leaves an aircraft carrier – straight up.

Rather warmer than he had been upon setting off, Albert feared his temperature would drop sharply if he hung around too long – the breeze coming off the sea was cold. Pushing off once more, he let Rex lead him into the caravan park.

There was a small booth to the right with a shop and a washhouse where Albert guessed visitors might do some laundry or get a shower. He believed caravans were fitted with showers, but maybe not older models. Whatever the case, nothing about the experience appealed to him and both the booth and the shop were clearly closed for the day.

There were one or two caravans illuminated from inside, each with a car parked next to them.

"I bet that makes the hill easier," Albert grumbled. A quick count suggested there were close to a hundred caravans for him to pick from. Pursing his lips, he approached the nearest hoping it would have a name or some identifying mark on the outside to tell him who owned it.

He didn't want to go door to door checking each one, but finding nothing on the first he wished that had been an option.

Rex's nose was working, but then it always was. Like always he put little thought to where his human wanted to go; the point was to go somewhere because it was an interesting thing to do. However, now they were high above the town below and his nose had once again picked up the scent of the man he found on the beach, he questioned if that was why the old man brought him to this spot.

Certainly that made sense. If the dead man had been murdered, then they were investigating again. That was what they did after all.

With Albert stymied for a way to progress, Rex chose to head for Karl Fielding's caravan. To him the destination stood out like a Christmas tree on a dark night – all lit up and impossible to miss. The man's scent was in the air, so to find the right one, all Rex had to do was head in the general direction and turn toward the source of the smell when it got stronger.

"Where are we going, Rex?" Albert asked though he made no attempt to stop his dog from leading the way.

When Rex stopped outside the door to a caravan on the right side of the field, and then proceeded to paw at it, Albert chose to accept it as another example of his dog being some kind of canine genius.

"Is this Karl's caravan?" he asked, "The man you found on the beach?"

Rex barked loudly once and danced a little - his human was being clever for once.

With a thoughtful expression on his face, Albert gripped the door handle and gave it a twist.

Silhouetted in the moonlight coming through the window opposite the door, a figure in the shape of a skinny man froze. He had a torch in his hand, the beam now aimed at Albert to blind him.

Caught completely by surprise, Albert spasmed in shock losing seconds he couldn't spare. Thinking Rex had led him to the wrong caravan and cursing himself for trying to treat his dog as an equal partner when Rex's nose was probably following the smell of a kebab, his first reaction was to apologise.

Rex hadn't known there was someone inside the caravan and didn't know if there ought to be or not. The man's smell was only apparent now that the door was open. Rex was in the right place, but nothing seemed out of the ordinary about the man's presence – humans cohabit all the time.

All this took about a second and a half, by which time the skinny form inside the caravan had chosen to bolt.

An embarrassed apology on his lips, Albert changed his mind when the skinny youth – he decided that was what he'd just seen – ran away rather than complain about the intrusion. Also, there were no lights on which was suspicious enough.

The torch was out of his face, but Albert's eyes could see very little now other than the glow the bright light left behind. Releasing Rex's lead, he shouted, "Stop him, Rex!"

Rex's thoughts were attuned to his humans. In his experience, people only run away when they are guilty of something, so his muscles were already propelling him to give chase when Albert's yell reached his ears.

Bursting into the darkened caravan, Rex skidding on loose paper spilled on the floor, slipped and fell. Trying to right himself, he watched the skinny youth go out the back window. Grunting a few canine curses, Rex jammed a paw against a bulkhead and finally got his paws back under his body.

The Perspex window had swung shut and following him out that way wasn't a great plan anyhow. Aiming for the door again, he found the way blocked by his human - Albert was coming in. Had it been anyone else, Rex would have catflapped their legs without a moment's thought.

The old man warranted more tender consideration.

Ducking left to get around his human's legs, Rex met with a pair of knees when Albert shifted the same way. They both performed the same manoeuvre at the same time to jink across to the other side of the caravan's tight entrance.

"Where are you going, Rex?" Albert complained, hopping down to the grass outside while trying not to fall on his rump.

The sound of a small-engined motorcycle sprang to life

on the far side of the caravan just as Rex cleared the door and started running.

"Rex! No!" Albert lost his dog for hours in Leeds when he chased after a pair of youths on a motorbike. The fire brigade brought him back on that occasion, but he would much rather avoid a repeat performance. Not least because he'd lost Rex for twenty-four hours not forty-eight hours ago.

In the same way that Albert had learned to watch Rex and try to interpret his dog's actions and noises, Rex had learned to trust his human. They had been travelling together and in each other's constant company for three months now; long enough for their bond to deepen. Add to that the multitude of scrapes they found themselves in, a few life-or-death experiences, and getting separated far too many times, Rex heard his human's shout and slowed to a halt.

His breathing was fast, but he held his breath to get a good sample of the air. Each motor vehicle has its own unique smell. Less individual than that of a person, it was still relatively easy for Rex to discern the tiny nuances from one to the next.

The motorbike left behind a trail of noxious gases Rex's nose sampled and stored.

Albert caught up to his dog, picking up his lead from the ground and patting him generously on the shoulder. The motorbike, a scrappy-looking red dirt bike, had just reached the road. The rider didn't slow down or bother indicating as he cranked the throttle and shot down the hill toward town.

"Well done, Rex. Thank you for not giving chase."

Rex huffed a disappointed breath and checked to make sure his human was okay. Satisfied, he turned around – there was something on the ground behind him that didn't belong. His eyes couldn't see it, but to his nose it stuck out like a fluorescent light due to its harsh chemical smell.

To get to it he had to start back toward the caravan which was fine with Albert – he planned to confirm Rex had indeed found the right one and then have a good look around it. He was marching to the door when Rex's lead went taut.

Albert turned to find Rex looking at him. His head was bowed with his eyes up. Under his nose and between his front paws something shone in the moonlight.

Rex dipped his head to pick it up gently in his teeth.

"What have you got there, boy?"

Albert came down into a crouch, holding out his left hand to take Rex's find.

"Urrgh! Tastes horrid," spat Rex, dropping the object though he missed Albert's hand unless one counts the blob of dribbly dog saliva.

Albert held up his hand, a grimace distorting his face. Rubbing it on the grass to an accompanying, "Ewwww," sound, he rid himself of the worst and picked up the object.

"It's a book of matches," said Rex, wagging his tail happily.

Albert turned it over in his fingers. "Well, I never. Do you know what this is, Rex?"

Rex rolled his eyes. "Yes. I. Just. Told. You. What. It. Is."

Holding it in front of Rex's face, Albert explained, "This is a book of matches. They used to be everywhere a few decades ago. You don't see them much now, but they were all the rage as a marketing gimmick in the seventies and eighties." The matches were held inside a shiny folded cardboard case that displayed a name and logo. Albert recognised the name at least – El Mango. The logo was a pair of mangos in a bra, the leftmost strap of which was teasingly hanging down as if said bra was about to be removed.

Albert was holding the book by its edges to avoid smudging any fingerprints it might hold. It had just left his dog's mouth so he wasn't holding out much hope, and he had no fingerprint kit or a lab to analyse it. For that matter, it probably wouldn't be admissible as evidence anyway, but decades of procedure were hardwired in deep enough that he wrapped it carefully in a handkerchief before depositing it inside his jacket.

Levering himself upright, both knees cracking in protest more than once on the way, Albert turned to face the caravan.

Hooking Rex's lead to the door handle, he said, "You keep guard, Rex. I'll not be long." With a ruffle of the fur around his neck, Albert went inside.

Rex sat by the door, the sea breeze ruffling his fur. Poking his nose into the caravan he drew in a sample of air. The scent he knew as Karl Fielding's dominated the interior as expected. The same blend of cinnamon, allspice, nutmeg, and herbs hung in the background behind the smell of his aftershave and general body odour.

Karl Fielding's was not the only human scent in the place. There were two others Rex could discern. Each unique, though not too dissimilar. Yawning deeply, Rex chose to lie down and wait for his human to finish.

Thankfully, when Albert found the light switch, which was not by the door where it ought to be in his opinion, the caravan was flooded with light.

Looking around, his first thoughts were for the general condition of the caravan. Not exactly dilapidated, had Albert owned it, he would have sent it to the crusher anyway. No one was going to rent it and were they to do so, they would reverse back out the door and demand their money back before even putting their bags down.

Décor and condition aside, it appeared to be weatherproof. With the door open it was just as cold inside as it was out, but the temperature was of no concern as Albert set about tossing the place.

The first piece of paper bore Karl Fielding's name – enough to convince Albert once and for all his dog's nose was a marvel to behold. The letter in his hand was a bill for ground rent on the caravan, a tidy enough sum that looked to have gone unpaid. There were other items of mail on the floor, most of which had either paw or boot prints on where the skinny youth and Rex had trodden.

Cupping his numb fingers around his mouth to blow some warmth into them, Albert was about to give up when he spotted the bin. Tucked under a bench seat built into the side of the caravan, a wastepaper receptacle was half full of something.

What he could see were bits of roughly torn paper. Good quality paper. The kind your Great Aunt Judith would use to write letters in the 1930's. Thinking it was probably nothing, Albert picked out a few pieces for the sake of being thorough.

He tried to read it, determining in a matter of seconds that it was a legal contract of some kind. He found the name 'Fielding' on one piece and the name 'Garside' on another. The information meant nothing and was filed at the back of Albert's mind in case it proved of interest later.

For a further five minutes, Albert opened and closed drawers, checked cupboards and looked around. Finished inspecting the small space he drew two conclusions: the man he'd startled was looking for something. It wasn't drugs because Rex would have alerted at the first whiff, and Albert found no money other than a few loose coppers in the bottom of a drawer. That meant the intruder had taken the money or there never was any. Or the intruder was after something else. In which case, since Albert found nothing of interest, the man probably made off with it.

The second conclusion was more interesting and was in two parts. On the door to the caravan there was a line of what he believed to be brown boot polish. There was a tin of it in one of the drawers – the good quality Kiwi stuff – plus a pair of brushes; one to put it on and one to buff it off.

Karl Fielding only had one shoe when Rex found him on the beach; the other could be anywhere, but it was brown and though battered from being churned around in the sea, it still looked to have been polished recently.

The line on the door was at waist height. A person using their foot to open or close the door would toe the bottom part, not lift their leg to their waist and karate kick it. It would be easy to ignore were it not for the second thing: The pillowcase on the bed was missing.

The bed had been slept in which is to say the covers were thrown to one side as though a person had recently exited them. The sheet and bottom pillow had matching covers and the duvet was a neutral combination of green and yellow gingham. Of the top pillowcase there was no sign, but the pillow itself remained.

It was incongruous and it made Albert's nose twitch enough for him to take out his phone and call the police.

Staged Suicide

By the time he spotted a squad car heading up the hill, Albert was getting cool. Warm when he arrived at the caravan park due to the steep hill between it and town, the gentle breeze coming off the sea ensured he didn't stay that way.

It would have been snug inside the caravan, but aware he'd entered it without permission even though he had a story to (sort of) excuse his actions, he doubted waiting inside for the cops would aid his explanation.

He wasn't expecting to see officers he knew, but was pleased to recognise Constables Massie and Pearson when the car turned off the main road to stop by the caravan park's entrance.

"Mr Smith," said Constable Massie, a frown wrinkling her brow. "You get around."

Choosing not to respond to her jibe, Albert clicked his tongue at Rex and started walking.

"It's this way."

He had to wait while they parked the car and donned

their hats, but heading to the Fieldings' caravan, the expected questions started.

"How did you identify which caravan belonged to Karl Fielding?" asked Constable Pearson.

Albert talked as he walked. "I have a dog. He led me to it." Suspecting they might challenge or question his claim, Albert carried right on talking. "The caravan belongs to both brothers, actually. They were left it by their father when he passed a few years ago. It's fallen into disrepair but I believe this is where Karl Fielding stayed last night after he returned home from his spell in captivity to find his girlfriend had moved a new man into his house."

He stopped and swivelled his feet around to face the cops. Expecting to see shocked looks on their faces, he was not disappointed.

"You're going to ask how I know so much already," he stated. "You probably know this already, but I used to be a detective."

"Used to be Sherlock Homes, more like," quipped Massie. "How can you possibly know so much about the situation? It's only been a couple of hours since we last saw you."

Albert checked his watch. "Almost four, in fact, Constable Massie. More than enough time to ask a few questions. Why do I get the impression no one else is asking them?"

Massie raised her hands in defence. "Hey, we're just beat cops. We go where dispatch tell us. It's lots of managing traffic when there's been an accident, standing around to keep the peace at events in the summer ..."

Albert waved her to silence. "I was a beat cop too," he smiled. "It was a little while ago now, but I doubt much has changed." Getting to the point, he said, "The point is Karl

Fielding returned home to find a man living in his house. His 'girlfriend'," Albert made air quotes around the word, "assumed he'd absconded with another woman and moved in a man she was already sleeping with. His first name is Milo. He's not very nice. Has a tattoo on his head."

"Sort of like a dinosaur claw curling around his left eyebrow?" asked Pearson, pointing to her own face to indicate where she meant.

Albert nodded. "Yes. You know him?"

"Milo Anderson. He's a turd that should have been flushed long ago. Petty crime mostly. Done some time, but nothing that would discourage him from doing it all again. I'm surprised you got away unharmed if you met him. He's well known for dishing out a swift backhand."

Albert smirked and patted his dog. "Rex bit hold of his wotsits."

"Wotsits?" both ladies raised their eyebrows in question.

Albert felt the term employed ought to make it obvious enough and wasn't in the habit of discussing men's particulars in front of young women.

Massie cupped a hand between her legs. "You mean ..."

"Yes. Wotsits," Albert fought and lost to a smirk which spread across his face. "He didn't seem to want to play after that."

Massie said, "I'll bet. I'll have to remember that manoeuvre."

Pearson cocked an eyebrow. "What? You're proposing to ..."

Realising what she had said, Massie's cheeks flushed, and she choked. "Lord, no! Ewwww, could you imagine!"

To move things along, Albert indicated the caravan. "Dispatch told you I interrupted an intruder when I arrived?"

"Yes." Massie removed a torch from her belt. "I guess we'd better have a look around. You didn't go inside, did you?" she asked as an afterthought just as her feet got moving.

Albert wasn't going to lie. "I did. Rex went in after the man/youth. He went out of a window and escaped on a motorbike. Afterward, before I placed the call, I went in to confirm Rex had the right caravan. I noticed a few things, but I touched very little." He chose to be convenient with the truth at that point having only touched things using a handkerchief as a barrier. "I'm afraid I did not see the intruder's face or catch the license plate on the bike.

There being nothing more to say, the constables opened the Fieldings' caravan and proceeded inside. The light was off; Albert left it that way, but it stung his eyes once more when Massie flicked the switch.

He didn't want to bias their inspection, but said, "Everything is pretty much how I found it. There's a couple of obvious clues you'll no doubt spot."

"Okay," echoed out from inside.

Waiting in the doorway because the caravan would be crowded with three, Albert pivoted and sat, lowering his bottom to sit on the step. Rex tucked into his arms, letting his human scratch absentmindedly at the fur on his neck and head.

A few minutes elapsed, the ladies inside the caravan chatting back and forth. Albert was sort of half listening but mostly not as he thought about what he'd stumbled across this time. Everywhere he went there seemed to be a crime to solve. It was kidnap or murder, extortion, money laundering, theft ... you name it, on this trip he and Rex had found crimes to solve like moths to a flame.

It wasn't a good thing.

He'd disturbed a young man. He believed it was a young man from the glimpse he caught. Admittedly, it could have been a woman. She had an androgynous figure if that were the case — no hips or bust, or it could be an older man in his thirties perhaps. However, the motorcycle was that of a teenager with a lack of guts and very little money invested. Whatever the case, Albert didn't see a face and would not be able to identify the person unless he saw them on the bike again.

Whoever it was, it wasn't Milo Anderson, Heather's current love interest. What had the kid been doing at the caravan? The mess inside suggested he was looking for something, but conversely, he might have been there to remove evidence. The pillowcase for instance. A killer returning to the scene of the crime might be a terrible cliché, but that didn't mean it didn't happen.

The killer could have discovered the body had been found and raced back to make sure there was nothing to tie them to the crime. Had he believed the body would wash out to sea?

Albert's musings were interrupted by the constables looking to exit the caravan. Using the doorframe to pull himself up, Albert cleared their route and turned to face them.

No one said anything, each party waiting for the other to speak.

When it became awkward, Albert asked, "How did you get on?"

The ladies exchanged a glance.

"Welllllll," said Massie, stretching things out.

"We didn't find anything," blurted Pearson. "I mean, we found letters addressed to Karl Fielding, but other than that …"

Massie took her turn, "You said you found clues? Clues to what?"

"Yeah, and what clues?" asked Pearson, clearly at a loss.

Albert made sure to sound kindly when he replied, "Did you notice the missing pillowcase?"

Massie said, "Um."

Pearson did a little better. "Yes. So what?"

Albert flipped his eyebrows and continued. "Well, when I add it to the fresh waist-high scrape of boot polish on the door ..." he waited for the cops to look for themselves, "I think it means Karl Fielding was killed in his bed. The killer got blood on the pillowcase so took it with him. He had to carry the body, whether already dead or just unconscious, out of the caravan and in so doing left a scrape mark on the door when he struggled out." Albert mimed carrying a body over his shoulder.

"Hold on," Pearson argued. "If Karl Fielding was asleep in his bed, he wouldn't have been wearing shoes."

Albert agreed. "But if you were going to fake his death and make it look like a suicide, you wouldn't have him wandering around naked and barefoot in the storm you had last night." Seeing the ladies were swaying, but not entirely convinced, Albert said, "A crime scene kit will find blood splatter in two seconds flat."

Suicide or Murder

DS Rogers arrived twenty minutes later. Albert was starting to get cold and had to move around and shuffle his feet to keep the blood flowing. They couldn't go inside the caravan to get away from the breeze, which had picked up and cooled by several degrees, and the only other place out of the chill was the washrooms.

Hoping he could leave shortly, Albert hung back to let the constables do the talking.

They met DS Rogers at their squad car when he parked his silver Ford Mondeo next to it. Albert couldn't hear what they were saying but the detective's body language told him everything: he was not happy.

Marching at speed toward the caravans, DS Rogers jerked an arm to point at one.

"This one?" he demanded, his tone terse.

Constable Massie said, "No, Sarge, the one next to it."

Albert got an annoyed glare and nothing more as Rogers swept by and into the caravan. The light came on inside again and the sound of the detective stomping about inside preceded his exit less than twenty seconds later.

"Explain again," DS Rogers fired at the uniformed cops whose call resulted in his forced departure from his nice, warm house. He wasn't happy and they were going to know about it.

The constables were his juniors, but they were cops and not about to be cowed by anyone.

"There's a mark on the door that matches the shade of boot polish on Karl Fielding's shoe," explained Constable Massie, her tone deliberately patient. "And the pillowcase is missing. Why would the pillowcase be missing?"

DS Rogers balled his hands on his hips and looked at the grass. "That's it? That's all you've got. You've let some daft old man fill your head with spy novel nonsense and now you both think you're Basil Rathbone?"

Pearson checked with Massie before asking, "Who?"

Rogers ignored the question. "It's a suicide! He came home, found his girlfriend living with someone else, got drunk and decided to end it all. It's a short walk from here to the cliff."

Albert selected that moment to speak. "You are going to check for blood spatter though, aren't you, Detective Sergeant Rogers? Anything else would be remiss."

Rogers snorted a tired laugh. "Anything else would be ... That's what you would do, is it? Oh great and wise Albert Smith, super sleuth to the nation, how would we ever manage to solve a crime without you to guide us?" Rogers chose to ham it up, overacting the moment to further disrespect his elder.

Albert folded his arms and waited, a quizzical brow suggesting he could not decide whether to be amused by the detective's antics or feel sorry for the fool.

Switching back to his annoyed voice, DS Rogers challenged Albert directly.

"I've no choice but to get the crime scene guys out here now, you've seen to that. If I can find a way to charge you for wasting police time, I will. Give me one good reason though … just one to make me believe the kid you 'supposedly' saw," it was the detective's turn to make air quotes, "wasn't just poking around for something he could steal and sell on."

Albert's smile was loaded with apology. "Because he used a key."

DS Rogers' expression froze. "What?"

Albert pointed to the door. "There is a key in the door."

"It's Karl Fielding's key," DS Rogers replied with a sad sigh like he was explaining the obvious to an idiot.

"No. His keys are hung on a hook inside the door."

Closest to it, Constable Massie looked inside. "There *are* keys here."

Albert didn't really want to drive the point home, but his knees were aching from all the standing around and he knew if he stayed out in the cold much longer he was going to feel it deep in his bones the next day.

"The keyring has two other keys on it. I'm willing to bet neither open the door to Karl Fielding's house. The intruder I disturbed fled on a bike – you can find the churned earth on the other side of the caravan - and left his keys behind. Whoever that was, they knew Karl Fielding well enough to have a key to his caravan or knew where to obtain one. Hours after he is declared dead, someone is back where he spent his last hours, snooping around in the dark. Are you getting suspicious yet?"

Albert made certain not to sound critical; he would gain

nothing from it. Too old to be bothered scoring points, he just wanted to bring the detective onto his side.

Huffing with exasperation, but no longer arguing, DS Rogers called for SOCO to attend his location.

Feeling like he'd put in a day already *and* had steered local law enforcement onto the right track, Albert begged a lift back into town. The walk going downhill might be a jolly sight easier, but it was no more attractive for it.

Massie dropped him outside the Hope and Anchor which, as a local, she assured him would be the best place to go for a quiet nightcap.

She could not have been more wrong.

Marine Reptile

The public house was distinctly more full of customers than Albert expected on a Monday night this late into the season and the crowd at the bar were in fine form, laughing and having fun. It was as if a rugby club had chosen to stop by for the night. Not that they were all burly men. Far from it.

"What's going on?" Albert asked one man as he made his way toward the door. He had his phone in his hand and looked to be about to make a call, something the noise in the bar would not permit.

The young man, a spotty-faced youth of about twenty, grinned on his way past. "Big dinosaur find!" He was gone and out the door before Albert could clarify, but the response told him enough.

The fossil hunters along the beach, the ones he never got to because Rex found Karl Fielding's body, had made a noteworthy discovery. Looking at the crowd now, their clothes were grubby with mud and dirt on the knees and up their trouser legs and most of them had an academic look about them – harmless, but worryingly intelligent.

There were other bars in town, and they were bound to be quieter than this one. However, there were tables free near the windows and he could tuck himself away there just as well as anywhere else. Albert was stopping for a nightcap, nothing more.

Or so he planned.

He was halfway to the bar when someone recognised him.

"Here, it's that fella off the news." One man nudged the chap to his right with an elbow, jogging his pint which spilled over his hand to drip on the floor. The man with beer on his hand chose to flick it in the other's face, necessitating a 'conversation' to ensue.

Albert steered away from them, but the damage was done, and a ripple spread through the bar as more and more punters turned to look at the famous face walking between them.

Trying to carve a path through a sea of faces in what was now an almost silent public house – silent except for the two playing argy-bargy over the spilled pint – Albert felt a mounting pressure to say something.

"Hello, everyone. I'm just stopping in for a nightcap. I understand there was a dinosaur discovery today," he aimed away from himself as a subject in the hope they might want to talk about that instead.

"Barman, get this man whatever he wants," called a man with shaggy blond hair swept to one side in a rough parting. "It's on me."

His offer of a drink was repeated by at least a dozen others, but the first man was directly in Albert's path, standing with one boot on the brass footrest at the edge of the bar. He looked like a 21st Century Crocodile Dundee but with more muscle and better clothes.

It was the professor Albert locked eyes with at the beach.

Reinforcing his offer, the professor said, "Join me and I'll tell you about this century's greatest fossil find."

Rex wagged his tail at the assembled patronage. "I'm up for some crisps if anyone is buying. Or some pork scratchings. I don't mind. Both would be good, actually."

"Well, hey there, buddy," slurred a Basset Hound, trotting through the forest of legs to get to Rex. He had grey fur around his muzzle and on his ears to denote his advancing years.

Rex looked his way, took a sniff to confirm what he knew and greeted the resident dog.

"Evening. This is your place? I'm Rex." Rex had smelled the deeply-ingrained dog ownership the moment he walked through the door.

The Basset Hound fetched up next to Rex where he dropped his back end unceremoniously to the floor with a slight thump.

"It shhure is. I'm Tailshpin. That'sh my human sherving drinks. What can you tell me about the bones?"

Rex had been half listening to the Basset Hound, half watching Albert because they were in a pub and that ought to mean a snack. Now Tailspin had his full attention.

"I'm sorry, what? You just said bones."

Tailspin belched, a combination of red wine and various ales. Rex chose not to breathe for a few seconds.

"Had a few have we?"

Tailspin giggled. "Always. Perksh of the job. People shpill their drinksh. Or they leave them unattended which ish the same as an invitation wouldn't you shay?"

Rex liked a drink himself, though his recent brush with red wine inebriation had dented his enthusiasm.

"You said something about bones," Rex reminded his new friend.

Snapping back to the present with a jerk, Tailspin said, "Yeah! That'sh right. What do you know about the bones?"

Rex blinked. "I don't know anything about any bones. I thought you did? I feel like I took a wrong turn in this conversation somewhere."

Tailspin checked his memory and backtracked a little. "Right, sorry. You're not with thish lot then?"

"No."

"Okay. Well you won't have to lishen for long to understand – all they talk about is bones. Giant bones."

Rex, always ready for a tasty bone on which he could gnaw, began to salivate.

Above his head, Albert ordered a gin and tonic with a thank you. He wanted to sit and rest out of the way in a quiet corner, but it was only right that he make conversation for a brief period since the professor was being generous. Anything less would be rude. Besides, he was genuinely interested to hear what had been found.

He asked for a packet of crisps and some water in a bowl for Rex, the Crocodile Dundee fossil hunter once again insisting they go on his tab.

With Rex on the floor munching crisps and a friend to share them with, Albert noted, he turned his attention more fully to his new companion. Extending his hand, he said, "Albert Smith. I guess you already knew that though."

The man broke a smile. "I think everyone knows who you are right now. How much of what they are saying in the papers is true? Did you really spend months hiding from the police while conducting a secret investigation into a clandestine underworld figure to then storm his underground lair and set free a village of captives?"

Albert liked to think that he was modest by nature. Bragging about what he might or might not have accomplished would be brash and vulgar. However, once again the ears of those in the pub were attuned to hear his answer and conversation had all but ceased.

Letting a little grin wrinkle his lips, Albert gave a shy shrug and said, "Well the news channels have greatly overstated the events, but … kinda, yeah."

Conversation sparked up again, the fossil hunter taking a healthy swig of his pint before placing it on the bar.

"You're undoubtedly wondering who I am and who all these youngsters are. I'm a university professor teaching palaeontology. These are my students."

A tall, attractive woman to his left reached around him to offer her hand to Albert. "Hello, I'm Claudia, his wife. When there are fossils to discuss, he forgets I'm here."

"What?" the professor laughed and took another draught from his glass. "As if that could ever be true my cherry-blossom."

Someone caught Claudia's attention; they had a question for her, and she turned away to speak with them.

Listening to the conversation around him for the last couple of minutes, Albert could not have missed that it was unlike that which one might expect to hear in any other public house.

There was a lot more Latin than usual for a start. Of course, given that the base amount of Latin in most pubs across the nation would be nil, that wasn't saying much. The pub's clientele were excited and noisy, but they were not drunk. They were here for the fossils.

"So, Professor …" Albert let it hang, expecting the man to fill in the blank. However, he seemed disinclined to give his name. Albert inclined his head and dropped another crisp. It didn't reach the floor. "Your wife is a Palaeontologist too?" he asked, switching tack.

The professor laughed. "Claudia? No. No, my wife tolerates my obsession, but she is a novelist. The joy of that is she can take her work anywhere so will accompany me whenever I dash off to a new dig."

"And that brought you here? So what was the big dinosaur find? The find of the century, I believe you called it. It appears to have your students rather animated."

The professor nodded to the bartender to refill his glass and without asking ordered another for Albert who already had three gin and tonics that magically appeared after he picked up the first one.

"You're sure this is of interest?"

Albert nodded. It was.

"Well, to start with it's not a dinosaur. It's a prehistoric marine reptile." Seeing Albert's face cloud, the professor proceeded to explain. "Dinosaurs lived on the land. Pterosaurs lived in the sky; they are not dinosaurs either, they are flying reptiles. I could go into the details of why, but the point is this coast is known for producing some of the most complete marine reptile fossils ever found. Mary Anning discovered the Ichthyosaur and the Plesiosaur just a few hundred yards from where we are standing. That was two hundred years ago, and many more unique fossils have been found here since."

"Yes, I know of Mary Anning. She sells seashells and all that."

The professor smiled, pleased he had an educated ear to bend. "That's exactly right. So my team work at the Natural History Museum in London but, of course, we have connections here and at other sites around the world. When we heard of the landslide, we came running."

Lyme Regis Layover

Albert could feel the excitement radiating off the professor of palaeontology. Drawn in by his story, Albert asked, "So what did you find?"

The professor lifted his glass to his lips before pausing, a question forming on his brow. He put the glass down again.

"That, my dear Mr Smith, is precisely the question. I can tell you for certain it is a new species. There's nothing unusual in that; new species are found all the time. However, what I believe we have from initial inspection, is an almost complete, or," he sucked in a deep breath like it was too much to hope for, "what might actually be a complete skeleton of a new species and that would be incredibly rare."

"But you don't know what it is?"

The professor's grin spread from ear to ear. "No. Glorious isn't it. This dig will keep us busy for months if not more than a year. It might not be the only creature the landslide exposed. What we do know, beyond that it is something completely new, is that it is huge. I mean like sauropod huge."

Albert jinked an eyebrow. "Sauropod?"

"Diplodocus, Brachiosaurus, the big plant eaters of the Jurassic. The vertebrae we found today measured three yards across."

Albert tried to do the math in his head, but had to give up and just give a low whistle. Whatever they had found, it was one big dinosaur. No, marine reptile, Albert corrected in his head.

"Say, what's your dog's name? Is it ... is it Rex? Do I have that right?"

Albert sipped his gin. "Indeed."

The professor stroked his chin thoughtfully. "This would be the king of all the oceans. I estimate it to be the biggest thing that ever swam. That would make it '*the king*' or '*Rex*' in Latin."

"You're going to name it after my dog?"

The professor picked up his drink and took a sip. "Yes, I might just do that."

Dem Bones, Dem Bones

With his human propping up the bar and forgetting the promise he made to be in bed early, Rex continued to conspire with the Basset Hound.

"They keep mentioning 'the museum'. Did you hear it that time?"

Rex nodded. "I did. What does that mean though?"

Tailspin jumped to his feet in excitement, staggered a little to one side and giggled when he bounced off someone's leg.

"Are you kidding?" he barked. "The museum ish right around the corner! I walk pasht it every day. That's where the bones will be and that's where we make our shcore."

Rex didn't follow. "Big score?"

Tailspin checked over both shoulders before whispering, "There's a way into the museum. Only a small animal can get in, but I've got that covered. They open the window to let the rest of us in and Bob's your uncle?"

"Is he?" asked Rex, more and more confused by the second. "I never met my dad, soooo how do you ..."

"Issh jussht a figure of speech," Tailspin moved the conversation along. "Lishen to what I'm shaying, old pal. If you schtick with me, there's a bounty of bones to be had. This lot," he flicked his eyes at the sea of humans around them, "are planning to bring the bones they are finding back to the musheum. I've recruited every dog that came in here tonight. I know, I know, you are wondering why the generosity. The truth is I can't do it all by myself. I'm not as young as I used to be. Plus, I get the impreshion there will be more than enough to go around. What do you shay? Are you in? We could do with a big fellow like yourself on the team."

Rex closed his mouth and considered the offer. Bones sure did sound good. The way Tailspin talked about it, the adventure would be like getting locked inside a butcher's shop at night. In reality though, tempting as it was, Rex wasn't prepared to leave his human's side.

Upon hearing the news, Tailspin expressed his disappointment. "That human of yours doesn't look too sprightly. How much trouble can he get into without you by his side for a few hours? Surely, you can just give him the slip?"

Rex wasn't going to get drawn into an argument. "Sorry. It's a generous offer, but he needs me."

"Needsh me," Tailspin repeated, sniggering to himself. "All right, I remember when I used to think like that. You be a good dog and stay by his side."

"Thank you. I will."

"Buuuuut, if you do change your mind, meet me and the rest of the gang behind the pub when the moon rises over the cliffs tomorrow night. Got it?"

Rex logged the information but had no intention of

keeping the appointment. "Behind the pub when the moon next crests the cliffs."

Tailspin was already wobbling back around the bar, calling over his shoulder, "You'll regret it forever if you don't. Bones, Rex, giant bones. The stuff of legends."

Rex laid his head down on his paws and tried hard not to imagine what that might be like.

All the while his dog was chatting with Tailspin, Albert could be found at the centre of a tale about his travels around the UK. Badgered into telling the 'real' story, not the one on TV, Albert took them all the way back to his decision to set off around the country.

Stood with his back to the bar so he could address the crowd pressed in all around him, Albert found that each time he twisted to collect his drink another one had appeared. There were now four on the bar waiting for him and he'd already put three away.

Dangerously, his normal inclination to resist had been eroded by the buoyant jubilation in the bar and by the first two drinks now firing their alcohol around his bloodstream.

He took another sip. "That was when I met a woman called Tanya," he revealed. "She's still out there somewhere; they didn't find her in the Gastrothief's lair."

"Is that your next mission then?" asked a voice from the front row of the crowd.

Albert looked at the young man who posed it. In his early twenties, the man had a little acne around his jawline and bushy black hair that hid his ears.

"Next mission? Goodness, no. Thank you, but my days of adventure were never intentional. I will be heading home tomorrow in all likelihood and there I will stay. If I never see Tanya again it will be too soon."

Prompted to continue his story by the professor, Albert

begged the assembled audience hold questions for later and got back to his tale.

Some time later, Rex was awoken by a tug on his lead: they were leaving. They were not going back to the bed and breakfast though. Oh, no, Albert had a very different destination in mind.

El Mango

The pub was due to close soon and a goodly proportion of the fossil hunters had already retired for the night including the professor and his wife. Albert, feeling a little unsteady on his feet, though he had sufficient sense to hand out several of his remaining drinks for the younger and more tolerant to imbibe, had been about to head to his bed when an altogether different plan emerged.

Some of the younger academics were heading to a club that would be open until after midnight. The venue in question was El Mango and while Albert had no desire to witness young women shaking their goods to a baying crowd, he was curious to explore the connection between Karl Fielding's death and the young man he caught raiding his caravan. The book of matches linked the kid on the dirt bike to the club and it was all he had to go on so far.

That the young man on the motorbike might be Karl's killer resounded in Albert's mind, banging away like a drum with a single insistent message: you won't sleep until you know. Truthfully, Albert believed he would be asleep seconds after his head hit the pillow. However, it was also true that accompanying a group of men AND women in their twenties and thirties would look less suspicious than wandering into a strip club all by himself – something he doubted he was brave enough to do anyway.

Rex didn't mind where they went. He slept whenever they stopped moving and rarely got to a point when he felt he needed to rest. He'd dozed for an hour in the pub, had food in his belly, and was happy to be out for another walk. They were with other people too and that was also nice.

Winding their way around what passed for a town centre, Rex's nose picked up a familiar scent: that of the motorbike he'd chased from the caravan park. It was faint, and it wasn't something he could follow, but it had passed by their current location not so long ago.

It wasn't far from the pub on the seafront to the gentlemen's club tucked down a seedy side street three roads back and the walk took less than ten minutes. Having never been inside a gentleman's club other than in pursuit of a case back when he was a paid police officer, and then it was more commonly during the day, Albert was unfamiliar with what to expect.

Consequently, the topless young lady dancing inside a cage just behind the entrance door took him by surprise. Gawping at her, his thoughts entirely along the lines of, 'My goodness, she must be freezing,' he was fortunate enough to realise what he was doing before anyone thought to comment.

Not that they would, for the fossil hunters were all doing precisely the same thing. Noticing how the eyes of the young men were universally ogling the almost naked lady, Albert thought it safe to assume they were not admiring the young lady's enduring spirit.

"You can't bring that dog in here," insisted a neckless man mountain in a black suit. Stood to one side of the entrance he raised an arm to bar Albert's path.

"He's my assistance dog," Albert replied confidently. "I can't go in without him."

One of his new friends latched onto Albert's statement.

"And that means none of the rest of us are coming in either." There were more than a dozen eager punters in Albert's little group; good business for a Monday night at any time of the year.

With a nod from the man taking entrance fees at a desk inside, the doorman changed his mind, but growled, "Just keep him under control."

There was a small cover charge to pay, which surprised Albert; he expected it to be higher. He found out why inside when the round of drinks he offered to buy cost an eyewatering amount.

The club was dimly lit and there were a few customers already lining the main stage. They did not look up when Albert's group filed in; as men they were transfixed by the busty young lady cavorting and grinding mere inches from their faces.

Albert didn't know where to look, but it was going to be anywhere other than the venue's main attraction.

Taking off his coat for it was warm in the club and he was starting to perspire, he folded it over his left forearm. He'd ordered himself a sparkling water - there was enough alcohol in his system already – and now that his companions were finding places to sit, Albert set about looking for someone he might quiz. Now that he was here though, he wasn't sure what questions he might ask.

Initially, he wanted to speak with Karl Fielding's daughter, but that was until his gin-addled brain woke up to the fact that she wouldn't be working tonight. By now she would have been made aware of her father's death, so even if she was due to appear, Albert was certain that plan had been cancelled.

There was a girl behind the bar. He thought of her as a girl because she looked so young, but dressed in just her underwear which he noticed even though he tried not to, she had a woman's figure. Albert's wife, Petunia, once looked much the same.

Looking around for one of the male members of staff – much easier to talk to than one of the scantily clad women – Albert spotted a likely looking chap on the other side of the room. Making his way between the booths arranged to face the stage, he was halfway there when the kid with the acne and the bushy black hair stepped into his path.

Flanked on each side by more than half the palaeontology students, they were grinning at Albert with excited, knowing smiles.

"Come on, Albert," said the kid with the bushy hair. "We've got a surprise for you!"

"A – a surprise?" Albert found himself moved along like a stick caught in a river. The students herded him past the bar and around the stage where yet another young lady was removing her bra. "What sort of surprise?"

Someone behind him said, "A really good one," with a snigger.

Someone else said, "Don't worry about your dog. We'll look after him until you are done."

Rex didn't like all the humans so close to him. Attached to his human as he was, he felt hemmed in, and they were clumsy with their feet at the best of times. He did not want to get one of his paws squished under a big boot.

He needn't have worried for he found he was suddenly

being taken to one side. Looking about, Rex saw his human going in a different direction. Confused, he twisted his head to see who was holding his lead. It was one of the female humans he met earlier in the pub. It was easy to tell she was with the group as they all smelled of dirt where they'd been digging in it. It was on their clothes and permeated their skin.

Turning his head around once more, he got to watch Albert vanish from sight through a door marked 'Private Sessions'.

"A lap dance?" Albert blurted. "I don't think so lads. It's a lovely gesture, but I'm a bit old for all that. One of you should have it instead."

The students, high on the giddy excitement of fossil hunting and making decisions based on the amount of alcohol in their bodies, had clubbed together to pay one of the ladies to perform a private dance. In their heads, they were doing something special for a man the nation was currently hailing as a great and selfless hero – someone to admire. It was something any of them would have gladly paid for if they had the cash.

Albert argued, but the lads weren't taking 'no' for an answer. They all but pushed the protesting old man into the private room and closed the door with him inside.

"Won't be a moment. Make yourself comfortable,' drifted out from a door on the adjacent wall, laced with a husky tone that was intended to strike at a man's libido.

As if such a thing were necessary.

It disturbed Albert that his heart chose to beat so hard in his chest. It wasn't excitement though; he had no desire to wait for the owner of the voice to make her appearance. He tried the door again, but when it opened, the lad outside looked back at him with such generous eyes that Albert found himself saying, "Just checking none of you want to take my place," even though he knew the answer already.

Closing the door again, he turned around to find a woman in her mid-twenties stalking toward him. She stood well over six feet with her six-inch heels and towered over Albert. Her figure was that of a swimwear model – honed and toned muscle beneath soft skin. She wore a bra and knickers spun from such gossamer thin silk Albert wagered he could swallow them both without needing a glass of water.

Coming closer, she said, "You should sit, sweetie. Your time is already ticking."

Albert didn't intend to employ profanity but that was what happened. Unable to retreat, unwilling to stay where he was to endure what many might consider a pleasurable experience, he chose to leg it instead.

Ducking around the woman, who shouted, "Hey!" at his departing back, he ran through the only door available.

It led him into a changing area where mercifully, though there were numerous ladies' undergarments and skimpy costumes on display, there were no actual women.

Aiming to loop around and collect Rex before making a hasty exit from the establishment, Albert opened what he hoped was a door leading back to the club only to find the cool air of night beyond. The door led into a courtyard at the back of the premises. He was shutting it again when he stopped.

Snatching it open once more, he confirmed what he thought he'd seen and drawn as if by a magnetic force, he stepped outside. The door closed behind him though he failed to notice he was now locked out because he was staring at the small-engined, red dirt bike that fled the caravan park just a few short hours ago.

Pausing to listen and check around, Albert made sure there was no one watching. It had to be the same bike. Though he'd failed to catch the licence plate at the time, there couldn't be many bikes similar in such a small town.

Standing over it, Albert could feel the warmth radiating off the engine. Stuck under the mud guards, both front and rear, he found fresh mud and grass where it had churned the ground to escape.

This time Albert noted the licence plate and feeling the cold seeping through his clothing, shifted his coat to put it back on. He had one arm in when he heard a crunch of gravel. The sound sent a shockwave of adrenaline through his body. Like lightning lighting up his synapses, he spun around to face the anticipated threat only to find he was already too late.

The punch, wild though it was and lacking in both power and experience, caught Albert on the chin. He toppled backward, his consciousness fighting to stay in control. He might have stayed upright and awake were it not for the motorbike. His hip caught the handlebar and already off balance, he fell. His head hit the wall and he knew nothing more.

The skinny figure swore and moments later the red dirt bike tore out of the courtyard and into the street, narrowly missing a collision with a truck carrying scaffold. To a blast of horn, Albert's attacker ripped back the throttle and left his latest victim behind.

Dog on the Loose

Rex wasn't happy with his current situation. His paws stuck to the floor every time he took a step. That was a minor gripe though. What he really didn't like was the absence of his human. Had the old man cried out for help when they were separated, Rex would have known how to react. He hadn't though and Rex believed the new humans they met earlier in the pub were now some kind of temporary addition to his pack.

They seemed unbothered about his human's absence, which had been several minutes already. Too long in Rex's mind. He gave it a few more seconds, watching the door the old man went through. A few seconds, but no more.

Rising to his feet, he tracked his lead back to the hand holding it. The girl who had it first was no longer there. She excused herself to attend the restrooms more than a minute ago and a chunky ginger-haired man had the duty now. He wasn't paying a whole lot of attention to Rex. His eyes were on the trio of blonde girls dancing right in front of his nose.

Judging shock to be the best tactic, Rex bunched his legs

and ran. The lead snapped out of the ginger man's hand, almost breaking his wrist when it momentarily caught. Free to go, Rex ran to where he last saw Albert.

The door didn't open. It was one of the annoying ones with a handle, and it was locked on the other side though Rex didn't know that. Back at the stage, the ginger-haired man was on his feet and giving chase, his colleagues berating him for failing to keep hold of the dog.

The club's staff – men in suits with more muscle than brain – missed the dog shooting through the room at knee height but saw the young lads. Assuming they were up to something, they hustled to intercept.

Rex heard the thundering of feet and chose to go in the opposite direction. His human was beyond the door he couldn't get through, but maybe there was another way around. Running presented itself as a sound policy, so that was what he did with the addition of barking to get his human's attention.

Rex wanted to follow the old man's scent, but it was in the air and all around, no stronger in one direction than any other. He kept running, nudging at doors with his nose. By now the club's doormen and the gang of mildly inebriated palaeontology students had untangled themselves and all were looking for the German Shepherd.

Rex heard someone shout something and sensing it was aimed at him, he batted another door with his shoulder. This one gave and he shoved it wide while barging through it. Finding himself in the ladies' changing room, Rex's nose caught a shockwave of perfume and product scents that tried to overpower his nose.

Hidden among those smells he found the unmistakeable odour of Albert Smith.

Completely still, Rex barked again, his tail wagging in

anticipation. No response came and the sound of people in pursuit was getting closer. Frustrated, he set off again, bounding to cover more distance but not running flat out so his nose would have a chance to track his human.

He ran past the door Albert had gone through not five minutes earlier and two distinct smells stopped him dead. The first was the hard whiff of exhaust, the same chemical profile the dirt bike left behind at the caravan park. The second was a smell Rex was all too familiar with: blood.

Catching the scent in his nose, Rex attempted to reverse course without bothering to stop. Momentum chose not to permit such a manoeuvre. His paws went one way, his back end went another, but it was only momentary. Scrambling to get his feet back beneath his body, Rex shot forward. Careening out of the door and into the cold air outside, he once again stopped dead.

Lying on the ground to his front, propped against the wall at an awkward angle, his human, Albert Smith, leaked blood from a head wound.

Canine Protection

"You'll have to wait for animal control to arrive," PC Pearson blocked the paramedic's path. "The dog goes for anyone who tries to get near the patient."

The paramedic, a balding man in his fifties called CJ by his colleagues even though his name was Ivan, peered into the dark courtyard behind the strip club.

"He looks harmless enough. Have you tried talking to him?"

Rex was lying across Albert's chest to keep him warm. When he licked the old man's face in a bid to revive him, an uncoordinated hand flopped ineffectually in the air to bat him away. It told Rex his human was still alive at least.

Albert had slumped further though, falling sideways onto his side and then rolling onto his back. The ground was cold, and Rex remembered only too well his human's battle with hypothermia in Keswick. When the doormen from the club burst into the courtyard moments after he found Albert, Rex turned on them.

Someone had hurt his human and until he knew who it was and paid them back in full, the rest of the world would be well advised to give him some space.

"I keep telling you not to go off by yourself," Rex chided Albert's unconscious form, angry at himself for not being more insistent about staying by Albert's side.

The doorman chose to stay back. The dog was outside now: hardly their problem at all, but they couldn't ignore the old man; that sort of thing brings bad publicity. The palaeontology students approached Rex too thinking they would be greeted as friends, but Rex wasn't letting anyone near his human. Not until the medical service people arrived.

Rex knew paramedics from his time in the police. They would arrive to patch people up and that had included him on a couple of occasions. They were easy to recognise from the smell, so when CJ appeared with his big bag of medical supplies, a colleague right on his shoulder, Rex wagged his tail and offered them his friendly face.

CJ remarked, "He looks friendly enough to me," and pushed past PC Pearson.

Rex got to his feet and stepped out of the way so they could get to Albert.

CJ dropped his bag and knelt on the ground. With a quick pat for the dog and a request that he sit – Rex obeyed instantly much to PC Pearson's disgruntlement – he proceeded to assess the victim.

With a light being shone in his eyes and hands touching his skin, Albert began to come around.

"Wassat?" he slurred.

"How much have you had to drink, sir?" asked CJ's colleague, Kareshma. That the old man had been drinking was not in question and the conclusion of a drunken fall an easy one to reach.

Albert mumbled, "Charlie Oscar fifty two Papa Papa Mike."

Kareshma repeated her question.

Hearing his human speak, Rex got back to his feet and tried to get involved.

"How's he doing? Is he all right?" Rex nudged his head through the gap between the two paramedics.

Kareshma, not a dog person, shoved him back with an elbow and flared her eyes at PC Pearson.

"Can you do something about the dog? Where are animal services?"

Pearson came forward. She liked to think she was a dog person – she grew up with pugs, but the giant German Shepherd was something else and she'd seen what one could do to a person if they chose to bite them.

Tentatively, she gripped Rex's collar to haul him back a foot, giving the paramedics room to work.

"What's the verdict?" she asked. "One too many? Got all excited having a lap dance and didn't have enough blood left to operate his brain?" She already knew from the palaeontology students that the old man had been in one of the back rooms for a private session and one only needed to get near enough to check his breathing to smell the gin.

CJ rocked back onto his heels. "Concussed most likely. We need to take him in. He'll need monitoring for the night."

"Charlie Oscar fifty two Papa Papa Mike," Albert slurred again. His eyes hurt to open, and his tongue felt too big for his mouth. He heard Pearson though, and she needed to know. "Killer," he managed to mumble.

The odd collection of words might have been dismissed

by many, but Pearson knew what Albert Smith was trying to say. Dropping to a knee, she took his left hand in hers.

"Was that a vehicle registration number?" she asked, her voice soft and encouraging.

"S'right," Albert managed. "Bike." He tried to open his eyes again, his eyelids snapping shut the instant light crept around them. It had been like pushing a knife through his brain and he decided to not try it again.

"Were you run over, Albert?" PC Pearson had a hand poised near her radio to make a call and used his first name since she knew it.

Rex tried to nudge his way through the press of humans again. The old man was coming around and Rex wanted to be there with him.

Shoved back again, he danced around their backs to get to Albert's head.

"Tell them" Rex barked. "Tell them about the man on the motorbike!"

Pearson angled her head back to the mouth of the courtyard where Constable Massie controlled the strip club's clientele. Both staff and clientele had congregated outside to watch. The girls had coats wrapped around themselves to ward off the cold, though Pearson doubted such a tactic would be particularly effective given how little they wore underneath.

Albert's brain was foggy and the effort of forming a coherent sentence and then wrestling his tongue around it proved too much. Feeling drowsy again, he managed to recite the vehicle registration number one more time.

"Nah, he's out again," reported Kareshma. "I'll get the gurney; we need to move him now. Can't you do something about his dog?"

The last comment was aimed at Pearson. She was on

her radio, getting dispatch to look up the VRN Albert Smith managed to mumble before he lost consciousness again. Hoping the old detective would be okay, she hooked a hand through Rex's collar and pulled him back again.

Rex watched and waited, nervous when they loaded his human onto a stretcher. The bed on wheels then popped into the air, legs extending below it like magic before his eyes. Suddenly, he couldn't see the old man. He was above Rex's head.

Prancing onto his back feet to get a better look as they led him away, Rex had every intention of going with him. He protested the instant he realised PC Pearson was holding him back.

"Hey, what are you doing? I need to go with my human. He's been attacked. I'm his protection." Rex wriggled and fought to break the hold she had.

This wasn't Pearson's first unruly dog though. Swinging her right leg around and over, she planted her feet either side of Rex's ribs and twisted his collar in both hands just before Rex attempted to back out of it.

Cooing at him to calm down, she was fighting an uphill battle to achieve anything of the sort. Then animal services arrived.

Risking letting go with one hand, she waved for them to hurry up. The dog was big and strong and she wasn't going to be able to hold onto him for much longer.

"You're going to go with these gentlemen now, okay? They will give you a nice, warm place to sleep and something to eat, okay? It's just until the morning, then maybe we can sort out something better for you. It's just until Albert gets out of hospital."

Rex took one look at the approaching animal services guys. That was all he needed. They were not the first ones he'd ever encountered, and he doubted they would be the last. Either way, he didn't like the sound of PC Pearson's plan and had a much better one of his own.

Lunging forward to throw Pearson off balance before she could get her other hand back on his collar, Rex immediately twisted his whole body to turn it around. In so doing, the thumb of the one hand still gripping Rex's collar snagged on the clip for his lead. It fell free, coiling on the ground by his front paws.

Pearson said, "Waaaaaaah!" as she fell against the wall. Rebounding with her left shoulder, she tried with all her might to keep her legs either side of the dog. Expecting it, Rex threw everything into reverse and before the eyes of a disbelieving crowd he aided Constable Pearson in performing a near perfect forward somersault.

Fingers still gripping his collar, her hand went between her legs at speed. Her head followed and physics did the rest.

Failing to land the gymnastic manoeuvre on her feet, she smacked into the unforgiving ground with her rump instead. Uttering an expletive, she got to watch the dog shoot past on her right as she questioned if her arms were dislocated or not.

Rex bared his teeth and ran headfirst at the animal control guys.

Larry and Chuck were seasoned pros and had been on-the-job partners for more than ten years. If a person were to ask them if there was anything they feared to tackle, they might joke about bears and alligators before replying that the world was yet to invent the animal they could not contain. It came as a shock to them both when the seemingly placid German Shepherd went berserk and chose to charge directly for them.

More shocking was the mutual and unspoken decision to hug each other for comfort in their final moments. When the dog veered around them at the last moment, their collective sigh of relief highlighted their proximity.

Afterward, they agreed the incident never happened and was not to be discussed at any point ever.

Recruiting Help

Dashing out into the street past the shocked legs of the bystanders watching, Rex was following his nose. His human had gone in this direction; his scent lingered still. The sound of a door thunking shut came just as he rounded the last of the gawping humans.

It was the ambulance and Kareshma was already on her way to get in the passenger door. Constable Massie shouted for Rex to stop and the animal control men were giving chase. He wanted to follow the ambulance, but knew he wouldn't be able to keep up. Moreover, someone was going to catch him if he tried, so he did the next most obvious thing: he ran.

It wasn't flight without thought though; Rex knew where he was going.

Three minutes later, he arrived back at the Hope and Anchor public house. Pawing at the back door and hoping Tailspin would hear him, Rex thought through his plan.

His human had been attacked and the exhaust fumes in the alley were from the same dirt bike he chased at the caravan park. The scent in the alley was from the same human he found in the caravan they visited, the one where the human he met in the Gastrothief's lair had been living.

Karl Fielding was dead now, and it was clear to Rex his human was trying to figure out who was responsible. The old man was out of action for a while, but Rex had confidence he could solve the case by himself. It wouldn't be the first time.

He didn't have a lot of clues to follow, but there were a few things. The motorbike for a start. He could search the town for it. It was kind of a long shot, he knew, but that task would be combined with tracking the skinny kid who rode the motorbike.

The kid was almost certainly the killer; that just made sense. He was at the caravan, and he ran the instant Rex found him. Then he attacked Albert and that had to be because the old man tracked him here. Rex was always impressed with the way his human was able to find people. It amazed him at times, not least because he never once employed his nose to find them.

Wanting to start the search now, but believing it was a good plan to employ some local noses to aid his quest, Rex set off. He thought Tailspin was the perfect dog for the job – he already bragged about how he knew all the local canines. It was late, but maybe he was still up. Spy hopping on his back legs to check what was on the other side of the wall, his eyes confirmed what his nose could not and he leapt the low wall with a run up to land in the pub's back garden.

Tailspin had not heard Rex clawing at the door to get in, and wasn't about to answer it anytime soon. In fact, he was lying on his back in his bed, all four paws twitching in the air as he drunkenly snored, farted, and dreamed.

Mercifully for Rex, Tailspin's human, the landlord of

the pub, was just finishing up for the night. Returning from letting the last of his staff out to make their way home, his last job was to put his dog out to relieve himself. It was that or come down in the morning to a yellow lake on the kitchen tile.

Unceremoniously woken from his sleep when the landlord lifted him into the air, Tailspin's tongue lolled to one side and his jowls covered his eyes until his paws hit the rough concrete outside.

"Don't take too long," warned the landlord, closing the door again to trap the cold outside.

Rex was behind the door, the unexpected sight of him almost giving Tailspin a coronary.

"Good grief, Rex. Give a little warning next time, won't you?" Tailspin complained, walking away from the small puddle his fright left behind. "What are you doing back here so soon, anyway?" The Basset Hound wandered a few feet to 'water' a patch of lawn.

Rex wasted no time beating around the bush. "I need your help."

With one back leg lifted into the air, Tailspin had to rely on the other three to remain steady, a feat a sober dog can perform without thinking. Tailspin lurched to one side before getting his paws back under control and had to try again.

The back door to the pub opened again. "Come on, Tailspin, I want to get to bed," complained his human.

Deliberately taking his time and heading across the garden to sniff something, the Basset Hound asked, "What do you need help with?"

Again Rex got straight to the point, "Solving a murder."

Tailspin shot his head around to stare at Rex, questioning if he was serious. He forgot to allow for his inebriation though and had to close his eyes when his eyeballs seemed to keep going.

When he felt that he could, he sought confirmation. "A human murder?"

"Yes. I found a body on the beach today. He'd been in the water, but my human says he was murdered, and he's usually right. Just a short while ago, a skinny man, quite young like an adolescent puppy, attacked my human. I think he is the killer and I have to stop him before he can get away or kill again."

"Why? Why do you care if he gets away? I mean, I appreciate that he hurt your human and all, but is he likely to do it again?"

"That's not the point. It's what my human would want. It's what he was doing when he got attacked. He solves crimes. It's what he does. At least, he tries to. It's quite sweet, actually. I have to give him a nudge so he stays on the right track, but he gets an A for effort."

Tailspin accepted what he was hearing. The German Shepherd would prove useful when they went after the bones. If he needed to pander to Rex's needs between now and then, it wasn't a problem. Just so long as he didn't want to get started right now.

"I'm ready when you are," Rex pointed out, keen to get going.

Tailspin started back toward the house. "And I'll be ready right after breakfast."

"Wait, no, we have to get started." Rex wasn't going to beg, but he knew time was a critical factor.

Tailspin's jaw opened wide, a yawn forcing his eyes closed. "Sorry, Rex, I need to sleep off this evening's little visit to the bar. It was rich pickings and I need a little nap now. We'll pick it up in the morning, okay?"

"No, not okay. Not okay."

Getting in Tailspin's way, he blocked the Basset Hound's route inside.

Grinding to a halt with a groan, Tailspin argued, "It's too late to do anything now. You go if you want. The whole town will be in bed at this hour."

The backdoor opened, the landlord calling for the pub dog to get inside.

"You coming?" asked Tailspin. "You can crash here tonight if you like."

Grumpily, Rex snapped, "No, thank you. I have a crime to solve."

Tailspin hopped over the doorstep and went inside. The landlord, his sleepy eyes barely open, failed to even notice the German Shepherd standing outside.

With a parting comment of, "Suit yourself. Come back when you've accepted there's nothing to be gained by losing sleep. I'll let you in if you can manage to wake me," the back door closed, and Rex was left outside in the cold.

Bakery Empire

Greg Garside couldn't stand when people changed their minds. Specifically, he hated when people agreed to a deal and then changed their mind about it. It wasn't right. It ought not to be allowed. An App, that was what the world needed. There were Apps for everything now. He needed an App to record people's decisions.

'Yes, I agree to sell you my bakery and have you absorb it into your franchise.' The moment the words were said they ought to be legally binding. The App could record it along with the person's fingerprint or something.

Greg crossed the room to see if his phone was broken or still in one piece. It got to endure the venting of his frustration when he threw it at the wall a few seconds ago. Knowing his temper, Greg had a military-style hardened case on the device. It had protected the delicate electronics this time.

Rage bubbling just under the surface, he felt like throwing it at another wall to see if he could break it with a second attempt, but dumped it on the kitchen counter instead. It wasn't his phone he wanted to hurt, it was Daniel Fielding.

They had a deal.

Now they didn't.

It made Greg's blood boil.

A successful baker in his own right, he learned the ropes from Daniel and Karl's dad. The brothers were younger than him and he'd been working there for almost five years when the elder brother, Daniel, left school and took a full-time post in the family business.

Greg got that it was a family business, but it was one he helped to shape and grow. That's how he saw it, but when the brothers were given shares in the company and he was not, it was clear he was never going to succeed if he worked for someone else.

The bitter disappointment and frustration started a fire in his belly that was to be the forge from which an empire was built. Storming from Fielding's bakery that fateful day, he set about opening his own place. He was going to take everything he knew and beat them at their own game.

He would put them out of business, robbing their customer base by doing everything the same but better.

He couldn't though. The Dorset Knob. That was the barrier to his success. Not only had Mr Fielding, senior never revealed the ingredients and baking technique he used to get them so crunchy, he then went and trademarked the name. No matter what he did, Greg couldn't produce a biscuit that matched theirs. Even when he came close, guessing how to get it right with his own experience and intuition, he couldn't market them as Dorset Knobs.

He called them Dorset Dicks and everyone laughed. He called them Lyme Regis Nobblers, and got mute disinterest. If he wasn't selling a Dorset Knob, he wasn't in the game.

A year after opening, Greg Garside closed his bakery in Lyme Regis and filed for bankruptcy. Some might have accepted defeat at this point, but he wasn't the kind of man to lay down and die. Far from it. Knowing the trade and the local area, he knew Sid Hepworth in Charmouth was a good decade past retirement age. He borrowed more money (you could do that sort of thing back then), made a sensible offer, and bought Sid's bakery in the centre of the seaside town. One stop along the coast from Lyme Regis, but far enough removed that he wasn't losing to the Fieldings every day, he carved out a market and expanded. A year after rebranding Sid's old place as 'Greg's', he opened a second place, this one in Seaton. Less than a year after that it was Axminster. Now his empire stretched from Southampton in Hampshire to Plymouth in Devon with almost a hundred stores operating seven days a week.

More than thirty years had passed since he quit working for old man Fielding, but not a day went by without the anger he felt resurfacing. The fire in his belly refused to die and he knew he would never be happy until the Fielding brothers were crushed beneath his boot.

Twice more he'd opened one of his stores in Lyme Regis and twice more he'd been forced to close up because everyone went to the bakery they knew.

He tried to buy Fielding's Bakery a half dozen times over the years, his offers getting higher and more ludicrous with each iteration. They just wouldn't sell. It embarrassed him that as the undeniable king of baked goods in the southwest, he didn't have a store in his own home town. If they would just sell, he would change the name above the door and that would be that. The staff could stay on. Oh, there would be a certain satisfaction in sacking the Fielding brothers, but being their boss, well that held a different kind of joy. One that he could revel in for years.

More than that though, if he bought their business, he would own the Dorset Knob. The Fieldings sold it from their one tiny shop in Lyme Regis. If Greg Garside owned it, the famous product would be spread across every last one of his outlets and the secret recipe would be his and his alone.

The problem had been Karl. Karl Fielding would not sell. The older brother, Daniel, had wavered, but even when Greg leaned on the one brother he believed he could convince, Karl was Daniel's equal partner and wouldn't budge.

The thought of killing Karl had crossed Greg's mind more than once, but only in an abstract way; he'd never put any thought into how he would do it.

Then Karl up and vanished.

At first that was nothing to get excited about. However, when a few days stretched into a week and he still hadn't returned, Greg, like a shark circling a stranded boat full of sailors, paid Daniel a little visit.

Daniel's health wasn't great which worked in Greg's favour, and he would happily exploit any advantage he could find.

Daniel agreed to sell. If Karl didn't return from wherever it was he had mysteriously disappeared to, he would sell. The money was significantly more than the place was worth, but Greg could afford it and was happy to pay – Lyme Regis would be the jewel in his crown.

"Think of Karl's daughter," Greg had pushed Daniel to see the bigger picture.

That had been two days ago on Saturday evening. Greg

was so happy walking home that night he almost danced and sang.

Less than twenty-four hours later, Daniel was on his phone revealing Karl's magnificent return. Karl hadn't vanished of his own accord, he'd been kidnapped by some maniac and taken to Wales. His rescue and that of forty more people from an underground bunker was all over the news.

Daniel wasn't going to sell after all.

Greg wanted to kill him for reneging on their deal. They shook hands and everything! Killing Daniel wouldn't solve the problem though. Killing Karl, well that was another matter entirely.

But Karl's 'suicide' didn't reset the deal. Daniel was too distraught to discuss it. He wasn't too distraught, however, to say that he planned to keep the family bakery going now. To honour his brother! The whole plan had backfired! The perfect murder - no one would ever be able to trace back to Greg Garside, yet it had worked against him.

There was only one thing for it: he was going to have to kill Daniel too.

Cinnamon

Rex wandered the streets and back alleys of Lyme Regis for two hours. He could have aimed his paws downhill at the seafront and gone straight to the bakery, but he hadn't because his mind was filled with a dozen other things: Would Tailspin help him in the morning? Was he better off waiting for his human to return? How would he know when the old man did return, and should he go back to where they were staying to wait for him?

In the end, when he accepted his strategy of walking around sniffing for something familiar wasn't going to work, Rex took a moment to orientate himself, then set off toward the ocean.

There was something about the smell of the bakery he wanted to check.

He might have ignored it had it not been for the scent of the kid on the motorbike. The kid left a trace of his odour on Albert. Rex's top lip curled at the memory of his human lying wounded on the ground.

Refocusing his thoughts, he concentrated on the scent

profile. It was cinnamon mixed with a raft of other ingredients such as nutmeg, allspice, and sage. That all played in the background to the kid's natural body odour, deodorant, and soap powder on his clothing, but the cinnamon scent had been present in the caravan too. At the time Rex believed it came from the victim, Karl Fielding. Now he wasn't so sure.

The only way to figure it out now was to get a better sniff of the bakery.

Plodding downhill and trying not to think about his human, for it made him mad and sad at the same time, Rex questioned why the kid on the motorbike smelled like the bakery. Did he work there? Rex didn't think so. Not unless it was in one of the back rooms. His scent had not been present when he went in with Albert earlier.

It had to be something else then and it couldn't just be because he murdered Karl Fielding, not enough of Karl's scent would have rubbed off for it to be that deeply ingrained. Not for Rex to still be able to detect it in the courtyard behind the strip club twenty-four hours after the murder.

Rex was still pondering the question when he arrived outside Fielding's bakery. The business was closed as he expected and there was no way in, he decided after five minutes of circling the fence behind the property. Poking his nose through the letter box at the bottom of the front door, he confirmed the cinnamon smell was still there.

The dormant bakery would spring to life in just a few hours when Pascal and Wendy, the early morning crew, would arrive to begin feeding the ovens. Starting at three o'clock six days a week and half past four on Sundays when they got a lie in, someone from the bakery had to be there to get that day's produce started. Everything was cooked fresh – a matter of professional pride and not like the mass-produced goods Greg's franchise kicked out from their central factory.

Removing his nose out from the letter box, Rex paused. There was something ... wrong was the, er, wrong word. Different perhaps, Rex argued. Yes, the cinnamon, nutmeg, allspice and goodness knows what else was in there, but the relative strengths of one against the other were off. Not by much, but enough that Rex's nose could tell the difference.

Fielding's bakery carried the same smell he found in the caravan where Karl Fielding had stayed. It was present at Karl's house when his human took Rex there, though in trace quantities only. What he could smell now was the same, but it didn't match the background scent the kid on the motorbike carried.

Not quite.

Perplexed, Rex wondered what to make of it.

One thing he did know was that he was wasting his time trying to achieve anything more before daybreak. The sun would be up in a few hours, but he needed to get some sleep and due to the simple fact that he was awake, he was getting hungry.

Rex thought about returning to the pub - Tailspin said he would let him in, but Rex wasn't convinced the Basset Hound could open the door or would even wake up. Besides, Albert might return at any time, so with a gentle loping trot, Rex made his way back to their accommodation.

There, he discovered he could not get in. It was as he expected, but the bed and breakfast had a covered patio around the back where Rex found a hidey hole beneath a bench. There he slept soundly until the door opened many hours later.

Lawn Ornament

"Cooo, you gave me a fright!" Mrs Beeler sagged against the doorframe to give her heart a moment to stop pounding. "What are you doing out here then?"

Locked inside the warm cocoon of a deep and dreamless sleep, Rex had awoken with a start when the door next to his head opened. Clambering out from beneath the bench seat, his abrupt appearance shocked the landlady almost as much as she startled him.

However, the smell of bacon wafting out through the open door killed all other thoughts in his head.

"Were you a bad dog?" Mrs Beeler asked. "Is that why Mr Smith shut you out here." Noting that the dog wasn't attached to anything, she remarked, "He was lucky you didn't wander off in the night."

Rex's focus might have been on the promise of bacon, but the 'bad dog' comment caught his attention.

"Bad dog? Really? I'm Rex the wonder dog. Ask the old man how many times I've rescued him from the brown, smelly stuff. Now, how about some bacon?" he added hopefully, offering his biggest doggy grin.

Mrs Beeler had a handful of bread crusts; Mr Beeler refused to eat them even though he was sixty-seven and really ought to have learned better by now. Her morning ritual included putting them out for the birds to find. Closing the door behind her to keep the cold out, she followed a set of six steppingstones across her lawn to the bird feeder where she left the crusts.

On the way back she encountered a small mound of Rex's, ahem, output with a frown. This was not what she expected from her guests. If she had her way there would be no pets allowed, but Mr Beeler had been right to reserve a room for guests with dogs. He advertised in a dog magazine – not a magazine for dogs, you understand, but one aimed at their owners. It brought in enquiries every week and helped to keep the income churning over.

Nevertheless, Mr Smith, national hero or not, was going to have to clean up the mess because she wasn't.

"Come along," she urged Rex inside. "Let's deliver you back to your master, shall we. I have a bone to pick with him."

Rex's ears pricked up. "A bone?"

Mrs Beeler continued to mutter, pausing at the kitchen door to poke her head inside.

"Keep an eye on the bacon, please, Tony. I don't want it to burn."

Tony Beeler looked up from his newspaper. "Why can't you do it?" Seeing his wife's expression, he slipped off his stool at the breakfast bar and went to check the grill.

"What sort of bone?" Rex enquired. "I ask because if there is some picking to do, I'd rather like to help. Or did you mean there are multiple bones and we get to 'pick' which one we'd like?" His stomach gave a meaningful growl at a volume Mrs Beeler could hear.

"Goodness, was that your stomach?"

"Yes. Now about that bone ..."

At Albert's door, Mrs Beeler knocked and called out. After her initial surprise at finding the dog outside and then her annoyance at the pile of poop on her immaculate lawn, her thoughts had turned to worry. Why would Mr Smith shut the dog in the garden and leave him there? It felt wrong and now that she was calling out to him and getting no answer, a rising panic gripped her belly.

The man was all over the news; his exploits so fanciful they were hard to believe, yet she knew they were true. They were calling him a national treasure, not least because simultaneous with catching a crazy member of the royal family in an underground bunker in Wales, the man won a huge pile of money betting on the horses and set up a fund to help those affected.

He was a legend. A legend she now feared had died in the night in her bed and breakfast. What would that do to the online ratings? Suddenly aware how selfishly awful her concerns were, she focused on her guest and called out again.

Thinking she was going to have to go back downstairs to fetch a key, a door behind her opened.

"He's not there," said the professor. He had his phone in his right hand and was partially dressed. "Sorry to interrupt. I could hear you calling for him, but he met with an accident last night."

Fearing the worst, Mrs Beeler's hand flew to her mouth.

"Oh, I don't mean ... I'm sure he's fine. He got a bump on the head, it seems. Some of my students took him to ..." The professor heard his wife cough, the noise conveying a simple message: stop talking. "Sorry, he's in the hospital. We're planning to check on him as soon as visiting hours start at ten o'clock. I see you've been looking after Rex for him."

Looking down at Rex when she suddenly remembered he was there, Mrs Beeler said, "Oh, ah, no. I found him outside actually. You say Mr Smith went to the hospital?"

"That's what I am being told. I have pictures of him being loaded into an ambulance actually. I guess that's evidence enough. Anyway, some of my students were with him and they say he got a bump on the head." What they actually said was they paid for him to have a lap dance and had to deal with the irate stripper who demanded to know why the old man had run away. They suspected he'd had one too many and lost his footing. The professor chose not to share that piece of detail.

Thrown by the news, which was the last thing she expected to hear, Mrs Beeler found herself staring into space as she fiddled with the pearls around her neck; an absentminded habit she'd had for years.

"Mrs Beeler?" The professor thought about waving a hand in front of her glassy eyes.

"What? Oh, sorry. You think Mr Smith will be all right?"

The professor gave a deep, two-shoulder shrug. "That's the advice I have. Like I said, Claudia and I met him last night and we are going to the hospital to make sure he is, in fact, all right."

Claudia, now dressed, came to the door, pulling it wide and sending her husband to finish getting himself ready for the day.

"To my knowledge he is here alone. Except for Rex, that is," she added, throwing a friendly smile at the dog.

Rex wagged his tail in response, still wondering where the bones for picking might be.

Gathering her thoughts and trying to put a positive spin on things, Mrs Beeler hoped a news crew might want to film Albert Smith in Lyme Regis. He had suffered an accident – that had to be newsworthy - but had chosen to convalesce at her guesthouse. They could 'accidentally' show her bed and breakfast on the television. She'd be happy to do an interview. Best not to let Mr Beeler take part though, he had a habit of saying the wrong thing. She could send him to the pub, her brain supplied brightly.

"Right," she clapped her hands together. "Well, I better be getting on with breakfast then. It will be ready when you are."

Left in the corridor when Claudia retreated inside her room and the landlady went about her business, Rex questioned what he was supposed to do next. The bone he thought he was going to pick failed to materialise and unless his nose was very much mistaken, which it rarely was, there were, in fact, no bones to be had.

He had a list of tasks in his head, all of which revolved around finding the killer and biting him. Rex rather hoped the skinny kid on the motorbike would run away so he could play chase.

More immediately pressing was his need to eat. Dinner was many, many hours ago and the crisps he ate in the pub were long forgotten. His breakfast was in the old man's backpack in their room. It might as well have been on Mars for he could not see a way to get through the door.

Praying Mrs Beeler was going to take pity on the poor hungry dog and feed him half a pig's worth of bacon, he angled his paws back toward the staircase and followed his nose.

List of Suspects

Albert woke in the night with a crushing headache of sufficient proportion that he willingly took the nurse's advice to 'Lie back down' and 'Try to get some sleep'. Sleep came, but he woke again some hours later with a dry mouth and a full bladder.

The headache wasn't gone, yet it had subsided to a tolerable level. Shuffling gingerly across the room in bare feet, he used the toilet without turning on the light and kept his eyes mostly closed so light entering them came through a tiny crack covered by his eyelashes.

In his head an unruly queue of questions vied for first place. It became a tie between 'How did I manage to lose Rex again?' and 'Why didn't I listen to my children and just go straight home?'

The latter of the two could be dismissed as pointless, yet there were other questions that needed to be answered. He'd found Karl Fielding's killer. Probably, he decided after a moment of thought. Lying back on the bed with his eyes closed, Albert ran through what he knew.

It didn't take long.

Karl Fielding returned home to Lyme Regis excited to be free and to get back to his girlfriend. Albert had a term for the type of woman she turned out to be. Though he employed it in his head, he didn't see her as Karl's killer. Milo could be. He was aggressive enough and had motive, but he struck Albert as too stupid to devise a plan that would make the death look like a suicide. Milo was all mouth and reputation. He would attack Karl … had, in fact, attacked him, and did so in public so people could see how tough he was.

Albert moved him onto the unlikely list.

It left the skinny kid on the dirt bike as the only player on the field. That didn't necessarily mean he was guilty, but he sure had some questions to answer. Not least of which was the reason behind Albert's attack.

The kid was at the caravan. That established a connection, but until Albert figured out who he was, there was no point jumping to conclusions.

Coming from a different angle, Albert thought about keys. The caravan had a lock on the door and a key in it. Karl's key was hanging on a hook inside, so the question, really, was who else would have a key?

Daniel Fielding for one. The caravan was their dad's so it stood to reason both boys would have access to it. That might not be the case, but it was a logical assumption for now.

Who else?

Albert thought about that for a while and found he came back to Milo Anderson. Milo was living in Karl's house. A spare key wasn't a hard thing to conceive. Albert had a spare of every key for his house and then extras with two of his neighbours 'just in case'.

Mrs Brown might have one. Not that Albert thought Mrs Brown was Karl's killer. Sticking with the idea that Milo at least had access to a key and knew where Karl Fielding might go, Albert moved the tattooed thug back onto the 'possible' list of murderers.

Daisy. The name of Karl's daughter popped into Albert's head like a magician performing a spell that involved a flash of light and a puff of smoke. She might have a key to the caravan and if she didn't, she would almost certainly know where to obtain one. A key to her father's house was a probable too.

Not that he suspected Karl Fielding's daughter. However, he remembered what Troy Macclesfield, the young man working in Fielding's Bakery said about Daisy's boyfriend. Troy held the opinion that her boyfriend was a 'total tool'. It was not a term Albert would have used but he understood what Troy had attempted to convey. Troy also suggested the young man in question wasn't afraid of a little violence and had recently been released from jail.

Albert didn't know his name, but 'Daisy's boyfriend' arrived firmly on the list of suspects. He would be about the right age for the kid on the dirt bike, Albert judged. Daisy was nineteen. The skinny kid on the dirt bike had to be about the same. Did he own a red dirt bike? Albert's memory of the previous evening was fuzzy, something he put down to his head injury because it couldn't possibly be anything to do with the gin he drank. However, he was certain he'd given the vehicle registration number to the police.

Maybe they already had the kid in custody.

"Mr Smith?" a voice called, rudely interrupting Albert's thoughts. He opened his eyes, regretted doing so immediately, and closed them again. The voice was that of the young nurse, a pretty, blonde woman in her thirties. She looked tired to Albert in the way only a nurse can: exhausted and overworked but with sick patients who deserved her best care. "Mr Smith, I'm sorry to disturb you. There are some police officers here to see you."

"Will there be breakfast?" Albert replied, asking a question he considered more pertinent than any the police might have for him.

"Um, yes. It's not coming to your room though. You were considered likely to be well enough to be discharged after the consultant's rounds so your breakfast is in the patients' lounge."

"I am allowed to go there?" Albert cracked his eyes again upon hearing people entering his room.

"No, Mr Smith," said DS Rogers. "You are not."

Bacon!

Rex took to whining pathetically when Mrs Beeler told him to shoo. She couldn't work out what to do with him. The obvious solution was to lock him in Albert's room; she had a key to open the door. But what if he needed to go potty again? Finding something unpleasant on the lawn is one thing. On her carpet was an entirely different matter.

It didn't bear thinking about.

She'd never been one for pets. Her sister had a rabbit when they were kids and the rotten thing peed on her the one time she held it.

"He's hungry," Mr Beeler pointed out, eyes never leaving his paper.

It had not occurred to her that the dog might want to eat.

"Can I give him bacon?"

"Damn skippy you can!" answered Rex.

Mr Beeler shrugged, an invisible movement behind his paper. "Don't see why not. Dogs will eat just about anything, including trash from the gutter."

Mrs Beeler pulled a face.

Rex whined again, really putting some emotion behind it this time.

"Why's he making that noise?" she asked.

Mr Beeler sighed and put down his paper. He'd grown up with dogs and would have dogs now if his wife would let him. Not just *a* dog, but dogs. German Shepherd wasn't on the list, but for no good reason other than there were so many to pick from and he preferred dogs with short hair.

Snagging a piece of bacon from the grill despite his wife's protests, he discovered it to be many degrees hotter than he expected. It was also stuck to the piece next to it and that one was stuck to the piece next to that and so on. Mrs Beeler always grilled bacon that way, cramming it in so she could cook more at once. It had never proven to be a problem in the past.

Flinging the piece of bacon he held, for his nerve endings assured him it had just melted through to the bony tips of his index finger and thumb, Mr Beeler succeeded in launching no less than six pieces of bacon at the dog filling the kitchen doorway.

Like a dolphin rising from the depths, Rex launched himself into the air.

Before Mr Beeler could get his fried digits into his mouth, Rex was inhaling the all-too-hot pig slices.

"Serves you right," frowned Mrs Beeler, bustling to the fridge with an audible, "Tut," to fetch more bacon. With the door open, she peered inside the chiller. "What else should I give him? I've got some leftover lamb here from yesterday's roast."

Still sucking his finger and thumbs, Mr Beeler offered to fix the dog something to eat. Roast lamb and some accompaniments would see him right.

Rex wolfed the lot down in a heartbeat and looked up expectantly for seconds. He wouldn't get them from his own human, but this chap ... well, he looked ready to please. He didn't get more lamb, but a bowl of raw eggs and milk was received with equal gusto.

Hunger and thirst suitably slaked, Rex made his way to the back door to be let out.

"There's a mess out there for you to clean up," Mrs Beeler's voice followed her husband.

"A mess? Why is it for me to clean up?" His grumbling came to naught as he knew it would, but in opening the door and looking around for a bag into which he could scoop the offending matter, he lost sight of the dog. A quick check later, Tony Beeler swore under his breath and trudged back inside to let his wife know Albert Smith's dog had leapt the fence and done a runner.

Accused

Albert believed what his ears were hearing, but at the same time, could not believe it.

"You are questioning me about my involvement in Daniel Fielding's death?"

"You were at Sunny Days Caravan Park last night were you not?"

"Any more rhetorical questions?" Albert sneered. "You know I was because you were there with me."

"Yes," DS Rogers smiled knowingly. "A clever alibi some might say."

Albert shrugged in agreement before saying, "Only if they were both blind and stupid."

His remark wiped the smile from the detective's face.

The body of Karl's brother was found at daybreak by a person out running their dog along the beach. Unlike Karl, whose body was trapped in the rocks and held there when the tide receded, the waves left Daniel's ruined corpse on the beach for all to find.

It sickened Albert to learn both brothers had died in

such a short space of time and a natural need to blame himself for not catching Karl's killer already landed on his back within seconds of hearing the news. What had he missed? Did this rule out Milo Anderson? It certainly appeared to.

DS Rogers clicked his fingers under Albert's nose, earning a scornful glare.

"You haven't answered my question."

"Which one was that? I ask, because honestly, I've a mind to refuse to answer any of them." It occurred to Albert that with one phone call he could have reporters lining up to ask questions. It would make the local police and DS Rogers especially look like absolute fools.

He wasn't going to do that though. Undermining the police, unless he knew they were guilty of something criminal, was not a step he would ever take.

"What were you doing at Sunny Days Caravan Park last night prior to calling for police assistance?"

Albert closed his eyes. Bored, hungry, and becoming increasingly annoyed, he wanted to find his clothes and storm out of the hospital – apparently they had been laundered and pressed while he slept as a special courtesy. Unfortunately, there was a constable positioned on the door to stop him leaving.

"I went there looking for evidence. You already know that. You were there."

"I know that's what you told me."

Albert backtracked to take the conversation in a different direction.

"Yesterday you were convinced Karl Fielding's death was a suicide. Can I assume that is no longer the case?"

DS Rogers chose not to make eye contact when he replied. "That is still being determined, but the medical examiner's preliminary findings suggest the cause of death was a massive blow to the back of the skull. There are tiny fragments of rock embedded in the bone that are consistent with the rock found on the beach."

"However …"

DS Rogers shot his eyes at Albert. "However, the rest of the damage to his body is post-mortem and the estimated time of death does not match that indicated on the smashed watch."

Albert let his head fall back onto the pillow.

"So we have a cleverly staged murder. Was there blood at the caravan?"

DS Rogers nodded his head. Albert felt like making him say it aloud, but there was little to be gained from grasping the upper hand.

"The registration number I gave Constable Pearson last night? Who owns it?"

DS Rogers had been feeling like he was standing on rocky ground with the wily old detective, but finding himself on steadier terrain, shot back, "No one owns it. It was last registered to a Nissan Micra that was deregistered and scrapped two years ago."

Albert pursed his lips.

"It was the same dirt bike I saw at the caravan park."

"Yes, the one being ridden by a tall, skinny youth whose face you conveniently failed to see."

A pulse of anger drove Albert to whack the table over his bed. There was nothing on it, but the sound made DS Rogers look his way. The cop outside craned his neck around to see what was happening.

"There is nothing convenient about it at all, man! Another person is dead, and you waste time here questioning me. Find the kid on the bike."

"A kid that only you have seen, Mr Smith. No one else. I think I know how clever you are. Karl Fielding died when you were still in Wales. But were you really still in Wales? It's only a couple of hours drive from A to B. You could have followed him here, whacked him on the head and ditched his body over the cliff. The best estimate for time of death would give you plenty of time to drive back to your bed and breakfast in Wales before anyone else would be out of their beds to notice you were missing. Then, last night, you killed his brother, performing much the same trick and doing your utmost to create a water-tight alibi. Having gone over the cliff, Daniel Fielding's body would be washed out by the tide, the time of death as murky as his brother's. You call the police, make up a story about a kid on a bike and for good measure have the imaginary suspect whack you on the head."

Albert shook his head in disbelief.

"We found the mark on the wall in the courtyard behind El Mango. You hit your own head against it, didn't you, then lay there waiting. Daniel Fielding died at some point in the night, and you have an alibi for most of it."

Albert waited for the detective sergeant to finish. When sure that he had, Albert looked him slowly up and down.

"They don't often stack stupid that high."

DS Rogers didn't respond with anger as Albert expected he might. In fact, Albert had to tip his hat at the detective's cool demeanour.

DS Rogers sucked on his inner cheek for a moment before beginning the formal arrest. "Albert Smith I am arresting you on suspicion of ..."

"Hold that thought," said a short woman in a grey suit as she entered the room.

DS Rogers jolted, "Ma'am?"

The woman held up a hand, her index finger aloft as she passed the stunned sergeant on her way to Albert's bedside.

"Mr Smith, I'm Detective Superintendent Alice Alverez. Please forgive DS Rogers, he was operating on old information." She left out the feverish analysis and effort that had taken place over the last few hours since she learned they had their sights set on the nation's latest and greatest hero. Wrongly accusing Albert Smith of a double murder when he was all the news channels and talk shows could talk about was going to get someone fired. They needed to be sure. And they were not.

"But Ma'am he's the only one with a connection to the victims. You agreed yourself ..."

"That's enough now, thank you detective sergeant," the superintendent advised in a tone that suggested shutting up was a very good policy and one to which he should adhere.

DS Rogers closed his mouth and waited.

"I wish to take this opportunity to thank you for your cooperation, Mr Smith, and to beg you to step back from the investigation now. I recognise you are clearly talented in getting to the bottom of such mysteries, but must insist this enquiry now be handled by those of us employed and equipped to do it."

Albert wasn't going to argue. He wasn't even going to beg that she find someone with more braincells than DS Rogers to front the case – a double murder twenty four hours apart would have half the police in the town actively engaged. Ultimately, he didn't get to say anything.

"Hello, everyone. Good morning, Albert," hallooed the professor as he barrelled into the room. He wasn't moving fast or speaking at a loud volume, he simply had an abundance of ... presence. He barrelled everywhere like a force of nature even when he was trying to be unobtrusive. His wife called him her 'Thunder Hippo' when they were alone.

Everyone in the room turned to look his way.

The professor looked at Albert's visitors, sized them up as police and not as he first assumed, doctors.

"You're here to tell him about Rex?" the professor guessed.

Albert's brow furrowed. "What about Rex? Where's my dog? What happened to him last night?"

DS Rogers knew he wasn't to blame; he was at home watching a US cop show when Pearson and Massie were losing the old man's dog. Those American cops had it so good. Always armed, always shooting people and getting into car chases. He never got to do anythi …"

"Rogers!" Superintendent Alverez barked, raising her voice as the man failed to respond the first two times.

"Ma'am?"

"What's the latest on Mr Smith's dog?"

Albert was already half out of bed, his feet dangling above the cold tile.

"Pass me that pile of clothing, please?" he pointed for the professor to fetch his clothes. They were neatly folded and placed on a chair in the corner of the room. His shoes, which looked to have been buffed, were underneath.

Placed on the spot, DS Rogers had to think quickly. "The dog? Um, so far as I know there have been no sightings since last night." He stopped talking again when his boss's eyes flared in threat.

Albert growled, "Unbelievable," but looked up when the professor started talking.

"I saw him at the bed and breakfast this morning. That was …" he shot his cuff to check the time, "ninety minutes ago, I guess. He was looking for you." he nodded his head at Albert.

"For me? Hold on, where are you staying?"

"Beach View Guesthouse. We checked in yesterday evening. There's a whole bunch of us staying there. It was all a bit last minute."

Albert didn't bother to comment; he was too busy putting his trousers on underneath his hospital gown. When he checked in yesterday lunchtime, he was the only guest in the place. Now it was full?

"You're going to tell me Rex is no longer at the bed and breakfast, aren't you?" Albert guessed.

"Yeah, sorry. We ... that's Claudia and I, were just getting ready for the day when we heard Mrs Beeler trying to get into your room. Apparently, Mr Beeler fed him some breakfast from the kitchen and Rex asked to go out. When Mr Beeler opened the door, your dog leapt the fence and kept going."

Showing concern she didn't really feel she had time for, but knowing it was right that she give support, Detective Superintendent Alverez asked, "Do you have any idea where he might have gone, Mr Smith? I can send units to look for him, but it would help if we can narrow down the range of their search."

Albert stuffed his left foot into a sock. "If I know Rex, and believe me I do, he'll be sniffing around trying to solve your double murder."

Rogers and Alverez exchanged a silent glance and the constable outside the door, who heard every word, craned his neck again to see if the old man was being serious.

Enter the Cat

The belly full of breakfast gave Rex a much-needed boost of energy. His human was yet to return, a fact that made him unhappy. Rather than dwell on it, he was going to do what he believed the old man would wish he could: solve the murder.

Rex had no idea a second death had occurred during the night, but would find out soon enough. In the meantime, he had enough clues to be getting along with.

His first stop was Fielding's Bakery where he hoped to get inside. They wouldn't welcome him, not without his human at his side, but Rex wasn't of a mind to ask permission or give opportunity for comment. He needed to get close enough to Karl Fielding's brother – Rex could smell the sibling connection yesterday – to be able to discern the tiny nuances between his smell and any others. The cinnamon-laced blend he found in the caravan required deep analysis.

Powerful though his nose was, Rex was zeroing in on infinitesimal details. How much cinnamon, the ratio of cinnamon to allspice et cetera. The skinny kid left his scent in the courtyard behind the strip club and the bike was there. It was enough evidence that Rex placed the kid in pole position on his suspect list. Truthfully, the kid was the only suspect, but Rex was keeping an open mind.

He didn't want to bite the wrong person.

However, arriving at Fielding's Bakery, Rex encountered a scene he'd not anticipated: It was crawling with police.

Three cars were parked half on half off the pavement directly in front of the bakery's windows. Two were squad cars, silver with yellow and blue police livery. The third was an unmarked pool car being driven by a young, keen, and newly qualified detective constable. Judy Marsh's advancement to the criminal investigation division was a matter of barely contained pride and she had to keep her mouth shut around her former colleagues in uniform lest she become insufferable.

DC Judy Marsh saw the dog looking into the bakery from across the road. She blinked twice, a bell ringing urgently in the back of her head. Something about the dog struck a chord.

"That's Albert Smith's dog!" she blurted, abandoning the grilling of Troy Macclesfield to run toward the door.

Rex saw her coming. He didn't know she only wanted to help. The incident at the strip club and the very presence of Albert Smith, a man all over the news, had gone around the station like a wildfire on a dry prairie. Everyone was asked to be on the lookout for the dog. Albert Smith was wanted for questioning in connection with the two recent deaths, but Judy knew that was being taken care of.

Right now she just wanted a few points for being the one to secure the old man's dog.

Rex backed away, unsure what his next step should be.

To investigate the murder and track down the kid on the dirt bike, he had a few options to explore, but the bakery was his best starting place.

He barked at the woman leaving the bakery, "I just want to sample the scents inside. Can I do that? Or are you all going to get excited because I don't have a human with me?" Thinking the daft bipeds should take the day off and let him figure things out, Rex huffed an annoyed breath when he saw two cops in uniform coming his way. They were already in the street and being directed by the woman leaving the bakery.

Able to see the inevitable consequence of hanging around, Rex pivoted off his back legs and ran. The humans shouted and whistled, begging him to stop, but Rex was on a mission and had a new destination in mind.

He pushed his speed to something close to maximum for a few seconds. It put distance between him and the police. Once content he was out of sight, he turned hard left to leave the seafront. Lyme Regis, like many British coastal towns, is a maze of backstreets and alleyways. Rivers run down through it to the sea carving channels two yards below the level of the roads and streets. Rex ran alongside one such waterway, his tongue lolling from one side of his mouth. At a flat, pedestrian bridge, he crossed to the other side and continued onward, climbing away from the ocean before looping back around to arrive at Tailspin's pub.

The indirect route wouldn't fool a dog, of course; his scent could be followed like a neon sign. Humans wouldn't have a clue where he went though and that was the point.

Arriving at Tailspin's garden, Rex stood on his back legs to check his landing, then jumped onto and over the wall much as he had the previous evening.

"Whoa there!" cried Tailspin, startled by the German

Shepherd's sudden appearance. "I said tonight, remember? We meet tonight when the moon crests the cliffs. We can't go yet, there's too many humans around."

Patiently, Rex asked, "Do you not remember our conversation last night? I told you I had a murder to investigate and that my human had been attacked, very possibly by the killer. You agreed to help me, but insisted we couldn't do anything until after breakfast. It's after breakfast."

Tailspin gawped for a moment, his eyes pointing upward into his skull, his memory failing to supply the information Rex claimed should be there.

"Nope, not ringing any bells. This was last night, you say?"

"Yes. The moon was high, your human was waiting for you to go back inside so he could get to bed."

The Basset Hound shrugged, aware that his memory went patchy when he'd had a few. The bar was busy the previous evening, he remembered that much. The busier the better because there were always unattended drinks he could snaffle, and greater numbers hid his activities more effectively.

"Okay, so what do you need me to do?"

Relieved, for he was half expecting the Basset Hound to opt for a return to bed, Rex said, "I need to track down a scent."

Tailspin raised an eyebrow. "Can you take me to it?"

"I doubt I'll have to. You're familiar with the bakery on the seafront?"

"The one next to the fish and chip shop?"

"That's it. It has a distinctive scent …"

"Cinnamon, allspice, nutmeg and the like, right? Strong enough to make you sneeze."

Pleased, Rex said, "Precisely. I encountered the same

scent when I went to the murder victim's caravan last night. There was a young male human there. He gave me the slip; jumped on a motorbike and shot off. The thing is the victim worked at the bakery so finding his scent in the caravan made sense."

Tailspin, not normally given to taking interest in anything that wasn't going to get him something to eat or something to drink and preferably both, was unable to deny the intrigue he felt.

"He took the scent of the bakery with him. That makes sense. It's a powerful odour. Would be hard to shift."

Rex agreed. "That's right. It would be on his clothing and in his hair. But here's the thing: the young male human I chased had the same smell. Almost."

"Almost?"

"Yeah. I didn't notice it until later when I found his scent again. It was on my human – he attacked him when we got separated." Rex found his jaw muscles tighten as he said the words. It was his job to protect the old man and Albert's injury did not sit well. "His motorbike was there too; I caught that smell first. The cinnamon smell, though, it was the same, but not quite. Trying to figure it out is making my tail twitch."

Tailspin accepted that Rex had his scents correctly identified without question. To a dog the smell of a human was as individual as a fingerprint only no equipment was needed, the scents stood out like neon signs.

"In what way was it different?"

Rex sat his backend down and twisted to get his back right paw up to scratch at his ear.

"The balance of spices," he concluded after giving it some more thought. "The victim's caravan smelled just like the bakery only less so, obviously. The kid I chased ... it was

... it was less cinnamon and more nutmeg for a start, but all the comparable strengths were different. Not by much ..."

"But by enough to notice."

"Who's this?" asked a voice from behind Rex.

Rex shot his head around, his top lip peeling back before his eyes located the owner of the voice. It was a cat. A rotund, grey Burmese cat with sky blue eyes.

"What do you want, cat?" Rex was poised to repel it, but the territory was not his to defend.

Tailspin waddled across to get in his way.

"Come on down, Penelope, this chap won't hurt you. Will you, Rex?"

Rex cocked an eyebrow. He'd worked with precisely one cat in his life and couldn't claim it had been a pleasant experience. He considered the species on a whole to be entirely self-centred and utterly untrustworthy.

"You know this cat?"

Penelope jumped down from the garden wall to take up a position on the lawn a few feet from Rex where she nonchalantly extended all the claws of her front left forepaw to inspect them like a warrior checking the edge of his sword before battle.

"This cat has a name," she remarked, her eyes never leaving the wicked looking sickles.

Tailspin grumbled, "It's too early in the day for people to be getting argumentative. I have a hangover that would kill a chihuahua, so if you want my help, Rex, it comes with a couple of extras. Penelope is one of them."

It wasn't worth arguing over, so Rex dipped his head at the cat.

"Pleased to meet you."

Penelope turned her head to meet his gaze. "Yes, I'm sure you are."

"Don't be such a cat, Penelope," mumbled Tailspin on his way to the garden gate. "If you would be so kind ..."

Rex's eyebrows performed a little dance. "We're leaving?"

Tailspin waited with his head pointing at the garden gate. "Not going to find your killer here."

The cat proved to be more athletic than its figure suggested, leaping lithely back onto the garden wall to then pad along to the gate. Leaning over, Penelope patted at the locking mechanism – a simple flip up hook holding a bar in place – until it popped free and swung open.

"Come along then, pup," chuckled the Basset Hound, trotting through the portal and turning right. "Let's see if I can't find your smell that's just like Fielding's Bakery only not quite." He was already out of sight behind the garden wall and Rex had to hurry to catch up.

The cat was coming too it seemed, the grey Burmese trotting along the line of garden walls until they reached the end of the street where she jumped down to talk at Tailspin's side.

"Should we stop for Reggie?" she asked.

Source of the Smell

Reggie turned out to be a Pomeranian. He'd moved into a house around the corner a few months ago and his owner hadn't gotten around to removing the cat flap in the back door yet. Consequently, he came and went as he pleased. He was another member of Tailspin's dinosaur bone raiding party set to get all they could from the museum tonight.

Reggie wasn't the only dog they collected along the way. Bruno the Dalmatian lived just three doors down. He was in the garden and saw the procession of pets going by. Penelope let him out too. Next was a one-eyed homeless cat who occupied an alleyway. He was twice the size of Penelope and looked to Rex as though someone had dipped him in muscle enhancer – his skin bulged and flexed when he moved. Missing half an ear and half his tail, Arthur the alley cat did not come across as someone Rex wanted to mess with.

"Where are we going?" Rex asked, wanting something

to say because Arthur kept giving him side eye with his missing eye and it was creeping him out.

Tailspin chuckled, "I told you. We're going to where we will find your almost like Fielding's Bakery smell."

Seeing no better option, Rex closed his mouth and carried on walking. It wasn't long before his nose caught the scent. His pupils dilated, a wave of excitement catching his breath. It was the same scent he encountered at the caravan and again in the courtyard behind the strip club: the same as Fielding's ... almost.

Wait though. It was just the cinnamon and allspice, the nutmeg and other flavours that ought to be playing background to the kid's smell. Where was the smell of the human? And why was the air filled with so many other incredible odours? He could smell bread and cakes, biscuits, pasties, pastry, sausage ... it was a long list, and it made his stomach tighten with the need to eat.

Squinting his eyes, Rex searched for any sign of the young human male, and lifted his nose to test the air for the motorbike. Neither were present.

He stopped when he heard Tailspin chuckling.

"You're wondering where the human is, right?"

Rather than answer, Rex said, "Where is the smell coming from? It's everywhere."

Reggie the Pomeranian sneered, "Something wrong with your nose? That's Greg's factory right there in front of you."

Bruno stared wistfully into the distance. "Sometimes I come here just to close my eyes and breathe in the air. It's the best spot in town."

At the end of the street was a large brick building. It looked new, which is to say no more than a few years old.

"I was just a pup when they built this place," reminisced Tailspin, the eldest in their pack.

Rex had to force his brain to focus on the investigation. Pushing food thoughts aside, he asked, "How many people work there?"

"Humans?" Tailspin confirmed. "Lots. More than I can fit in the pub for sure."

Rex gritted his teeth. He wanted to find the one person, the kid on the motorbike. He now knew where the smell came from, which could be considered progress, but it helped him not one bit. The detail of it didn't matter, the point was that Fielding's had a cinnamon-based product they baked which had a very distinct smell. It dominated the other smells and stood out to a canine nose. The factory to his front had a similar product. So similar in fact that even a dog could miss the subtle differences unless they were concentrating.

Someone from the factory left their scent in the caravan and then in the courtyard. Moving ahead of the pack, Rex continued toward the factory gates.

Tailspin called out, "Hey, where're you going?" He'd set off to show the German Shepherd the factory because a walk always helped with his hangovers and because he wanted to assemble the pack before the planned raid at moonrise. Seeing the factory was supposed to be the end of it. Now Rex was heading straight for the gates.

Without looking back, Rex said, "I'm going in to look for the bike. I could do with a distraction."

Honest Intentions

Albert refused to be rude to the nurses who were only doing their jobs in trying to keep him from leaving. They wanted him to wait for the consultant who would be doing his rounds shortly. That they would not commit to a time when that was likely to take place was enough to convince him to leave. They couldn't even state if it would be before or after lunch.

Apologising profusely, Albert insisted he had to go. He was dressed, the small wound on his head had been closed and covered, and he felt no ill effects from the blow the skinny kid landed, nor from striking his head against the wall.

The police were keeping quiet. Well, DS Rogers and the constable outside the door were. Detective Superintendent Alverez less so.

"I wish to know your intentions, Mr Smith. While I know I speak for everyone present when I admire the tenacity you demonstrated in apprehending Earl Bacon, I must warn against interfering in my investigation here."

Albert wasn't of a mind to listen, but being tailed through the hospital like a rock star with an entourage, he offered, "I'm a private citizen, Superintendent. I can go where I please so long as I don't trespass. I need to find my dog and who can say where that will lead me." The truth was that Albert had not the slightest intention of playing ball. To his mind the police in Lyme Regis had treated him unfairly since he first encountered them. DS Rogers had a mouth on him and to suggest he might be behind the murders ... well, he planned to find out who was just so he could rub their noses in it.

Besides, he really did have to find Rex and he wasn't entirely joking when he claimed his dog would be trying to solve the case. It had taken him a while to notice his dog's odd behaviour, but there was no doubt in Albert's mind that Rex was one in a million.

He was a former police dog, a job from which he was fired. Until that very moment, it had not occurred to Albert to find out why Rex got booted from the Metropolitan Police. However, Albert suspected he could guess the answer: he made them look bad.

Superintendent Alverez hurried forward to get the exit door, but instead of opening it as Albert expected, she held it shut, effectively trapping him.

"I must caution you to steer clear of the investigation into the deaths of Karl and Daniel Fielding, Mr Smith. I will not permit you to jeopardise the chain of evidence or to tip off anyone we may wish to question. Can I have your word that you will collect your dog, continue your planned vacation activities, and be on your way when you are done?"

Albert thought about lying directly to her face. He was

just about mad enough to do so. It wasn't in his character though, so he opted for the honest answer instead.

"No, you cannot. In fact, unless you arrest me, I'm going to find my dog and do everything in my power to bring the killer to justice. Are you going to arrest me?" It was a direct challenge. A line in the sand. Despite what the papers had to say, he was not a gambling man. Their opinion was based on his million to one win on the horses, a feat he could never repeat even if he tried.

Nevertheless, Albert felt safe in throwing down the gauntlet. He was yet to do anything wrong and threatening to interfere with an investigation was not the same as doing so.

Superintendent Alverez narrowed her eyes. Having her authority challenged was a rare thing. Ultimately, there was only one thing she could do.

"Sergeant Rogers. Watch Mr Smith like a hawk, please. I do not want him near my investigation."

A sound much akin to a teenager being asked to clean up their own mess escaped DS Rogers' lips before he realised he was doing it. A swift, "Yes, Ma'am," followed though it was obvious from the man's expression he was anything but happy.

The crackle of a radio interrupted anyone saying anything further and the voice of Detective Constable Judy Marsh came over the air. She reported the probable sighting of Rex outside Fielding's Bakery and that the dog had eluded her and other officers when she attempted to catch him.

Albert tipped his head at Alverez.

"See? He's using his nose to solve the case. He'll find the killer before any of us can." It was a happy statement delivered with a chuckle, but Albert was anything but pleased.

His dog was still loose in Lyme Regis – a place with traffic and other dangerous hazards.

The professor, still with the group having followed them down from Albert's room, volunteered his services.

"I can get you there, Albert." He whipped out a set of keys. "I'll call some of my students back from the dig too; they can help to look for Rex since it's largely their fault he's out there alone."

Pushing past Superintendent Alverez to get outside, Albert thought about his dog. This was far from the first time he'd lost Rex in a strange place. Usually, by the time he found him again, Rex had found friends.

Death to all Humans

"I'm too old to be running around getting into trouble. I don't move as fast as I used to, and I was hardly a bullet in my youth."

Rex looked at the Basset Hound. His ears drooped almost to the ground when he stood, forcing the dog to hold his head up all the time. When he lowered his nose to sniff, Tailspin had to stop walking or risk treading on his ears. His legs were stumpy, a bit like a dachshund's, but where a sausage dog could move surprisingly fast and corner on a penny, a Basset Hound could only lumber. Lumbering was top speed for that matter.

Rex didn't need Tailspin though because all the others were willing volunteers. Overly enthusiastic volunteers.

"It's been a while since I killed a human," growled Arthur, the alley cat. "Which ones do you want me to neutralise?"

Rex said, "What? I don't want you to kill anyone!"

Bruno's eyes were so wide Rex worried his eyeballs might fall from the sockets.

"I'm not killing anyone. Killing humans definitely falls into the 'bad dog' category."

"No one said anything about killing anyone," Rex pointed out.

"The cat did," argued Reggie, squeaking with excitement. "I've never bitten a human. What do they taste like?"

Arthur cricked his neck to one side and then the other, his vertebrae popping audibly.

"Like broken promises and missed opportunities."

The dogs took a second to consider Arthur's description.

"Is it anything like chicken?" questioned Bruno.

Penelope was clearly in love with the alley cat and ready to follow his plan over Rex's.

Arthur puffed out his chest and squinted his one good eye at each of the dogs in turn. "I say we kill the guard at the gate and keep killing until there is no one left to fight. We can turn this place into a bloodbath."

"I hate baths," said Bruno, missing the point entirely.

Rex might have face palmed if he were a human.

"No, listen, please. No one needs to hurt anyone. I just need a distraction. I want to look around the carpark, that's all. If the red motorbike is here, then the human I saw on it will be too. If it's not, then there is no point hanging around and we can extend our search radius. However, if I go through the gate, the guard will see me, and the humans will come to shoo me out again. I won't need long to look for the motorbike. Just a couple of minutes."

"So you want us to create a distraction," said Reggie, finally understanding.

"Killing the guard will do that, no?" questioned Arthur, murder never far from his thoughts. Cats get like that when they are abandoned by their owners. In his case, the people he lived with moved away and decided to not bother taking him. He almost starved to death, but in surviving he got tough. And mean. Really mean. Now, when a human looked at him in a way he didn't like, they lost some flesh.

Rex closed his eyes and was about to reiterate the point about letting the guard live when he heard the man at the gate cry out in alarm and start swearing.

While they had all been arguing over Rex's thoroughly simple plan, none of them noticed Tailspin wander off. Spinning around to look out from their hiding place behind a car, they found the Basset Hound with one back leg in the air and a horrified security guard dancing away from the stream of yellow liquid.

Guffawing now and struggling to breathe in his amusement, Tailspin dropped his leg and started running.

The guard's left trouser leg had a definite mark up one side and he was mad about it.

Launching obscenities at the Basset Hound, he left his post unattended to chase Tailspin down the road.

Just like that, the gate to the factory was unguarded and Rex could just walk in.

Penelope chose to run interference for Tailspin; she didn't want the guard to catch up to him and swing a boot. Arthur went with her. The rest followed Rex across the road, through the gate, and into the carpark beyond.

There were more than a hundred cars, Rex judged. Not that he could count that high. Like most dogs he knew numbers well enough to count his ration of bedtime biscuits and know if he'd been short changed. Otherwise, he counted one, two, some, many, lots. It was good enough for almost every situation.

"There's probably a separate place where all the motorbikes are parked," he said, setting off at a jog. Bruno, svelte, sinewy, and lithe, shot off ahead at a speed Rex couldn't match, but Reggie, his legs a blur beneath his fluffy body, stayed by Rex's side.

"What will you do if the motorbike is here?" Reggie enquired.

Rex knew the answer without having to think.

Eyes narrowed, he said, "I will find his scent and track him down. It won't matter if he's in the factory, I will find him."

Impressed and a little in awe, Reggie asked another question. "What then?"

"I'll bite him."

Reggie's mouth dropped open. That was right up there on the high end of the 'bad dog' scale of things you were not allowed to do.

"Won't you get in trouble? I heard they make dogs go to sleep forever if they bite humans." He was scared enough that a little trail of liquid followed him for the next yard.

"He won't be the first one I've bitten." Sensing his statement might be a little misleading, Rex added, "It's important to only bite criminals. If I'm right and the human on the motorbike is the killer, biting him will bring the police and hopefully *my* human. They will figure out the details and it will all be okay."

Reggie gasped, "Wow."

Meanwhile, Bruno, his brain wired like a hamster in an electrified running wheel much like any Dalmatian, bounded back into sight.

"The motorbikes are at the end, but there isn't a red one among them."

Cursing aloud, Rex continued onward to see for himself. Not that he doubted Bruno, but he wouldn't be the first colourblind dog Rex had ever encountered. Thirty seconds later he was cursing again. Bruno was right; there were motorbikes, but none of them were red and none of them smelled right.

His attempt to get a good sniff around at Fielding's Bakery had achieved nothing and now his quest to find the kid and motorbike was a failure too. Was it worth exploring the factory anyway? Maybe the kid owned a car as well and had come to work in that today?

Before Rex could consider his latest thought, a shout rang out. The three dogs turned to find two men in the security guard uniforms running their way.

Reggie cried, "Oh, no! We're bad dogs!"

"Only if we get caught!" Rex's bark jolted the other dogs into motion, a scramble of paws on tarmac the only sound as all three went from stationary to full sprint in a heartbeat. In the direction of the gate — the way they needed to go if they wanted to leave the factory compound — the original security guard was staggering back to his post. One leg of his trousers was torn to shreds making it look like he'd lost a fight with a shark, and there was blood on the left side of his face.

Rex thought to himself, '*At least he's not dead. That would take some explaining.*'

The guards did their best to block the way but there was too much space to cover, and the dogs were entirely too nimble and fast.

Reggie squealed the whole way, a continual, "Eeeeeeeeeee," sound that set Rex's teeth on edge. The guard on the right managed to touch Bruno when he shot by but that was as close as either man came.

The guard at the gate, slumped in his little box by the barrier, cared not which direction the dogs went. His colleagues were shouting for him to close the gate, a big electronic sliding contraption that would seal the dogs inside, but he made no move to do so.

He'd just been peed on and lost a fight to the biggest tom cat he'd ever seen. It had been like fighting six tiny ninjas all armed with multiple knives. He shuddered at the memory of it running up his back to land on his head where the cat from hell tried to burrow through his skull.

He needed to find a mirror and was on his way back into the factory to find one when he'd paused for a breather at the gate. Now there were three more dogs heading his way and the only thing he was going to do was hide.

Rex had his head down to streamline himself for maximum speed. The tiny Pomeranian kept pace despite his two-inch-long twig like legs and with Bruno going slow so they would all hit the exit together, they got to watch as their one remaining obstacle climbed up and onto the roof of his own guard hut.

Laughing to himself, Rex leaned into the turn, shooting under the red and white barrier at what felt like the speed of sound.

Then his heart stopped.

Angling into the factory gate, a large silver Mercedes was going to run them all over and there was nothing the dogs could do to get themselves out of the way.

Babysitting

The professor of palaeontology drove a tricked out blue pickup truck, its load bed stuffed with equipment. He drove sedately, right hand on the wheel, right elbow resting on the door and left hand atop the gearstick.

His wife, Claudia, had just been on the phone, confirming six of his students were leaving the dig site to meet their professor and Albert in town. They were all volunteers - their youthfulness notwithstanding, they regretted their poor decisions the previous evening and were looking to make amends.

The professor found a slot in a carpark on the western edge of the town centre not far from Fielding's Bakery. Albert wondered what would become of it now the brothers were gone. It seemed like a tragedy for it to close. What about their famous dish, the Dorset Knob? What would become of that? Did Troy know the recipe? Albert knew from his recent travels the lengths some would go to protect what made their special thing special.

DS Rogers was waiting for them when they exited the

professor's car. He'd tailed them from the hospital and though he wasn't happy about it, planned to stick to them like glue for the rest of the day.

The bakery was surrounded by and filled with cops – a double murder will do that. No one was buying the suicide theory now that forensics had turned up blood splatter at the caravan. Karl had been killed there and carried to the cliff: that was the new theory. It pained DS Rogers more than a little that Albert Smith had been able to call it right from the get go. It was one of the things that continued to make him suspicious.

Aiming for the bakery's front door, Albert's hand stopped in mid-air when DS Rogers nosily cleared his throat.

"Yes, Detective Sergeant?"

"You have no business in the bakery, Mr Smith," Roger stated firmly. "You are looking for your dog, are you not? I can assure you he is not to be found inside."

The professor, not one for holding back, voiced his opinion, "The dog was last spotted here, man! Surely Mr Smith is to be permitted to ask them which direction the animal went."

Albert wasn't sure about having his latest companion speak for him, but on this occasion the rebuke was better coming from someone else. Choosing to leave the ball in DS Rogers' court, he pushed through the bakery door.

"I'm looking for a Detective Marsh," he announced before his lead foot met the floorboards. When a young woman in a sharp suit looked up, he angled toward her.

Albert remembered the suits and how they said so much about the individual wearing them. The young and super-keen always wore the best ones. For them it was an indicator to everyone around that they were going places. A decade later some would still be wearing the same suit. Passed over for promotion, or simply discovering they did not have the aptitude or temperament for the job, their suits would be out of fashion, faded, and quite possibly have patches on the elbows.

In many ways Albert knew those were the better detectives. They relied on actual police work and solving crimes – doing the work. The ones still wearing the sharp suits were in it for promotion and trying to impress the tiers above them, who, quite incidentally, were also wearing good suits.

Albert found a way to combine both things in his career, but his reluctance to fully embrace the need to look good over being good stopped his promotion at superintendent. It wasn't something that preyed on his conscience.

The professor tucked himself out of the way by the door where he waited, not part of proceedings. DS Rogers did likewise, watching Albert with scrutiny.

Albert held out his hand to the young detective.

"Albert Smith," she gushed, genuinely a little in awe: the man was famous. "How can I help you?"

Albert checked over his shoulder to confirm DS Rogers was there and listening. He wasn't to involve himself in the investigation. Well, fine, he could figure it out without getting details from the police.

"I just wanted to ask about my dog. I understand you saw Rex earlier."

"Yes, that's right."

"Can I ask what he was doing?"

Judy Marsh's eyebrows did a little dance on her forehead.

"Um, he was outside in the street looking at the shop."

"That's all?" asked Albert while thinking, '*Rex came to the bakery. He wasn't looking for me, he was looking for a clue.'* "He didn't get inside?"

"Oh, goodness, no. I wouldn't have let him inside. With two deaths in two days my boss says we have to be extra thorough. It looks like suicide, but we need to be sure. The last thing I need is a dog in here contaminating the scene."

Albert had to force his facial muscles to resist smiling. He had not asked a single question about the crime, but was finding out plenty.

"Was he killed here then?" Albert chose to fire a direct question to see what DS Rogers would do. No reaction came.

Marsh sucked on her lip, unsure how to answer, but went with, "No, because it looks like he committed suicide by jumping off the cliffs."

Nodding to show he understood, Albert asked, "Has anyone at Daniel's house seen my dog, do you know?"

"I can certainly check. I think they are still there." Marsh volunteered, plucking a radio from the waistline of her trousers. In so doing she confirmed Daniel hadn't been killed at his house either. Had that been the case, the police would not be finished there yet.

Albert waited patiently while Marsh spoke to someone, using the time to look around the bakery's main room. There were no cakes or biscuits on offer today, no bread or buns and definitely no Dorset Knobs. The bakery had a background smell to it, cinnamon for sure and some other things Albert couldn't quite discern. Nutmeg maybe. But the scent was old now, dissipated and faded like old news.

Marsh dropped her arm to her side, the radio conversation finished.

"I'm afraid he hasn't been seen there either, Mr Smith."

Albert pursed his lips and nodded, his eyes still roving the shop.

"Can I ask, did Troy Macclesfield come to work this morning?"

"Yes. As you might imagine," Marsh volunteered yet more information, "I had to take him to one side to break the news and then have a constable escort him home." Marsh was especially proud to be able to assign tasks to uniformed constables. She didn't outrank them, but that was how it worked. It was as if the suit gave her an edge over her equals. This was an investigation and that meant she was in charge until someone senior turned up.

Okay, so DS Rogers was here, but he wasn't attempting to usurp her command. In fact, he looked like he was babysitting Albert Smith. With a start she kept to herself, Judy Marsh realised one of her bosses, Alverez probably, must have recruited the famous sleuth to help them.

All of a sudden, she wanted to ditch what she was doing and help him. The old man would solve the case in a flash, and she could learn something that might give her an edge.

"Sarge, have you got a second?" she flashed DS Rogers a smile.

Huffing a bored sigh, Rogers levered himself away from the doorframe.

Following Marsh to a back corner, he listened.

"I was wondering, Sarge … hoping I guess, actually, that you might fancy swapping. I could escort Mr Smith …"

"Yes."

"And … sorry, did you just say 'Yes'?"

"Yes. He's yours. I'll take over here. Help him find his dog. Don't let him interfere with the investigation. Have you got that?"

Marsh nodded her head, but she hadn't been listening.

Not really. She heard DS Rogers agree to handover the job of helping Albert Smith and her brain filled in everything else. She started to move, but DS Rogers snagged her elbow and held it tight in his hand.

"If you run into Alverez, you tell her you were out of your depth here and needed me. You are babysitting the old geezer, but only for a short while. Got it?"

Puzzled, Marsh nevertheless agreed. "I'll tell Alverez I needed you to take over. Okay." She wasn't going to do any such thing, not a chance. She was a strong woman on her way up. Tell someone like Alverez, a woman who already made it, that she was a frightened girl who couldn't cut it, and that would be career over. Doubting she would run into Alverez anyway, she pulled her arm free and tried not to skip when she crossed the room.

Albert saw Marsh grab her coat and had a quizzical eyebrow hitched by the time she arrived at the door. He shot one glance at DS Rogers who was swift to look away. Recognising what was happening, Albert took the gift and went out the door. Losing DS Rogers as a chaperone was a monkey off his back, but he soon found out getting Marsh instead was better than he could have imagined.

"So, what's your next move, Mr Smith?" asked Marsh. "Do you already have a theory about the killer's identity?"

Quickly changing what he was planning to say, Albert led with, "Not as yet. I need to find Rex. That is my priority. However, since we are discussing the deaths of Karl and Daniel Fielding, I suggest we need to look at who stood to gain."

The professor scrunched his face in disgust, "Who stood to gain? That's awful. You think someone will profit from their deaths?"

Detective Constable Marsh stayed quiet, interested to

hear what Albert Smith had to say. No one had ever boiled it all down so simply.

Albert was about to reply when he saw some of the professor's students coming their way.

"These are yours?" he asked, nodding his head to make the professor look.

The students arrived and were duly dispatched to look for Rex after they gave their professor a jolly good listening to. He was less than pleased to hear of their antics the previous evening. Well intended or otherwise, it led to Albert's injury and visit to hospital.

While they scattered in pairs to scour the town, Albert pulled out his phone and fiddled with it, entering an address he'd memorised: Brookes Lane. There he hoped to find Daisy Fielding, but he wanted to speak to a different person first.

"I need to speak with Troy Macclesfield," he aimed his statement at Marsh. "Is his house within easy walking distance?" Quite deliberate in his wording, Albert wasn't asking permission to go there.

The question caught Marsh by surprise, but she recovered quickly, raising her radio to ask a question and getting an answer almost immediately from dispatch.

"It's half a mile from here," she indicated the direction they needed to go. "Now, Mr Smith ..."

"Albert, please."

"Albert," Marsh smiled. Twisting as she walked to face Albert's companion, a tall, muscular, handsome man in his late thirties, she asked with a frown, "Did I hear those kids call you professor?"

"Yes. They're my third year palaeontology students. We are here for a dig. A section of the cliffs collapsed two days ago, uncovering a section of strata hidden beneath the ground for 135 million years."

"Gosh," said Marsh, unsure what else might form an acceptable response. "You don't look much like a professor." Her statement was worded carefully, or so she thought when the words were still in her mouth. In truth the man was such a hunk it made her worry she might be dribbling.

She blushed bright red though the professor was kind enough not to stare at her. Instead, he laughed, a hearty bold laugh that did nothing to help her infatuation. Even his laugh was manly.

"You know, I hear that all the time. I think it's probably a compliment."

Scrambling her brain and yelling at it to think of something semi sensible to say, she fumbled and mumbled until she remembered what she was trying to ask Albert.

"Albert, sorry," she gabbled, "I lost my train of thought there for a moment. You were saying about there being someone who would gain from the Fielding brothers' deaths."

Albert nodded and sucked on his teeth for a moment.

"The most common reasons behind a murder are ..."

"Money and sex," replied Marsh without needing to think. "Not necessarily in that order. And one could say love instead of sex. It's the act of betrayal of love that most often leads to murder. They used to call it crimes of passion, but that was just window dressing to make it sound less awful than it is."

"Exactly. Karl Fielding recently got kicked out of his home. You'll already know this, of course."

"Yes," agreed Marsh.

"Has Milo Anderson been quizzed regarding his whereabouts?"

"I believe he was picked up by DS Rogers last night in connection with Karl Fielding's death, but he was still in custody when Daniel Fielding died. I know Superintendent Alverez favours a verdict of suicide in Daniel Fielding's case. The coroner's report will confirm it soon enough, I guess."

"It was murder," stated Albert, inviting no discussion. "Both men were killed by someone clever. Someone with something to gain from their deaths. Someone with access to a key to their caravan at Sunny Days Caravan Park and knowledge of where and how to find them."

The professor had been holding onto a question for more than a minute.

"But who could possibly gain from their deaths?"

"They were successful bakers," Albert pointed out. "That might not seem like much to some, but that's the thing that ties them together. We need to dig into their past *and* into their current affairs to see if there is anything else. Were they in debt …"

Albert was throwing ideas into a hat and wasn't expecting Marsh to supply answers.

"No, they were doing really well. Neither had a mortgage. They owned the bakery outright and they both had money in the bank."

"So the motive isn't money," The professor tried to play along and looked at Albert to see if he agreed.

Albert wasn't giving a whole lot away. "Hard to say. We don't have a lot to go on."

The rest of the conversation was cut short by a squawk from Marsh's radio. There was a minor fracas at Greg's factory. A pack of wild dogs had just caused an accident and a security guard had been mauled by a big cat.

"A big cat?" repeated the professor, his face screwed up in disbelief. "Like a tiger?"

Albert only said one word, a broad grin spreading across his face. "Rex."

Man of the People

Greg Garside had very little troubling his mind on his way to work. The best thing about being the boss, in his opinion, was that he got to go where he wanted when he wanted. Who was going to tell him otherwise?

He employed over five hundred people. He was a member of more than a dozen committees in Lyme Regis and across Dorset where his name was synonymous with success and leadership. He was a man of the people, and they shook his hand wherever he went.

He was also a ruthless murderer, but that was a new development he chose not to dwell on. Not that it troubled him. Karl and Daniel Fielding would both still be alive if they had just chosen to be reasonable. He had been reasonable. Heck, he had been generous. Now they were dead and there was only one minor barrier left to overcome.

Daisy Fielding was the last surviving member of her family. Greg was glad the brothers hadn't churned out kids the way some people did; having half a dozen or more members of the next generation to wade through would be too much. One young woman though, that he could deal with.

She would sign the business over to him later today, he was confident of that. She wasn't a baker for a start, she was a stripper of all things. How her father must have felt about her choice of career Greg could not imagine. He thanked the Lord he had a son. A wayward idiot of a son, but a son, nonetheless.

Thinking about his kid, he picked up his phone again. He asked him to do one simple thing. One simple little, easy task and he hadn't heard from him since.

Did he get it done or not? That was all Greg wanted to know.

Greg's call went to voicemail where he left a threatening message and he followed that with a text to reinforce how badly his son would suffer if he didn't start responding soon.

Where the heck was he anyway?

Slamming the phone back into the cupholder by his left elbow, Greg's thoughts returned to Daisy Fielding. He knew the girl well enough; she would sell. He wasn't planning to give her a lot of option. She would sell or she would volunteer to commit suicide. It was that easy.

His offer would again be generous. If he waited until the business failed, he would get away with paying less. He felt certain it *would* fail now both bakers were dead. The secret recipe for their Dorset Knobs might have died with them and that was a risk he chose to take when he killed Daniel and tossed him off the cliff. The kid that worked there, Troy somethingorother, might know it, but Greg was doubtful.

It wouldn't matter. He'd already guessed the recipe and tested it until it was close enough. Over time, without the Fielding brothers showing off their superior Knobs, Greg believed his would be accepted.

Anyway, he would make the offer today, swooping in to save poor Daisy from the struggle of having to run the business her father and uncle left behind. Knowing the press might see it as a cunning businessman taking advantage of a young woman's grief was the reason why he had to offer way over what the place was worth. He was fine with spending the money.

Minding his own business as he plotted and schemed and congratulated himself on killing two men too stupid to see things his way, he began to sing. A familiar tune was playing on his radio – *Walking on Sunshine* – and that was exactly how he felt.

Tunelessly belting out the words at the top of his lungs, Greg Garside was paying almost no attention to the road when he swung his S Class Mercedes toward the gate of his factory. Three dogs shot into view, haring from right to left as they ran under the barrier.

Cursing in his shock, he had no braking time – it was hit the dogs or crash the car. In retrospect, Greg couldn't say why he chose to crank his steering wheel to avoid the hounds. Given a second to think about it, he would have run them all over with glee.

But crash he did. Whipping his steering wheel to the right, the nose of his car cleared the German Shepherd's tail by the width of a whisker. Greg got to watch the dog glance over its shoulder, man and dog locking eyes for the briefest of moments before the car mounted the pavement and its front bumper ploughed into the unyielding concrete that formed the entrance gate.

Thrown forward by inertia and then back by the exploding airbag, Greg caught a final flash of fur as the dogs vanished from sight.

A Scent with Meaning

Rex felt the car pass his tail, the horrifying thought of losing it enough to make him yank it between his legs. He stayed like that for the next ten yards, running awkwardly until his heartrate slowed and his brain assured him they were clear of the danger.

A man was exiting the car, screaming blue murder at the dogs though he had no hope of catching them. The breeze carried the man's scent, little eddies created as the wind passed under cars and around lampposts leaving pools of it behind. Rex caught the slightest trace in one nostril as he ducked between cars to cross the road.

It stopped him dead in his tracks.

Reversing back onto the pavement, Rex stared at the man, lifting his nose to more fully capture the smell. It wouldn't come though. He was too far away and the breeze too erratic.

The man continued to shout. Not at Rex though. He was shouting at the man in uniform. The guards were emerging from the factory gate, their eyes trained down the road where the German Shepherd continued to try to smell the man who almost ran him over.

"He's wearing a collar!" Greg Garside bellowed. "That means he's got an owner and his owner is financially responsible for the repairs to my car."

"And the gate," pointed out one of the guards, instantly regretting his volunteered statement when Mr Garside's face of thunder turned his way.

"Get the dog, you idiot. Get him now!"

Fearing for their jobs, the two security guys not bleeding from a cat attack set off toward the German Shepherd. Neither was running fast though, they both wanted the other to get there first.

They needn't have worried because Rex wasn't planning to hang around.

When Mr Garside turned to inspect the damage to his car, the wind chose to gift Rex with a fresh breeze blowing directly at his face.

With a noseful of air that lit his eyes with truth, Rex pushed off with his back legs, twisted to face the opposite direction, and left the guards in his wake. The other animals were waiting for him at the next street corner some seventy yards ahead.

He caught up before he slowed his pace.

"What happened?" asked Reggie. "One moment you were right next to me, the next you were nowhere in sight."

"Yeah, we thought you'd been captured," said Bruno.

Rex went around the cats and dogs intending to continue walking and have them follow him. His feet had other ideas though; they chose to stop when they saw Arthur the alley cat.

The scraggly feline was playing pat with something on the pavement, batting at it with a paw like it was alive.

"Is that ... is that a piece of someone's ear?" Rex asked, his tone incredulous.

Arthur spiked the quarter inch square piece of flesh with a claw and flipped it into his mouth.

"Yup," Arthur boasted proudly. "I like to take souvenirs."

All Rex could do was gawp; he had no words.

Jumping in to break things up during the momentary silence that followed, Tailspin said, "That was all very fun, Rex, but we don't appear to have learned anything. How about if we call it quits now and head to our respective homes for a power nap. I know I could do with one. Don't forget we are hitting the museum tonight.

Tailspin wagged his tail and grinned like an impish schoolboy. "Dinosaur bones, eh? Lots and lots of them. I for one have never tasted dinosaur and quite fancy a gluttonous nibble."

There was a hearty round of agreement from the other dogs which was not echoed by the cats.

Turning his attention her way, Tailspin begged to know, "You are still joining us, aren't you, Penelope?" His voice was close to pleading.

Penelope was cleaning a back paw and had to look up upon being addressed.

"Yes, Tailspin, but only out of morbid curiosity. And because you are paying me in sardines from your human's kitchen."

"Sardines?" repeated Arthur, instantly interested.

"But we need you to get inside and open the window."

"I am aware of that, Tailspin. However, you fail to comprehend that your problems and challenges are no concern of mine. I agreed to help you only when you sweetened the deal enough to make me want to."

Bruno huffed, "Cats."

They all heard a *snick* sound and looked around to find Bruno's eyes somewhat wider than they had been.

Arthur had a single claw extended. It looked like it could cut through steel. He held it against Bruno's throat.

"What about cats?" Arthur enquired, his voice filled with honey.

"Um, nothing," gibbered Bruno. "Love cats I do. Hang out with them all the time."

Arthur narrowed his eyes and made sure to drag the tip of his claw through Bruno's fur when he lowered his arm.

"Just as long as we're in agreement on the subject, pooch. Wouldn't want us to mistakenly arrive at a misunderstanding, now would we?"

"Goodness, no. Ha ha," Bruno laughed nervously. "That would be most unfortunate."

Rex shook his head to clear it.

"You can all do as you please. I just caught a sniff of the man who almost hit us with his car. His scent was at the caravan. I think." Rex had been too busy chasing the kid who went out of the window to get a proper sniff at the time. "I need to head back there and check it out."

Tailspin frowned. "Hold on. What caravan?"

Rex started walking. "I'll explain on the way."

Worrying Question

The professor asked, "Do we go?"

"It's not far," said Detective Constable Marsh. "A two minute drive to the factory, if that."

Albert looked in the direction she was pointing and shook his head. "Rex will be long gone by the time we could get there and it's a five minute walk to get back to the cars." To the professor, he said, "You might want to angle your search teams in that direction. Maybe they will get lucky and run into him."

"You're quite sure it's going to be your dog?" he sounded sceptical. "The report said a pack of dogs. Where would Rex find a pack of dogs to hang out with?"

Albert chuckled and shot an eyebrow.

"That is a great question and one I've asked myself more than once. He just appears with other dogs. Or cats," Albert added, recalling the rain of alley cats showering from the sky in Arbroath, each bearing a seagull to the ground as they fell. "I've stopped questioning the how of it."

"Sooo, you want to speak with Troy Macclesfield still?"

DS Marsh had one hand on the gate leading to his mother's front door.

They knocked and were greeted by the young man Albert met the previous day. He was looking glum and rightly so. Both his bosses had been killed, one after the other. His mum had offered to take the day off, but Troy knew they needed the cash, so he was home by himself wondering if he still had a job.

"They said Karl's death was murder," he explained as if his visitors might not know. "They wouldn't speculate on what happened to Daniel, but I'm guessing it must be the same thing."

"It's a terrible business," agreed Albert. "Was it Superintendent Alverez you were talking to?"

Troy nodded. They were in the living room of his mother's small, terraced house. Politely, he'd offered to make tea and was waved to sit. However, since tea sounded good, the professor was in the kitchen rummaging for mugs and teabags.

Troy occupied one armchair set into the corner of the room. He looked shrunken and withdrawn to Albert, not a patch on the young man he'd met the previous day. Of course, at that point Daniel was only just finding out about his brother and Troy had no idea there was anything amiss.

Albert held no doubt he was asking questions the bakery assistant had already answered, yet the young man took it all in his stride. Rarely looking up from a spot on the carpet, he promised he had no clue why anyone would want to hurt either brother, let alone both. Karl and Daniel Fielding were popular in Lyme Regis. They were active members of the town, taking part in charitable activities and donating money where they saw fit.

They treated him well and were talking about a more

senior role in a few years when they planned to reduce their hours and edge toward retirement.

"I'm not sure what will happen now," Troy sniffed. "I know I ought not to be thinking about myself, but I'm not sure if I even have a job to go to. I started there when I was fourteen. That was just so I could be near to Daisy," he admitted quietly. "I started there full time the day after I left school. I don't know how to do anything else."

Albert took a moment to think about Troy's quandary.

"Does Daisy now own the bakery, do you know? Daniel didn't have any children, did he?"

Troy didn't look up, but shook his head and shrugged. "No, Daniel never even got married. I think he might have been gay, but I don't recall seeing him with a boyfriend either. I guess the place must belong to Daisy now."

Albert looked across at Marsh. "How long until the police are finished with it, do you think?"

"What, for it to reopen?" She pushed her lips out in thought. "A couple of days," she tried to sound confident, choosing not to reveal this was her first case after transferring to CID.

To Troy, Albert said, "A business operates as a separate entity to the people within it. The business pays corporation tax, not the directors. I cannot speak in exact terms, but assuming the bakery is set up as a limited company, there is no reason why it cannot continue to operate and there is a big customer base, so I'm led to understand."

Troy mumbled, "I don't know the recipe for the knobs. Without that, the business is just another bakery."

Sensing he wasn't going to bring the poor chap any cheer, Albert changed tack, returning to questions he hoped might shed some light onto the reason behind the murders.

The professor arrived with steaming mugs of tea and some chocolate digestives he found next to the kettle.

"What about their relationship?" Albert asked. "The brothers worked closely, did they get on okay?"

Troy looked up. "I already told that Alverez lady about their big fight. It's the only one I ever remember them having."

A beat of silence preceded Albert's next question.

"What fight? What did they fight about?"

"It was Sunday morning. I had no idea Karl was back until I got to work and found him there with Daniel. They were both so happy to be back together, it was like he'd never been away."

"But they got into an argument?"

Troy's eyes were back on the carpet. "It was right around lunchtime. They were in the bakery at the back, I was serving out front, and suddenly I could hear Karl shouting."

"What was he shouting about?"

Troy shrugged, lifting his chin to meet Albert's gaze. "I don't know. Their voices were muffled by the door. He was angry though. I heard Daniel shouting too. The customers could hear them; I had to pretend like nothing was happening."

"Did it sound like it got violent?"

Troy shook his head without needing to consult his memory.

"No. Karl stormed out. He threw his apron on the floor and left without another word. The rest of the afternoon was quite uncomfortable; all of us dancing around the incident and not talking about it."

Troy continued talking, Albert probing with questions, but there didn't seem to be anything else to learn. Apart from the argument – the subject of which remained unknown – Troy had nothing to report. If the Fieldings were up to something murky or had a hidden past, Troy didn't know what it was. One thing Albert took on board was the reason why Karl Fielding hadn't chosen to go to his brother's when his girlfriend kicked him out. He was just as mad at him as he was Heather.

Albert sipped at his tea, but it was still too hot to gulp when he accepted it was time to leave the young man alone.

At the doorstep, he did his best to impart a little elderly wisdom: there really was no sense in worrying about his job. He was a talented lad and would find other employment in the same line of work if the bakery did close.

Troy nodded, his head and eyes still down, but he lifted them to look at Albert just when he was about to turn away. The look in his face made Albert stop.

White as a sheet, Troy blurted a question that had clearly just occurred to him, "Will the killer come after me?"

Albert placed a hand on the young man's shoulder and was about to say he had nothing to worry about when the full force of Troy's worry arrived. Did he need to worry? Why did the killer target the Fieldings?

Closing his mouth for it was hanging half open, Albert ran the ramifications of Troy's fear through his head. What if Troy was in danger? What did that mean?

"Is there someone you can be with?" Albert asked. "Until your mum gets home, I mean."

Troy gave a kind of half shrug. "I guess. Do you think I might be in danger then?"

Albert made sure to look positive and upbeat. "No, not at all. It's just a sensible precaution. If you have somewhere you can spend the day and be with other people, that would be better for you anyway. It will help to take your mind off things."

"Yeah. Yeah, okay. I guess that would be better than sitting here all day. I'll head to my mate's house. He's got three older brothers and they're all in a band. They won't be doing anything today except a bit of practice. I'll hang out there."

With a clap on Troy's shoulder, Albert moved out of the way so he could shut his mum's front door. He'd grabbed his coat already and was following them down the garden path to the pavement. There, he turned left and with a wave set off to find some company.

Two strides later, he turned around, the set of his features showing a memory had just surfaced.

"I just remembered something."

"Go on."

"Karl had something in his hand when he left. Daniel tried to get it from him like it was his and he wanted it back. Karl wouldn't give it up though."

Marsh asked, "What was it, Troy?"

"Oh, a piece of paper. Sorry, no, that's not right. It was pieces of paper. Thick, like a dozen pieces stapled together."

"A4 size?" Albert wanted a clearer image.

"Yeah. Like a letter or something." Troy shrugged. "Maybe that's what they were arguing about."

Albert quizzed him some more, but that was all Troy had. He was just a baker's assistant when all was said and done: not involved in the running of the business and not privy to information that might prove pertinent.

Waiting until Troy was out of earshot, the professor said, "I really ought to head back to the dig, Albert. Am I alright to leave you in Detective Marsh's capable hands?"

Albert gripped the professor's hand and shook it firmly.

"Thank you for your help today. Perhaps I'll see you at breakfast tomorrow," Albert added, remembering they were staying in the same guesthouse.

The professor said his goodbyes and left Albert with Marsh in the street outside Troy's house.

"Where to next, Albert?"

For once it was a question to which Albert had an immediate reply. "We need to speak with Daisy Fielding."

Uphill Slog

"How much farther is it, pup?" grumbled Tailspin. The dogs were an hour into their walk, their noses pointing uphill toward the headland and the cliffs for the last twenty minutes.

The cats were with them, but they were not walking. They refused. They were hitching a lift instead. On the back of one of the dogs. Not one of the dogs who was with them at the factory raid, but a new dog.

The pack grew as they wended their way through the back streets and alleys of Lyme Regis. For those in the know, this was a completely normal thing to occur. Dogs, being naturally inquisitive and happier with company, will always gravitate toward a pack. Just claim a bench at your local park and observe for a while to confirm this for yourself.

When a pack happens to pass by your garden wall, there really is no option to resist tagging along. The first to join was a Jack Russell called Jack, as most Jack Russells are. He wiggled under the gate at the back of his garden and fell in beside Bruno who he knew from visits to the park.

Next up was Jessie, a Bull Mastiff. Unlike most of the dogs, she could look over the top of her garden fence even though it was six feet high. The cats were riding on her back. Not because they had been invited or were welcome, but because she hadn't noticed they were there yet.

Bruno almost asked her about her feline situation, but caught Arthur glaring at him and chose to stay silent instead.

By the time they reached the town fringes, they'd also gained a pair of standard poodles, a brother and sister duo called Crash and Wallop, and a wire-haired schnauzer. Her name was Molly and she had news.

"You're investigating the murder?" she sought to confirm when Reggie revealed their ultimate purpose. However, she followed her question with another one that caught Rex's attention. "Which one?"

"Which one what?" Rex asked, his eyebrows twitching like hairy caterpillars on an electric fence. "You mean there's been more than one murder?"

Finding herself the sudden centre of attention, Molly mumbled, "Well, I think so. That's what Boris said on his way past this morning. He's a police dog. He lives next door but one with his human. They were setting out before breakfast this morning. I'd just been let in the garden and Boris said there was another body at the beach. It was the brother of the man who they found at the beach yesterday."

Bruno lamented, "I should have been a police dog. They get to lead such interesting lives. Apparently, Dalmatians don't make good police dogs, so it was never really an option."

Tailspin grumbled, "It was never an option because

you've got a hamster wheel where your brain should be, Bruno. Police dogs need to stay calm and be able to think clearly."

Bruno looked hurt, but with most of the other dogs in the pack sniggering, he didn't argue.

"I was a police dog," Rex admitted. "It's not nearly so glamorous as one might imagine." Focusing on Molly, he asked, "You're sure about this? A second death and it's the brother of the man who died yesterday?"

"That's what Boris said. I figure he probably knows what he is talking about."

Did that change things? Rex couldn't decide. He figured it had to be to do with the reason behind the first death, but Rex couldn't fathom human motivations any better than the dogs around him. Humans were beyond reason when it came to their need to kill each other. The killer targeted both brothers though, that had to mean something.

The caravan would have answers, or it would not. He wasn't going to find out standing in the street.

Setting off again, he checked they were going the right way.

"Aye, pup," grumbled Tailspin. "This will bring you out of town and into a field. If you're aiming for the headland, this is the fastest route, and it will keep us out of sight most of the way there."

Local knowledge was an invaluable resource and no mistake. Rex was glad to have the other dogs at his side. The cats not so much but he wasn't going to kick off about them tagging along. Besides, Arthur the psychotic alley cat might prove useful at some point.

Exiting another alley, the sunshine striking their eyes as it began its late autumn dip toward the horizon, they were spotted by a pair of palaeontology students.

Searching for Albert Smith's dog got boring quite quickly. It was cold out too, but they were students so their meagre funds wouldn't stretch to a nice lunch and a couple of drinks somewhere. Settling on a bag of chips to share, they'd found a sunny spot out of the wind to while a way a few hours. Their professor expected them to be scouring the town for a dog – a needle-in-a-haystack task if ever there was one. They couldn't return to the dig until Rex was found, so doing nothing – a time-honoured student hobby – got their vote with the added hope someone else would do the finding for them.

"Here," Archie nudged Derek. "Isn't that him?"

"Him who?" asked Derek, his eyes locked on the few strands of tobacco he was attempting to roll.

"The dog, Derek. The dog."

"What d ..." Derek looked up to see what had his companion all excited.

It did look like the same dog the old man had with him the previous evening. It was a German Shepherd though and one of those looked just like another so far as Derek was concerned.

"Rex!" Archie shouted and whistled, hoping the dog might come to him. Pushing off the floor and wiping his hands on his jeans to remove the gravel, he saw when the dog looked straight at him.

Derek looked back down at his roll-up just in time to see the breeze steal his last few wisps of tobacco. Tutting as he crushed the thin white paper between his fingers, he levered himself up too.

"You really think that's him? Where did all the other dogs come from?"

"I dunno, but that looks like him and I'm bored doing nothing. I want to get back to the dig. They might have found anything by now. I bet they have too," Archie was starting to cross the road. "I bet someone found another new species and the professor will name it after them. I bet it's Dave. I bet Dave gets to name his own dinosaur."

"Yeah, the Daveosaurus," chuckled Derek, not caring one bit if they found new dinosaurs or not. He only came on the trip because Kirsty Macphee was going, and she hooked up with Ryan Goldwing last night.

Jessie, still oblivious to the two cats riding on her shoulders, asked, "You know those two?"

The question didn't come with a name attached, but Rex assumed it was aimed at him since the humans were calling his name.

"Yeah. I was with them last night."

Both young men were whistling now, each with derivations of, "Here, boy. Come on, Rex. Let's take you back to Albert."

Rex wagged his tail just once. The wag was an automatic response to humans being friendly, but did he really want to go with them. He was on a mission now and though they claimed to want to take him back to his human, Rex figured he could find the old man for himself when he was ready. The last he saw of Albert, they were loading him into an ambulance.

Rex couldn't fill in the blanks to know what that might mean in terms of when Albert would be back, but he saw nothing to gain from accompanying the two scruffy-looking young men heading his way.

"I think it's time to run," said Rex. One of the humans was on his phone, telling other people he'd found Rex. "Definitely time to run."

"Run?" moaned Tailspin. "Again? We did running an hour ago after you stirred up a hornet's nest at the factory."

"Yup, running," Rex confirmed, barking to get the pack moving as he tore across the road to find the path bisecting the fields. It was precisely where Tailspin said it would be. "Come on, everyone. It's not far now!"

The Basset Hound voiced his opinion on the subject of running with some inventive language, but barrelled along at the rear within touching distance of the other dogs for a while.

Archie shouted, "Hey! Wait!" at the flurry of departing tails but gave up chasing after only a few yards. Derek hadn't bothered running at all. "Where were you?" Archie complained.

"On the phone," Derek mouthed.

Archie waited patiently, but when Derek ended his call and put the phone back into a pocket, Archie found his companion had not, in fact, been trying to coordinate the rest of the searchers.

"That was Baz," Derek revealed.

Archie whined, "I thought you were on the phone to the professor."

Derek scoffed over his shoulder, angling himself back to the town centre, "To tell him what? That we saw a dog and it might have been the one we're supposed to be catching? I'm sure that would go down well. Baz, Harry, and Mike are heading to a café and then the museum. Said they've been busking on the seafront and dancing for the old ladies. Made a few bob. Baz bought some ciders from an off licence. You hunt for the dog if you want, but you'll be doing it alone. Anyway, it will be dark soon and I want to see what was found today; the lucky beggars who stayed at the dig will be bringing their haul down to store and secure it in an hour or so.

Complaining most of the way, Archie followed Derek into town. Had they seen Rex or not? Neither really cared.

The dogs slowed to a walk when they were sure the humans chose not to follow. That allowed Tailspin to get his breath and catch up. They went at his pace the rest of the way, arriving opposite the caravan park with the sun arcing toward the ocean. Soon it would dip below the horizon where the cliffs stretched to the sky.

There was time enough to complete Rex's inspection of the caravan, but the excitement of their planned raid on the museum and its collection of juicy dinosaur bones sparked between the dogs like static electricity in a cloud. Checking for cars, Rex led the pack across the road and into Sunny Days Caravan Park.

No One Likes Cooper

Albert questioned the validity of visiting Daisy Fielding. The poor young woman had lost her father and her uncle in the last two days, the police undoubtedly visiting her to deliver the news twice in less than twenty-four hours. It would be a bitter pill to swallow for anyone, and so far as Albert knew, the young lady in question had no other family.

However, recalling what Troy Macclesfield said, she did have a boyfriend.

He deferred to Detective Constable Marsh to do the honours and ring Daisy's doorbell. Having her along allowed Albert to feel less like a nosy intruder. He suspected it also meant Daisy would be more likely to answer his questions and, since he only knew what road she lived on and not which house, Constable Marsh's assistance proved invaluable.

"I guess you've done this a lot," said Marsh, making conversation as they waited for someone to open the door. "Visiting the recently bereaved, I mean."

Albert gave a sad nod of his head. It was inevitable that he had to draw information out of people who felt and acted like their own lives had just ended. People who had lost spouses or partners or children – the ones who lost young children were by far the worst to manage – were in no mental or emotional shape to answer questions, but they had to if he was to catch the person or persons responsible for their misery.

Long retired from such a role, yet here he was again, facing the door of a woman he knew to be in pain.

A shadow fell across the door, someone moving inside and coming closer. Through the frosted glass, Albert could make out the shape of a young woman. However, when she answered the door a moment later, her face was not set with the anguish he expected.

"Daisy Fielding?" Marsh questioned, showing her identification.

The woman gave a slight shake of her head. "No, I'm Tamara. I work with Daisy. We heard about her dad and then about her uncle and we came over. She needs someone with her and Cooper's nowhere to be found as usual."

Tamara had already backed away from the door, inviting those outside to enter.

Following Marsh inside, Albert asked, "Cooper is Daisy's boyfriend?"

"He's her something." Tamara dropped her voice to a whisper, closing the front door. "She's been dating him forever when she could have anyone. Okay, so he's the heir to an empire, but hanging on for that fortune to drop isn't worth the hassle and heartache."

Clearly it was a subject Tamara wanted to discuss or at least an opinion she wanted to get off her chest.

Albert thought it to be a distraction; Daisy's layabout,

delinquent boyfriend hardly the ... hold on though. Daisy might have a key to her father's caravan. That would mean the boyfriend, Cooper, would have access to it. Was he a skinny kid with a dirt bike?

"Who was it, Tammy?" a voice called from deeper in the house.

"It's the police." Only when the words left Tamara's mouth she questioned if the old man could still be employed. Too late, she hurried behind as the female police officer led him into the living room.

Self-trained to be observant, Albert noted the downstairs layout. A narrow hallway led past a dining room/office – he saw a desk with a computer. Stairs ran perpendicular to the hallway in the centre of the house leading to a bedroom at the front and probably two at the back. The living room was at the rear of the house with the kitchen accessed through it.

Arriving behind Marsh, Albert looked at the young ladies lining the living room. His cheeks warmed when he recognised two of them. They had clothes on now at least.

Tamara was an absolute knock out and had answered the door wearing an outfit that many might describe as provocative. Her skirt showed a lot of thigh and her neckline was nothing of the sort since it plunged most of the way to her navel. The other ladies were similarly attired as if this were a kind of offstage uniform.

Only one stood out, a woman around whom the others were fussing. She wore a pink sweatsuit from Pink by Victoria's Secret, plus thick woolly socks pulled almost to her knees. A box of tissues sat half empty and gainfully employed on a side table next to her where she curled into one corner of a sofa.

Albert introduced himself.

"Wait," interrupted Daisy. "You're the fella on TV. The one who saved my dad from that crazy Earl."

"Something like that," Albert admitted. "That's why I'm here. I'm terribly sorry for your loss."

Daisy sniffed and reached for another tissue. After blowing her nose, she asked, "What brings you to Lyme Regis, Mr Smith?"

"I came because your father invited me. I was going to try his Dorset Knobs. Now I find myself unable to move on until I know what happened to him." Albert wanted to know about Daisy's boyfriend. Was Cooper the same kid he saw at the caravan? The same kid who knocked him out behind the strip club? The question was there on his lips ready to be asked, but he knew he needed to gain her trust first.

Daisy's eyes, deep blue, huge, and framed by a symmetrical face about which glorious blonde hair fell in perfect ringlets, locked on Albert's.

"You're trying to solve my dad's murder? Why? What's it to you?"

It was a fair question. Albert indicated to his left where Constable Marsh sat. "I want to help." It was close enough to the truth and the girl would gain nothing from hearing about Albert's desire to throw the solution in DS Rogers' face. "It's nothing more than a case of two minds being superior to one, but your question leads me to ask who might or could be behind such a terrible act."

Daisy looked from Albert to Marsh and back again. "I already told the police all I know. I don't know anything. I haven't really spoken to my dad in the last two years."

"Why is that, Daisy?" Marsh asked.

Daisy scrutinised her hands where they lay folded in her lap.

"It started to go wrong when mum got sick. Dad couldn't deal with it. He was angry and he would drink."

Marsh jumped in again, "Was he violent?"

Daisy shook her head, a definite motion that carried the truth.

"No, he was just ... he just wasn't there, you know." She looked up for the first time in over a minute. "Cooper was. We were both fifteen and he was sweet. He had his own problems, you know?"

"Your father disapproved?" Albert guessed. It wasn't much of a leap. Karl Fielding felt like his world was unravelling and his fifteen-year-old daughter was carrying on with a boy everyone described as a criminal layabout. Wanting to keep his precious daughter close, he'd laid down the law and in so doing succeeded only in pushing her away.

Tamara volunteered her opinion. "We all did."

Daisy snapped her head around to glare across the room.

"Oh, come on, Daisy. You know how we all feel," Tamara thought perhaps it was time for some tough love. "He's no good for you. He's only just got out of jail and where is he now, huh? Where is he? Your dad was murdered, and Cooper hasn't even showed his face to give you comfort."

Through teeth that were grinding together, Daisy growled through her pain. "You can leave any time you want, Tamara. That goes for the rest of you," she added, getting to her feet to face her friends. "Do the rest of you agree with her?" It was a simple question and a direct challenge. "Huh, Becky? Which is it? Do you think I should dump Cooper too."

"Weeelll, Tamara has kinda got a point," Becky did her best to edge around the question.

Daisy screamed, a deep angry sound of intense frustration. Jabbing an arm toward the door, she ordered, "Get out! All of you. Get out!"

Becky tried to calm her friend. "Babes, we're on your side …"

Overwhelming emotions stealing her rage before it could get up to pace, Daisy's voice was quiet when she spoke again.

"I want you all to leave. I cannot do this right now. I have too many things to think about. None of you know Cooper. None of you know what his life is like."

Tamara made a scoffing noise. "It can't be that bad. Look at who his dad is."

Daisy shot Tamara a glare that made her take a step back. "Get out. Now."

Daisy's friends needed no further encouragement. They grabbed handbags and coats, hustling to get to the door with apologies to their host and requests she call them when feeling ready to talk.

They were good friends doing their best in a difficult situation. Maybe they were right about Cooper and maybe they were not, but it was clear to Albert they had pushed too far at the wrong time.

Daisy waited until she heard the front door close. She had her back to Marsh and Albert and didn't feel like turning around to face them.

"Can you leave too, please?" she requested. "I need … I need some time to myself."

Albert rose to his feet, encouraging Marsh to do likewise. "Of course, Daisy. Just two more questions, please, and we will be out of your hair."

Daisy wanted to argue, to insist they leave straight away, but they were trying to find the man responsible for her father's death and she was emotionally aware enough to know the root cause of her anger was born of having failed to reconnect with her dad. That was no one's fault but her own. She loved her dad, but when things got tough, he wasn't there for her and she'd put off fixing things. Now she never would, and it hurt.

Twisting in her socks to face the old man, she asked, "What do you want to know?"

"Your grandfather's caravan. Do you have a key to it?"

The question surprised Daisy. DS Rogers quizzed her endlessly the previous evening and Superintendent Alverez came back for a second round not more than two hours ago. Neither had asked about the key.

"Somewhere," she replied. "I haven't been up there in years. The police said that's where ... that's where it happened."

Albert nodded. "Most likely, yes. Can you check to see if you still have it?"

"The key? Um, okay, sure." Daisy's feet moved seemingly of their own accord, guiding her to the hallway leading from the front door. "If they are anywhere, they would be in here."

Albert took a step so he could see what she was doing. A thin console table sat against one wall, the drawer now open as Daisy's delicate fingers rummaged through it. Unable to find what she wanted, both hands were employed to scoop a portion of the contents. Dumped on the surface of the table, she rooted through them, frowning deeply.

Albert took out his phone. "Would they look like this?" he asked, holding up the screen. Part of becoming more familiar with his phone was the ability to access and employ the camera. He'd taken photos with it before, then struggled to find them - the stupid thing had too many Apps. Last night, when he was going through the caravan, he'd taken shots of anything that looked important.

Daisy squinted from three yards away, coming closer when she needed to see the image in finer detail.

"That's the door to the caravan," said Daisy, her voice filled with confusion. "And those are my keys. When was this taken?"

Albert didn't answer her question. Instead, he took his phone back and placed it in his pocket. With a twist, he plucked a photo frame from a shelf at head height. The picture showed a couple enjoying a day at the beach.

Daisy was wearing a bikini. The young man cuddling her, his arms around her shoulders, had on a t-shirt. The setting and their clothes were irrelevant though. The important part was that Albert recognised both faces.

"This is Cooper?" he confirmed.

"Yes. Why are you asking about him? Why does everyone suddenly have so much interest in my boyfriend. I don't know where he is." Her words were clipped, angry, and barely below a shout.

"Neither do I," replied Albert, calmly replacing the photograph on the shelf where it had left a small line in the dust. "What I do know is that I disturbed him in your grandfather's caravan last night."

"You're lying!" Daisy's rage was instant.

"And he attacked me outside El Mango last night!" Albert rammed his delivery home, raising his voice to match Daisy's. He'd caught a glimpse of the kid's face when his fist landed. It hadn't registered until he saw it again in the photograph.

"No! I don't believe you! Cooper would never hurt anyone!"

"He put me in the hospital last night, Daisy. He was at

the caravan, and he ran the moment he saw me. He had your keys, Daisy. Why would he have the keys to your grandfather's caravan?"

Daisy's mouth opened and closed, no words forming.

"Your father didn't like him, Daisy. Your father didn't like him and I'm sure that was reciprocated. What aren't you telling us?"

"Nothing!" Her response was a distraught, snot-filled denial. "Cooper wouldn't hurt my dad. He wouldn't hurt anyone."

"He's a criminal," Albert pressed, his voice softer as he let off and tried to rein Daisy in. "You know that's true."

"But he's not violent and it's all silly stuff. Mostly it isn't even his fault. I know you are looking for answers. I want them too. You're looking in the wrong place though. Cooper isn't a killer. He doesn't have a violent bone in his body."

Albert removed his flat cap to show Daisy the dressing on his head. "He was violent enough last night. What was he doing at El Mango, Daisy? You weren't working last night, surely he knew that."

"I ... I don't know," Daisy fumbled for an answer. "It's not like him to just vanish like this. Despite what my friends think. He must have been looking for me."

"Why wouldn't he just call or text you?" asked Marsh, speaking for the first time in more than a minute.

Daisy didn't have an answer to that question and there was no time for Albert to ask any more. An insistent thumping at the front door made everyone jump.

"Miss Fielding? Daisy Fielding? Are you in there? This is Detective Superintendent Alverez. There have been reports of raised voices."

Albert uttered some choice words in his head and

watched Constable Marsh go around Daisy to answer the door.

Alverez looked shocked to find one of her own people inside the house.

"Marsh what are you doing? Why aren't you at the station collating evidence from the bakery. That is the assignment I gave you, is it not?"

"I swapped with DS Rogers," Marsh replied, her answer dutiful and honest, but the tone in which it was spoken acknowledging that she believed her boss was not about to approve.

Things went downhill from there.

Suicide Note

Alverez chewed out Marsh on the spot, her voice quiet but no less intimidating without the volume. Albert caught the young detective's eyes as she obeyed her superior and left. His confident nod was intended to impart that she had done well and should be proud. Whether she understood the message or took comfort from it he could not guess.

Stepping in to defend her would have been worse - she had to be able to stand alone and hold her own.

Daisy expressed her disbelief that he was able to enter her home when he was not, in fact, working with the police as he claimed.

"I never actually said that," Albert pointed out.

Alverez shot back, "I'm sure you implied it."

"Regardless, Superintendent. I have identified the person who assaulted me last night. The same person who I disturbed in Karl Fielding's caravan while the police were still ..." Albert stopped himself because his voice had grown in volume and Daisy was still within earshot. Speaking quietly, he said, "While your officers were evacuating Karl Fielding's body from the beach ahead of the advancing tide. It's Daisy Fielding's boyfriend. He lives here with her, he just got out of the nick, and he had access to a set of keys to the caravan." Albert didn't need to state, '*He's the killer*', the implication was there. Of course, Albert knew all he had was some circumstantial evidence.

Detective Superintendent Alverez listened anyway, and when Albert claimed to know his assailant, hooked a thumb at a waiting sergeant.

"I want everyone to be on the lookout for Cooper Garside. Arrest on sight. Mr Smith identified Garside as his attacker."

The sergeant said, "That's going to violate his parole. He's only just got out." With a beaming smile, he added, "He'll serve proper time for this one. Another toerag off the street."

Daisy heard what was said and went nuts. "You all need to leave him alone!" she screeched, tears cascading down her cheeks. "He's never hurt anyone. He's the victim! He didn't kill my dad and he didn't kill my uncle!"

"Then what was he doing at your dad's caravan?" Albert pinned her with a question. His voice was kindly, not aggressive, but she had no answer to give either way.

Alverez had no patience to prolong the debate. She had her own theories and Cooper Garside fit with none of them. Pulling Albert away from Daisy's front door and into the street by dint of gently but firmly tugging his jacket sleeve, she made sure they would not be overheard before she started talking.

"Mr Smith, I am this close," she showed him a forefinger and thumb that appeared to be touching, "to arresting you. However unpopular that might be given your pseudo celebrity status, I will do it if I find you anywhere near this investigation again."

Albert folded his arms across his chest in an act of defiance.

"You have caused that poor young woman distress she could have avoided and distracted my officers ever since you arrived yesterday. Enough is enough, Mr Smith. You might be a first-rate detective, but you are way off the mark this time."

Hitching an eyebrow, Albert said, "How so? You have identified the killer?"

Alverez pressed her lips tightly shut. When her boss heard of Albert Smith's involvement in the case, he was clear they were not to arrest him. Such an act in the wake of his success with the Gastrothief case and at a time when he was all the media could talk about would embarrass the entire department. She was under orders to tolerate the old man's busybody nature. He didn't need to know that though.

Well, there was one way to shut him up.

"Yes, thank you. Daniel Fielding killed his brother. We found evidence at his house earlier today. The rock used to crush Karl Fielding's skull was in his garden. It had been cleaned but there were still traces of blood on it. Forensics have it now for testing, but preliminary findings suggest it is an exact match for the fatal dent in Karl Fielding's skull. He also had a key to the caravan where his brother was staying and left a suicide note confessing to his brother's murder. They had a fight at the bakery only a few hours before Karl was killed. His remorse proved too much. It's a closed case, I'm afraid. I came here to break the news to Miss Fielding."

Albert listened to it all with utter disbelief. He knew emotions could be faked. Heck, he'd seen it himself, but

Daniel's distress when Pearson and Massie broke the news seemed so genuine.

"Why? What reason did he give for killing his brother?"

Alverez sighed. "Daniel wrote that he wanted to do something new with his life. He wanted Karl to buy him out or to sell the company to a new owner. They could both retire and not have to get out of bed at three o'clock every morning. Daniel wanted something new, and Karl refused to let him. In the suicide note, Daniel claims he had been begging his brother for years and just couldn't take any more."

"Was the note handwritten?" Albert pushed to find a hole in her reasoning, though he felt like he was clutching at straws.

Alverez shook her head, an expression of sad frustration.

"No, Mr Smith, it was not. Nor was it signed by Daniel Fielding's delicate hand. No one writes their suicide note by hand in the 21st century Mr Smith. No one."

Albert had no words. That he was wrong about Cooper didn't bother him; he'd been wrong before and suspected the kid only because the clues led him in that direction. What bothered him was not his own errors, or that he might have caused unnecessary upset to Daisy, but that he still didn't believe it.

Karl Fielding was excited to be a baker. Albert never got a chance to speak to his older brother, Daniel, so could not comment on how he might have felt. They owned the business together. If Daniel wanted to sell his half, he could have done so and wouldn't have needed his brother's permission. For that matter, if the early mornings bothered him, as the co-owner, he could have taken a step back and given Troy or anyone else the extra hours and the early starts.

"It doesn't add up."

"I'm sorry, what?"

Not intending to voice his thoughts aloud, Albert backtracked quickly.

"Oh, nothing. Sorry for all the mess. I suppose you would like me to go now, yes? Any sign of my dog?"

Think Thin

The pack crossed the road successfully; traffic was light at that time of day. It would pick up shortly as the commuters returning from their jobs flooded back into the town, then drop again as people settled in for the night.

Rex wasn't thinking about cars. His mind was one hundred percent stuck on the confusion of scents he wanted to unravel. The factory smelled like the bakery, but not exactly like it. His nose picked out the same subtle differences he found in the caravan. It meant nothing at the time and Rex excused himself because he'd been trying to chase and bite someone.

Now he wondered if perhaps it meant everything.

The dogs didn't need to be told which caravan they wanted. Of course, they could have just followed Rex, but the tang of cinnamon, nutmeg, allspice, and the rest was there for them all to smell. Even the cats could track it.

Tailspin arrived next to Rex where he stood staring up at the caravan and let his backend slump to the ground.

"Well, pup, you dragged us all the way here. What now?

How do you propose to get into that caravan? Time's a wasting, sonny. That moon will be up before long and I for one do not plan to miss out on my ration of dinosaur bones."

The how to get in was a good question, but not one Rex was able to answer. Not with a solution he'd already prepared. Thinking on his paws, he walked around the dilapidated mobile home. It sagged in one corner, the plastic windows were almost opaque with age, and the tyres would need to be replaced if it was ever to be moved. None of that registered in Rex's head. He was looking for a way in.

At the back of the caravan, Rex stopped to look up. The skinny kid had gone out through the back window when Rex went after him. It hinged from the top and slammed back down, almost smacking Rex in the face.

He bounced up on his hind legs, nudging the window with his nose. It moved. It wasn't locked.

Looking around, he spotted what he needed. "Um, Penelope, can you do me a favour?"

Penelope offered Rex a look that suggested he'd just asked if she would like to eat yesterday's hairball.

"I'm a cat," she pointed out. "Cat's do not do favours for dogs."

"You're helping Tailspin later, aren't you?"

"That's different. He's bribing me with sardines. Do you have sardines?"

"I can help," volunteered, Reggie. "What do you need me to do?"

"I need to get this window open and hold it there."

Reggie's enthusiastic smile froze. "Oh, I don't think I can do that."

"No, the task requires a cat's agility and a cat's paw," Rex agreed.

Arthur jumped down from Jessie's shoulders.

"I will do it on one condition?"

Rex had a feeling he knew what was coming.

"You are chasing a killer, no?"

"That's right."

Arthur twisted his head to the left and then to the right, causing it to crack with a bone-chilling sound in each direction.

"When you corner him, I get to deliver the death blow."

"Well I wasn't planning to actually kill ..."

"Those are my terms, take them or leave them."

Rex rolled his eyes and huffed out a breath.

"Okay, Arthur. You win." Turning away, Rex added under his breath, "*You psychopath.*" Focusing his energy on the task at hand, he called the larger dogs to assemble under the window.

With Jessie, Bruno, Crash, and Wallop all standing on their hind legs with their front paws against the wall they looked like they had just been roused by the cops and were about to be patted down for weapons.

Arthur climbed onto Jessie's head and with an evil *snick* sound of his claws extending, hooked the edge of the window. It jammed instantly.

Growling and swearing under his breath, Arthur wriggled and fought to get the window open. The problem was one of flexibility. The window needed to be levered from both sides at the same time.

Rex said, "Penelope?" the single word a question to the cat refusing to take part.

"Oh, all right," she did nothing to hide her lack of

willing participation but clambered up Bruno's back to get into position.

"Ouch. Ooh, Ouch. Um, could you use slightly less claw, Penelope?" Bruno winced and begged.

"Yes, Bruno, I could, but then I could be on the ground and not climbing to help you daft mutts with your stupid plans."

She arrived on his shoulders, balancing precariously as she reached out with an unsteady paw.

"I'm not sure I can do this," she wailed. "I don't feel safe."

Arthur called across the divide, "You can do it, my little kitten. I will be there to catch you should you fall."

The dogs couldn't see Penelope's heart melt, or her eyes dilate, but Rex did get to watch her reach out and hook the other side of the window. Together, the two cats were able to lift the Perspex flap high enough that a dog could get its nose inside.

Now it was Reggie's turn.

"You can do this," Rex whispered encouragement. "Believe in yourself."

"Yeah, I can do this," the tiny Pomeranian yipped. "Why am I doing this?"

"Because it is the right thing to do." Before the fluffball had time to question Rex's wisdom, he barked, "Go!" in Reggie's ear and watched his little twig legs explode into action.

With a three yard run up, Reggie raced across the grass, leapt onto Wallop's back and bounced in through the half open window. Rex might have cheered if he knew how.

The Pomeranian reappeared a moment later, panting excitedly as he peered out. Standing on the bed where it mounted under the window, he had to climb onto the windowsill itself and use his front paws to push the Perspex sheet as high as it would go.

This was the moment of truth. Rex knew he could fit, the hole was big enough for him. That didn't make it an easy jump though. With Reggie holding the flap of window, the rest of the dogs and both cats cleared his path.

Muttering to himself, "This is a bad idea," he gave a grunt of effort and went for it. Rex's mind was prepared for pain. In all likelihood he was going to scrape his back on the top of the frame as he went through and that would hurt. Or he was going to catch his undercarriage on the bottom lip and that didn't bear thinking about. Or neither would happen and he would break a leg landing awkwardly in the dark on the uneven floor inside.

Driving off with his back legs, he stretched out with two front paws, making himself as long and thin as possible.

"Think thin! Think thin!" he repeated, forcing his eyes to stay open.

With back legs tucked against his belly and ears flattened, he sailed through the hole and into the caravan, not so much as a claw or a hair touching the top or bottom.

The dogs outside watched in awe and though they would never admit it, both cats were impressed.

Inside there were a dozen things Rex could hit. A foldout table, the leg of a chair ... he missed them all, his front paws touching down on the rubber matting where he was able to arrest his forward momentum and come to a complete stop.

He stayed motionless for a second, barely able to believe he'd pulled it off. It was the right moment to say something cool, and with that in mind he twisted around to face Reggie.

The little Pomeranian was on the bed, his tail wagging madly and Jessie the Bull Mastiff was looking in from outside, reporting what she could see to the other dogs.

In the confined space, Rex's tail caught the edge of a cantilever lamp which swung on its axis to knock into a saucepan on the caravan's tiny hob. Just as Rex curled a lip to deliver what he hoped would be a classic line, the saucepan dropped on his head.

Reggie winced. "Are you all right?"

Moment lost, Rex squeezed his eyes tight shut until the pain passed. "Yeah." Remembering he was there to check the scents; something he doubted would be possible from outside, Rex kept his eyes closed and started to sniff.

Rex knew precisely what he was looking for. Karl Fielding's scent dominating the enclosed space. That was to be expected. His mix of body smell, products, diet, and the underlying, yet strong odour from his bakery all combined to create a scent so distinctive no dog could fail to identify its owner. However, the kid's smell was here too. A trace of soil from his shoes combined with oil from his bike. The stench of petrochemicals from the exhaust that permeated his clothing and inevitably left a taste behind wherever he went. Inside the kid's odour, the same lingering bakery smell pervaded. Cinnamon and spices, the same as Karl Fielding's yet just that little bit different. Rex spotted it early on, but not when he first entered the caravan. That was an error on his part and one he was doing his utmost to fix.

Digging deeper now, Rex bumped his head on the edge of a chair. His eyes were still closed as he moved around the caravan, sniffing deeply here and there to hold and sample each scent.

Was it here? Had he imagined it?

His nostrils twitched and he had to take a step back to recheck a spot. Snorting in his amazement and losing the scent, Rex had to go again, sniffing and finding. This time he savoured the scent. It was confirmation.

A third person had been in the caravan recently. As recently as the previous day, Rex judged. Not only was there the scent of a third person, it was someone Rex could identify: the man who almost ran him over.

There was more. The third person's scent profile was so close to that of the kid, they had to be related. Father and son, Rex guessed, though he knew human relationships and packs to be more complicated than that.

Opening his eyes, Rex lowered his backend to the floor and gave himself a moment to think. The skinny kid was involved, there was no doubt about that. He was here last night *and* attacked his human. When Rex found him, the young human was going to feel his teeth.

But that didn't make him the killer. There were two bodies now, the man Rex knew from the Gastrothief's lair and his brother who Rex got to smell at the bakery when they went inside.

If it were possible for a dog to grasp the concept of gambling, Rex would have bet the third man, the man who almost ran him over, was the killer. There had been something about him. His scent was here anyway. He'd dragged the pack all this way to confirm it and knew they were itching to get back to the museum and the bones.

A rumble vibrated through Rex's belly at the mere thought of food. Breakfast was so long in the past he couldn't remember what he ate. It was time to go. He had a good idea who the killer was now. What he really needed was his human back at his side. Together they would be able to solve it.

Lyme Regis Layover

The only question in Rex's head as he clambered awkwardly back out through the caravan's back window, was where the old man might currently be.

What's in a Name?

Alverez told Albert there had been multiple sightings of his dog but none by her officers since Marsh spotted him outside the bakery this morning. A large German Shepherd apparently caused an accident outside Greg's factory where it appeared to have staged a raid with several other dogs and at least one cat.

That sounded just like a Rex escapade to Albert. It meant his dog was probably okay. Certainly Rex was fine a few hours ago when the incident occurred. He didn't like being separated from his dog, but there was little he could do about it until Rex found his way back to him.

In dismissing Albert, Superintendent Alverez instructed DS Rogers to deliver him back to his bed and breakfast. Albert was expected to stay there until morning at which time Alverez expected him to leave Lyme Regis. The instruction was delivered carefully since she couldn't charge him or limit his freedom to go where he pleased, but she expected the old man to comply, nevertheless.

He didn't.

Albert was hungry. Lunch failed to occur and the whole point of a bed and breakfast is that you only get - can you guess? – bed and breakfast. There was no evening meal on offer and though he was sure his hosts would provide a cheese sandwich if he begged, his plans did not include staying at the Beach View Guesthouse.

Forced to wait twenty minutes because DS Rogers was parked across the street watching the door to see if Albert would attempt to leave, Albert waited another five to make sure the idiot detective sergeant was truly gone before setting out.

It irked him enormously that he had to sneak around to solve a crime, but not as much as where he knew his feet were taking him next.

The name Garside was stuck in his brain and he wasn't sure why. He'd only just learned it was the last name of Daisy's boyfriend, but a niggle in his brain kept insisting he already knew it. Cooper Garside, the skinny kid with the red dirt bike that wasn't even legally registered was hip-deep in the double murder. Alverez could say what she wanted because Albert wasn't buying a word of it. The more he thought about it, the greater the holes in her explanation.

Daniel Fielding murdered his brother with a rock from the beach and then took it home to place in his garden? Albert met plenty of idiots during his time in the police, but never any so dumb they would choose to take incriminating evidence home with them.

It was just one of a list of discrepancies, all of which could be ignored if examined in isolation.

Ruling out Daniel Fielding and the concept this was a murder and not suicide left Albert with Cooper Garside as the only name on his list of suspects. He didn't believe that either though. For a start, Albert questioned the kid's ability to carry either man to the cliff. Neither Karl nor Daniel were big men, but they couldn't have been far short of two hundred pounds either. Maybe Cooper Garside was stronger than he looked, but even if he could lift Karl Fielding, it had to be more than a hundred yards from his caravan to the cliff and there was a barrier in the way to stop people straying too close.

Karl was killed in the caravan and wasn't dragged across the grass; Albert would have seen the marks. That meant he was looking for someone else and due to that fact, Albert found himself trudging back toward the infernal caravan park at the top of the infernal hill.

He stopped at a petrol station to grab something to eat – it was the best he was going to get unless he wanted to delay his investigation. There, he found a counter serving a selection of warm pasties and sausage rolls. Behind the counter, a proud sign boasted, 'Greg's'. On one side, a large man with a broad smile stood proudly superimposed in a baker's apron.

"I'll take the steak and stilton pasty, please?" Albert requested when the young man serving prompted. "Are these local?" he asked, more out of conversation than curiosity.

"Can't get much more local," the young man chuckled. "They're made at the Greg's factory in town." Placing the pasty into a paper bag with a pair of tongs, he inclined his head to indicate the man on the sign. "That's Greg Garside. He's famous about these parts."

If there had been a clock in the petrol station's little shop, this would have been the moment when it chose to stop ticking. Time had not, in fact, slowed down, Albert's brain was simply working at twenty-five times its previous speed.

"That's Greg Garside?" Albert handed over a ten pound note without noticing he'd done so.

The counter clerk opened the cash register, idly remarking to himself that the old man was the first person through the door today with cash. Everyone else used a card.

"That's right," he confirmed.

"Any relation to Cooper Garside?" Albert couldn't take his eyes from Greg Garside's image. He asked the question but already knew the answer. Tamara said Cooper was the heir to an empire. It meant nothing at the time and his attention had been on other things. Now he understood what she meant.

The clerk looked up and shrugged. "I just serve the pasties."

Albert was backing toward the door, his need to get to the caravan suddenly infinitely more urgent when the clerk called him back.

"Your change?" he held aloft a five pound note and some coins.

Albert kept going. "Keep it." There was no time to waste.

Taking a bite from the pasty and revelling in the hot meaty filling and warm comforting pastry, Albert sucked in a breath and told himself the slog to get back to the hill was doable. Sure his knees and hips hurt already. Okay, so his lower back and ankles were aching. He could muddle through.

He wasn't a regular church goer. He never really had been. Petunia always went; she liked to be part of the community, but Albert worked half the Sundays God sent and when he had the opportunity and the sun was shining, he preferred to spend his Sunday mornings peacefully gardening. Or reading the paper.

However, though he might not think of himself as overly religious, Albert was swift to say a prayer and thank the Lord when a taxi pulled up to the pumps just as he was stepping out of the shop.

The driver jumped out, eager to fill his tank.

"Any chance you can run me up the hill?" Albert waved a fresh ten pound note in the air.

"Which hill?"

"That one. See that caravan park about a mile from here?"

The cabbie was on his way home. His dinner was already going cold according to the latest text from his wife, but a fare to Weymouth at the end of his shift took him way over his intended return time while simultaneously netting him a decent wage for the day. A two minute detour for another tenner wasn't going to make things any worse.

Five minutes later, his tank full and his backseat empty once again, he spun his car around and headed back to Lyme Regis and his stone cold meal.

Albert looked at the caravan and wondered how he was going to get in. The challenge of entry without a key had only just occurred to him. Too late to do anything about it now, he resigned himself to figuring it out.

The caravan was locked as he felt certain it would be – the police would have been diligent enough to secure it when they finished scouring for evidence. On his hands and knees, Albert checked all the little cubby holes, nooks, and crannies until he accepted there was no spare key tucked away waiting to be found.

Unwilling to be defeated now that he was here, he considered breaking one of the windows. It wasn't something he wanted to do, but could justify it to himself easily enough – the police were going to let a killer go free.

Probably.

He needed to see inside the caravan. That was if the thing he wanted, the thing he saw yesterday, was still there.

Looking around for a brick or a rock, he found what he needed after a few moments of searching. Taking a twenty pound piece of sedimentary rock from a collection outside another caravan – one that looked to be inhabited – Albert approached the back window of Karl Fielding's temporary home.

Hefting it with both hands, he paused to look around. It was a bit late, he realised, to be checking the coast was clear, but just when he was about to smash the rock down, he spotted dirty paw prints on the bedding inside.

They were two different sizes. Blinking in question, his eyes caught sight of the window latches. They were in the open position. Albert lowered the rock, cradling it against his chest to hook his fingers under the window.

It lifted with no resistance.

Dropping the rock, he swore and clapped his hand over his mouth. He'd dropped it on his toes.

Given a moment to recover and walk it off, Albert thought about how to now gain entry. A younger man would vault up and through the aperture without thinking it was a feat at all. Albert needed something to step on first. His legs just weren't as springy as they used to be.

He found a large cooler back at the same caravan from which he borrowed the rock. Eighteen inches of additional height proved to be enough and with a grunt and roll, Albert found himself on the bed. Only for a moment though; a man had been murdered there.

Turning the light on felt like a risk, but he did it anyway

for the sake of expedience. Moments later he found what he was looking for.

Unlocking the door from the inside and leaving it that way – there was nothing of value inside to bother stealing, Albert hotfooted it back to the road and stuck out his thumb. The car he hoped to flag down sped right on by, but undeterred, Albert started walking. Another car would be along soon. Maybe the next driver would be more generous.

It was light enough, he noted, to be able to see where he was going. With the vanishing of the sun almost two hours ago, the sky had been dark ever since. Now the moon filled it, cresting the rise of the cliff to fill the sky.

Dem Bones

The Lyme Regis Dinosaur Museum wasn't the only such attraction in the town. Famed for being one of the bigger seaside destinations on the Jurassic Coast with fossils in abundance if one cared to hunt for them, several buildings had been repurposed during the twentieth century to cash in on the year-round interest.

Fossil hunters would cross oceans to get to a site that promised good fossils. It was the reason behind the professor's rush to get his students in place. By getting there first, he was able to scour the site and claim the best finds. Of course, the nature of the hunt for fossils dictated a newcomer might find something new and extraordinary twenty yards from the edge of their dig, but that was how the game was played.

In the lee of the museum sat a storeroom. Basically a steel-sided industrial unit, it was twenty yards deep by eighteen wide and another twenty-four yards high. There was a door and window on one side and a larger window on the other. Many years ago, one of the curator's assistants had accidentally gouged a hole in the back wall with a forklift truck and chose to cover it up with a heavy crate rather than reveal his error. The hole wasn't big, but it was big enough.

Tailspin looked up at the sky. A huge semicircle of moon now hung as if balanced on the edge of the cliffs. Light from it shone down to illuminate the alley where he and his vastly oversized pack were now gathered.

His plan was for a small incursion, a select group of dogs he already knew, plus one or two others such as Rex because he suspected they might run into some humans – the bigger dogs were there to act as a deterrent while the smaller dogs stole bones for the pack to pick over at leisure once they all escaped.

If there were no humans and they could take their sweet time, so much the better.

The way in was too small for almost any dog to squeeze through. It was one of the primary reasons Tailspin recruited Penelope. That she was a cat and had no interest in a bone on which she could gnaw might be seen as an obstacle to many. However, to Tailspin cats were easy to work with. Their very selfishness dictated they could be bought.

He would deliver on his promise of sardines; they were on the menu in the pub every day. Obtaining some would be difficult, but at the same time, his agreement with Penelope hadn't stipulated when he would deliver.

Vibrating with excitement, Reggie was also small enough to fit through the gap in the panels at the back of the museum's storeroom and did so, rushing through ahead of the Burmese cat. Arthur followed, suspicious he might be missing out if he returned to his usual haunts. So far today, hanging out with the dogs had proved amusing.

Lyme Regis Layover

Head down so he could peer through the gap, Tailspin gave commands.

"Right, now you need to head around to the other side and let us in."

Penelope's voice echoed its boredom from inside the steel sided storeroom. "Yes, I know. I've done this before, Tailspin. I can operate the handle to let you all in." Her voice grew fainter as she moved deeper into the storeroom.

"Is there anyone in there?" hissed the Basset Hound. His ear was up against the hole, and he jumped out of his skin when Arthur shouted from an inch away.

"Not so far!" the alley cat chuckled, amused by his own antics.

The 'how they get in' part of the plan was yet to be explained, so it was with curiosity that Rex asked, "Penelope is going to open a door?"

"A door?" Tailspin shot Rex an incredulous look. "How's she going to open a door? She's a cat. There's a window on the other side. She climbs on a bench and pulls the little handle thingy."

Trying to picture it in his head as he followed Tailspin and the others around the building, he asked, "Okay but how do we get in from the outside. Surely the window is above our heads." What he really meant was how would Tailspin get in. A window at head height would be no problem for most of the dogs. However, the elderly Basset Hound was far from athletic.

The solution presented itself before Rex got his answer. They were around the back of the storeroom now, shielded from moonlight, streetlight, and public view. Perhaps that was why someone had parked a car there.

The Volvo looked past its best years because it was. Tailspin could not remember a time when the car wasn't there.

It belonged to the museum curator, not that Tailspin knew or cared about the vehicle's ownership. The big estate car had refused to start one day and promising to fix it later when he had the time, the curator pushed it out of sight. That was ten years ago.

It sat two inches lower than it had because the tyres were completely flat, but rust on the bonnet made climbing onto it and then the roof an easier proposition for the less athletic.

The pack arrived just as Penelope pushed the window open.

"Can you smell that?" asked Tailspin, enticing his crowd. "Bones."

Rex watched the Basset hop through the window while thinking to himself that he couldn't smell bones at all. What he could smell was rock and dirt. Plus dust. A little grease and ...

"Oh, my word! Look at them all!" cried Bruno.

"Have you ever seen anything so magnificent?" asked Reggie.

Losing track of what his nose was trying to tell him, Rex bounded through the window to see for himself. He was hungry and while a bone might not necessarily sate his appetite, it was a whole lot better than nothing.

"They're a bit hard," observed Jessie, the Bull Mastiff.

"And they taste more like dirt and rock than meaty marrowbone," agreed Wallop.

Rex bounced down to the storeroom floor. His eyes were adjusting to the dark, but he didn't need a lot of light to see the stacks of bones. They were everywhere. Partially assembled dinosaurs intended for display and the remaining bones to be used filled one corner. Shelves to his left held more bones, these much smaller and arranged carefully with labels.

Or at least they had been. Wallop and Crash got to them before Rex was through the window, knocking the fossils in every direction as they fought to find the biggest and best bones.

Thirty seconds into their incursion, the dogs were already questioning if they might have missed something vital.

"Um, Tailspin, I don't wish to be critical," Reggie worded his criticism carefully, "But these bones, aren't bones. They're rocks."

There was a moment of silence which was broken a second later when Arthur and Penelope could contain their mirth no longer.

Laughing uncontrollably, the cats struggled to catch their breath.

"You really ..." Penelope managed to say. "You really ... It became too much and she descended into hysterical giggles once more.

Rex wasn't a fan of cats at the best of times. They were always filled with pompous attitude and superiority. None of which he felt they could justifiably claim. Being forced to tolerate them now was grating against his soul.

Arthur might tear a chunk out of Rex's ear if he went for the remainder of the alley cat's tail, but that was a price he was starting to feel might be worth paying.

Finally getting her laughter under control, Penelope had to wipe away tears when she finally completed her sentence.

"You really believed you were breaking in here to find a hoard of juicy bones. I've had to hold onto that laughter for more than a day. How do you lot manage to walk and wag your tails at the same time?"

Tailspin was as angry at the cats as anyone else, but he wanted to know what he'd missed first.

"They were all talking about bones. Why would I think they were anything else? If these are supposed to be bones, why are they made from stone?"

Penelope groaned, "Because they're fossilised, nitwit."

Reggie tried the word on for size, "Fossilledised? What does that mean?"

"Foss. Ill. Ised," Penelope said it phonetically. "Dinosaurs are creatures that died out millions of years ago. Their bones have been in the ground ever since. Calcium and other minerals in the soil leach into the porous bones as the soft tissue of the creature rots away. Over time, the bone dissolves, leaving the hardened minerals behind. That's how you get fossilised bones. How do none of you know that?"

A better question, Rex believed, was how a cat knew so much about the subject, but he didn't get to ask the question because the museum storeroom's main door opened and light flooded in.

Humans were coming.

The Contract

Albert kept his pace at a fast walk. He wasn't up to running, not at his age, and certainly not after the miles he'd already completed today. The lights of the town beckoned, and it wasn't far to go. Three hundred yards or so to the first houses. To Daisy's house though, that was more than a mile. Fifteen minutes if he hurried, so hurry he did.

Was his haste important? Well, he wouldn't know until he got there. Not that he believed the young lady would be pleased to see him.

He would have called the police, but yet again his phone was dead. He spent the night in the hospital with his phone's battery dwindling in the pocket of his coat – the one item the lovely orderlies did not clean for him. He'd not been anywhere near his charger since, so when he needed it, as so often happened, it was as dead as a doornail.

The one caravan at the park that appeared to have life in it - the lights were on at least – did not have anyone at home, so his hope to call the police from there was dashed too.

Would Alverez listen even if he could get to speak to her? That was a good question.

Stuffed into his coat pockets were the torn-up pieces of paper from the caravan's wastepaper bin. It was evidence but it wasn't what one might call conclusive. Yet again, as he had been almost since arriving in Lyme Regis, he was reacting to a hunch. The way he viewed things might be different to how another person viewed them, but he had what he believed was a contract for the Fieldings to sign their bakery over to Greg Garside, a man Albert now knew to be the father of the suspicious, delinquent, criminal, scumbag, Cooper Garside.

Garside. He saw the name when he first picked out the pieces of paper from the trash. It meant nothing at the time, and he'd forgotten it completely until he walked into the shop at the petrol station.

That he found Greg Garside's son in the caravan further cemented Albert's belief the two of them were behind the double murders. It took some reassembling to piece together enough of the torn pages to figure out what he was looking at. Along the way he found a piece where Daniel Fielding had signed his name.

The date next to Daniel Fielding's signature was three days ago.

A full day before Daniel Fielding knew his brother was still alive.

One might concede that this suggested Karl's return ruined Daniel's plans to sell and gave strength to the story Superintendent Alverez wanted to believe. But what if it wasn't just Daniel's plans that were ruined? What if Daniel had been leaned on to sell?

To Albert, it was equally easy to believe Greg Garside wanted the bakery. The figure he offered in the contract was eyewatering. Surely more than the business was worth.

Albert's hypothesis went thusly: Karl's disappearance at the hands of the Gastrothief created an opportunity for Greg Garside to lean on one of the brothers, the one he knew to be more susceptible to persuasion. Karl's return scuppered Greg's plans and upon discovering Daniel had signed the contract, he and Karl argued – the fight Troy overheard. His mind changed, Daniel withdrew from the plan to sell, and Greg reacted by removing the barrier to his success. Then he framed Daniel for his brother's murder and staged Daniel's suicide.

The killer dispatched his son to retrieve the contract when he recognised the link it presented. It was Albert's blind luck he picked it up yesterday. That the police had overlooked it was sloppy. It should have been gathered as evidence, but Albert could see they found an explanation that fit and stopped looking for a different one.

The sound of another car coming down the hill behind him almost made Albert raise his arm to thumb a lift. It wasn't worth bothering now; he was so close a driver would be dropping him off within seconds unless they conveniently happened to be heading for Daisy's house.

The car chose to stop anyway. Its four way lights flashed into life as a warning to other motorists and the driver angled into the side of the road, parking with two wheels on the grass.

Perplexed, Albert wondered what they could want until the driver clambered out.

"Albert, what are you doing out here? Where are you going?" asked Detective Constable Judy Marsh.

"Judy! Boy, have I got something to show you!" Albert jogged to her side.

Marsh held out a hand, palm showing to ward him off.

"I'm in enough trouble already, thank you, Albert. I don't think I can get involved any further."

Albert paid her concerns no mind. "Greg Garside is the killer, Judy. He was trying to buy the Fielding's bakery."

Not hiding her exasperation, Marsh screwed up her face when she said, "What? What are you talking about, Albert? Superintendent Alverez sewed up the case hours ago. Daniel Fielding killed his brother before taking his own life."

Albert whacked the roof of Marsh's car and dug out a handful of torn up contract.

"No, he didn't!"

Marsh looked at the scraps of paper, her eyebrows raised.

"Um, that's just some litter, Albert."

Impatiently, he explained what she would find if they pieced it back together."

"Albert, that doesn't mean anything," she groaned. "An important local businessman wanted to buy a thriving company. He probably planned to convert their name and success into his own. Everyone in Lyme Regis knows he's opened two shops here only to see them fail because everyone had been going to Fieldings for decades. You can't erode that kind of loyalty."

Albert shook his head, tired of having to do things himself.

"Can you take me to Daisy's house? Please?" he added, his voice close to begging. "If Alverez is right then Daisy has nothing to fear, and Greg Garside will be writing her a fat cheque any day now." He paused to make sure Marsh was listening. "If I'm right, then Garside has already killed two people and has one young woman between himself and something he dearly wants."

Marsh groaned again. She was supposed to be going home. She had a date tonight. Not that she really felt like going out, not with her boss's words still ringing in her ears. She was going to mess up her private life too.

With a sad nod of her head, she said, "Get in."

Cooper Garside

Rex peered out from behind a large wooden crate. A shaft of moonlight from the door cut through the darkness inside the storeroom like a knife. But only for a moment. Light from overhead strip lamps, blinking as they came to life, invaded the shadows, chasing the night into the corners and under shelves where all it could do was lurk ready to reclaim the storeroom the moment the lights went out again.

The shockingly sudden intensity of the light stung Rex's eyes and forced to squint for a moment, he ducked back out of sight.

There he let his nose and ears figure out who had just arrived.

The professor was disappointed with his day and trying hard not to let it show. Inevitably, hundreds of fossil hunters had arrived to scour the same area he wanted to preserve and carefully inspect. In his opinion, fresh fossil beds were of enormous scientific importance and ought to be protected. No such statute existed, so he, his colleagues and contemporaries were stuck battling Joe average and his desire to dig up a dinosaur.

Most of his students arrived with hangovers this morning, for which he knew he was at least partially to blame, and having sent half of them to help search for Albert's dog, well … they just didn't get a whole lot done in the period between sun up and sun down.

Anywhere else in the world he would have teams working around the clock to excavate his incredible find and to look for what else the exposed strata might hold. Here it was too dangerous. The cliffs were no joke and with two deaths in the last two days, suicides or otherwise, he was rightly cautious.

"We'll spread the smaller ammonites and such out on that table," Rex heard the professor say. His voice was strained in a way that made Rex think he must be carrying something heavy.

Peering out again, Rex saw there were half a dozen humans inside and a couple more still filling the doorway. He could smell them all; the familiar mix of dirt and outdoors, the sweat of the day and some spilled burger sauce on someone's clothes.

Sniffing deeply, as was his habit, Rex was trying to decide whether he should just announce his presence when another scent caught his nose.

Cinnamon.

With a jolt, Rex realised he'd been smelling it all along. It was hidden among the soil and dust, and it was only faint, but it wasn't the cinnamon that made Rex reveal his location. It was the human wearing it.

Bruno thought they were supposed to be hiding, so Rex's decision to expose himself made him question if he might have misunderstood the instructions again. He looked across from his cubby hole next to a giant dinosaur bone to where Reggie hid beneath a shelf.

"What's going on?" he hissed.

Reggie could only shrug.

Both dogs twisted their head to look back down the line where the rest of the pack, including the cats, were all tucked out of sight from the humans at the other end of the storeroom.

Resisting the need to growl, Rex padded into sight.

His unexpected presence terrified the first person to see him. Ryan habitually smoked recreational plant-based drugs and wasn't firing on all cylinders when the giant German Shepherd strolled into view.

Believing he was seeing either a werewolf or a prehistoric dog come to life from the assorted fossils in the museum's storeroom, he chose to scream. The high-pitched wail of fear made Rex and more than half the humans jump.

Standing closest to him, one of the professor's best students, Rebecca, slapped Ryan on the arm with enough force to knock him sideways.

"What's the matter with you?"

Her cry filled the air as the echoes of his terrified scream were still dying away but by then everyone had noticed the dog looking at them.

The professor said, "Rex?" He knew who he was looking at but needed a moment to process the information. "How did you get in here?"

Behind Rex, Arthur was making a fuss.

"We should stay out of sight," insisted Jessie who was finding it hard to stay hidden – even the biggest crates weren't big enough for her to hide behind.

Arthur wasn't listening. "Nah, I want to see. I was

promised a human to kill and there are humans here. One of them will do."

Crash and Wallop were freaking out. Swayed into joining in because everyone else was and it sounded fun, they had missed their dinner and now they were about to get into trouble.

"This is bad dog behaviour," whined Crash. "What are we going to do? What are we going to do?"

His own fears propelled by those around him, Reggie made a break for the door.

"I'm getting out of here! Every dog for himself!"

Tailspin shouted, "Noooo! Stay hidden you idiots! We can go back out the way we came in."

That might have been true if they hadn't been making so much noise and if Rex hadn't already been spotted. However, the dogs as a pack were panicked beyond reason and it was too late to prevent the stampede already ensuing.

Crossing the storeroom to get to Rex, the professor's feet faltered when a dozen assorted dogs exploded from behind a set of wooden crates behind Rex.

It wasn't just dogs, he noted in his amazement, there were cats here too. He spotted at least two, one of which was on top of the crates and coming straight for him.

Thinking fast, the professor barked an order, "Shut the door!"

Skidding, their paws scrambling on the polished concrete floor of the storeroom, the dogs rounded the corner behind Rex. They were heading for the door, planning to barrel into the night where they would return to their homes and pretend they had no knowledge of any reports of dogs running riot. Whatever their humans heard, it wasn't them.

Rex had other ideas. He had something more important

to do and the bedlam around him was an unwelcome distraction.

He watched the door close and was glad for it; he wanted everyone to stay right where they were.

Sucking in some air, Rex barked his loudest, "Enough!"

Hearing the voice of an alpha – every pack needed one – the dogs skidded to a stop.

The cats did not.

Penelope was at the window trying to let herself out again. Her day had been far more active than she liked, but the memory of the dogs chewing on bits of bone-shaped rock would stay with her for years. She heard Rex's bellow, but ignored it. She would have been out and gone in the next second were it not for the sound of Arthur's battle cry.

The professor saw the cat coming. It looked deranged. One eye was missing and its fur, a sort of dirty sandy colour, was missing in places to suggest the cat was diseased as well as demented. Unable to take his eyes from the crazed creature, his feet took a step back when the cat began to make an ungodly screeching sound.

Rex barked, "No, Arthur!" but his words went unheeded as the cat leapt.

Dogs, humans, even Penelope watched the scene unravel, no one making a sound as Arthur twisted his body to bring his back legs around. Flying through space with all sixteen claws extended (he lost two in a fight years ago) Arthur was going straight for the human's throat.

The professor, raised by a long-serving soldier and not unused to life in the wild where animal attacks could and did occur, side stepped the flying feline.

Unable to believe what was happening, Arthur turned his head, his eyes meeting the tall man's for a moment.

Then he was snatched from the air by a meaty hand that gripped the scruff of his neck.

The professor would have thought it impossible for the cat to make a worse noise, but was wrong.

The language spilling from the alley cat's mouth would have emptied a bar full of sailors so it was a good thing the humans couldn't understand the noises he made.

Holding the cat aloft, the professor pointed to a wire basket.

"Rebecca, could you empty that for me, please?"

With the struggling, swearing cat held at arm's length, the professor took the basket, lowered it over his hand, and let go, trapping the cat on top of a crate.

Arthur spun around to exact terrible revenge the moment he was free.

"He's biting the steel," Rebecca observed, mildly concerned the creature might be rabid.

With a heavy ammonite pinning the basket down, the professor backed away.

Less than ten seconds had passed since he first spotted Rex, but when he looked back at the German Shepherd, Rex was no longer there.

Rex was in the far corner of the storeroom, a part of the large space he hadn't explored so far. There, in a locker in which some cleaning supplies were stored, a figure hid.

Rex knew who was in there. It was someone he wanted to bite. The human on the other side was trying to be still and silent, as if either thing might fool a dog's nose. He could hear a dog sniffing at the edge of the door and was almost whimpering with fear.

Cooper Garside was terrified. Not of the dog on the other side of the door though that did worry him, he was terrified of his father. Their relationship had never been great, and had worsened as Cooper grew from boy to man. His father wanted a carbon copy of himself and did nothing to hide his disappointment at what he got.

Cooper's mother left when he was a toddler. That she left him with his father said enough about her that Cooper chose never to bother seeking her out even when his father beat him. As he often did.

Cooper could do no right, and growing up in the shadow of his father's success, he lived in a perpetual state of trying to find a way to please. Every now and then he would do something that might draw a smile or a word of encouragement. Conditioned to strive for those moments, he did anything his father asked.

It was rarely good enough.

He knew of his father's more violent side first hand, but was fourteen when he saw it inflicted on another person. Greg Garside wanted to buy a bakery in Yeovil. The owner didn't want to sell. Greg Garside changed his mind. It wasn't so much what he did, but the threat of that which he was not yet doing, a tactic Cooper knew only too well.

The sound of approaching feet took Cooper's breath away. When his bike ran out of fuel, he attempted to refill it only to find his debit card no longer worked. His father had turned it off. Trapped in Lyme Regis, he needed somewhere to stay out of sight.

Alone in the museum storeroom having snuck through from the museum itself when they were open, he was hiding from his father. He couldn't go home, not after his most recent failure. He lived with Daisy and his father would go there looking for him. More than anything, he wanted to keep Daisy safe from harm. If he wasn't there, then Daisy wouldn't have to protect him, and she wouldn't have to see her boyfriend cower in fear.

Hungry, scared, cold, and with nowhere he could go without endangering someone else, he'd been hugging his knees and hoping the world would simply end when the animals started to come through the window. He spotted the German Shepherd instantly – it was the same dog who chased and almost caught him yesterday. The same dog that stopped him from completing his father's latest task.

The feet paused outside the locker door.

"What is it, Rex?" asked a man, his voice deep and confident. "There's something in there?"

"Yes," said Rex. "The person who hurt my human. Please open the door so I can chase him."

Cooper had a knife in his pocket. He wished it was in his hand to use as a threat, but there was no way to contort his body to reach it, and before he could consider what else he could do, the door to the locker opened and bright light robbed his vision.

The professor spasmed in surprise to find a person in the locker. His first thought was that the dog had found another body. Then it moved.

Rex had his lips pulled back to show his teeth. The skinny young man before him had hurt his human. Made him bleed and if ever there was a reason to get bitten, that was it.

Growling at the form cowering in the tight confines of the steel locker, Rex couldn't bring himself to do it. The young human was pathetic. Too scared and feeble looking for Rex to consider attacking. It was more than that though. Despite the fact that he'd hurt Albert, Rex believed the human was innocent of the murders. His scent was where it ought not to be, but so was his father's – Rex continued to assume that was the relationship.

The professor offered the kid a hand to get up.

"You okay there?" he asked. His assumption was that he'd caught a fossil thief; the market was buoyant and lucrative. Now was not the time to pass judgement. Not yet. First to check the kid was okay.

Cooper accepted the offered hand – what choice did he have? It wasn't like he could close the locker door and pretend he wasn't there.

"I'm ... I'm okay," he managed to stammer, his eyes never leaving the dog. "I didn't mean to hurt the old man."

Rex narrowed his eyes at the mention of his human's injury.

The comment made the professor blink and give his head a slight shake.

"You hurt an old man?"

The palaeontology students were pressing in around him, all trying to see.

With a shout, Archie blurted, "Hey, he's on my phone! The police are looking for him!"

Shocked into motion, Cooper tried to run. There was nowhere to go and no chance he could get to the door, but he tried, nevertheless.

Rex moved to block his path and the professor snagged his collar before he got two feet.

With a rough shove that sent Cooper back into the locker door, the professor demanded, "What did you do?"

Rex tilted his head to one side, examining the young man. He didn't smell like a killer. He was too scared for a start and there was no blood on or about him. It was obvious to Rex's nose the kid hadn't washed in more than a day and his clothes stank of the bike and the grass and dirt from the caravan park. If he had killed the man in the caravan, Rex would be able to smell it. If not the blood of his victim, then at least the victim's scent on the kid's clothing. It wasn't there.

"Shall I call the police, professor?" enquired Rebecca, always looking to be seen as the responsible one among his students.

Cooper begged, "No! Please. I didn't mean to hurt him. I just needed to get away. I was trying to get to Daisy. I had no idea her dad had been killed."

The professor held up a hand to slow the kid down. Whoever the young man was, he had tears on his cheeks already and snot coming from his nose. He was a mess.

"Let's back up a bit, shall we? Are you telling me you are not in here trying to steal fossils?"

Rex looked up at the professor, one eyebrow jinked. "He's related to the killer. He's involved, but not in a way that makes him guilty. I don't think. I haven't got all the parts figured out yet. Keep him talking, will you?"

Cooper's face creased in disbelief. "Fossils? Who would want to steal fossils?" he asked, showing his ignorance.

"Okay, so why are you in here?"

Cooper cast his eyes to the ground where he found Rex ready to meet his gaze. He had to find somewhere new to look, but surrounded by the professor and his students, plus a pack of dogs, he was forced to give up.

Looking at the professor again, he said, "I'm hiding."

"From the police?"

"No. From my father. I think he might have killed Daisy's dad."

Rex barked, "A-ha!" The sound in the quiet of the storeroom made everybody jump. Reggie stepped away from the little puddle between his back legs and acted as if he had no idea where it might have come from.

The professor felt increasingly like he'd come in halfway

through a conversation, but then remembered Albert saying the name in connection with his investigation.

"Wait. Daisy? That's the name of the murder victim's daughter." Neurons connected in his brain. "You think your father killed him? Did he kill the brother too?"

Rex hopped from paw to paw. "Ooh, ooh, this is good. Full confession time. Blurt the truth, kid!"

"What!" Hiding from the world for more than twenty-four hours, Cooper had no idea anyone else was dead. "Daniel Fielding is dead too?"

Rex sat down again. "Drat. He doesn't *know* anything."

The professor nodded. "Both deaths look like suicide, but Albert didn't believe it. He said he knew Karl Fielding. I think you need to talk to the police, young man."

Cooper shook his head in a panic. "No, no police! They'll just arrest me. They always do." Cooper's mind was whirling, the news that both Fielding brothers were dead almost too disturbing to accept. However, it was the natural conclusion he drew from it that really shook him to his core. "Daisy! He'll go after Daisy next!"

Cooper tried to run again only to find his way blocked by the professor and everyone else. Too scared for what might occur if he didn't get to her, Cooper whipped out his pocketknife. A flick extended the blade.

"Get out of my way!" he yelled, threatening the air with his weapon. "I've got a knife!"

The professor had backed up a pace amid gasps from his students. Across the room, Arthur screamed blue murder and headbutted the cage. No one had noticed but it was slowly yet inexorably moving toward the edge of the crate on which it sat.

Reaching to his belt, the professor popped a press stud and pulled his own knife from its sheath.

"That's not a knife." The professor paused at that point, recognising the words from somewhere though the source eluded him.

"Um, yes, it is," pointed out Rebecca. "Yours is just bigger, Professor." Her comment on size drew a snigger from several students to make Rebecca roll her eyes.

Trying to regain control of the situation, the professor said, "Just calm down, okay? No one needs to get hurt. I'm going to put my knife away. I want you to do the same. If you are worried about this Daisy person ..."

"She's my girlfriend."

The professor nodded to acknowledge the kid's concern. "Let's go together. If she is in danger, it's no good to face it alone."

Cooper lowered the blade nervously. "We have to go now. It's not far."

Turning to Rebecca, the professor said, "Okay, you're in charge here. Unpack today's finds and label them. I'll be back ... in a little while." He was already forging a path toward the door, one hand on Cooper's right bicep to drag him along. His students moved out of the way to let him pass.

Rebecca asked, "You're taking the dogs, professor?"

He turned to see what she was talking about and found a trail of hounds hot on his heels. Led by Rex, there were more of them than he'd noticed before. Taking the dogs had not been his intention, but Rex had a look about him that said he was coming no matter what the professor had to say about it. He wanted to deliver Rex back to Albert anyway, so keeping him close was the only sensible move.

Starting toward the door again, he called over his shoulder, "I guess so."

Always Right

There was no space for her to park in front of Daisy's house, forcing Marsh to hunt for a spot further down the road.

"Wait here, Albert." She grabbed his hand when he reached to unclip his seatbelt. "I mean it. I'm going to check on Daisy and I will be back in under a minute. Do not get out of the car."

Albert said nothing, but dipped his head to show he accepted her instruction. He waited for Marsh to walk away, then craned his neck to see.

The vehicle behind them was a small panel van, the kind with opaque sides. It completely blocked his view of Daisy's front door.

He tried using the door mirror to spot Detective Constable Marsh returning, but there was no sign of her. Huffing an impatient breath, Albert unclipped his seatbelt anyway. Marsh had to be inside the house. If she returned saying everything was fine, Albert would send her on her way and walk back to his accommodation.

Lyme Regis Layover

He didn't think he was wrong about Garside, but he needed to find Rex. With Rex he could return and make sure Daisy wasn't in danger. Quite what he was going to do, Albert had not yet worked out, but a glance at the clock told him Marsh's one minute promise had already become three.

His feet twitched.

When the digital clock ticked off another minute, he exited the car. His heart thumped in his chest again, beating at twice the pace it ought to. Did the adrenalin prolong his life, or rob him of years by swiftly eroding the number of beats his ticker had left? He didn't know the answer, but it was only one of many thoughts swirling in his mind when he approached Daisy's place for the second time that day.

There were lights on inside, but no sign of movement. Remembering the layout, Albert knew the room at the front of the house was a dining room/office that looked to be infrequently used. If Daisy and Marsh were inside, they would be in the back.

He was about to knock on the door, risking Marsh's wrath and hoping for it, when he noticed the door wasn't fully shut. Gritting his teeth, his breath seething in and out, Albert nudged the door gently open to listen.

Not a sound came from within.

Cursing that he always had to be right, Albert stepped over the threshold.

In the hallway leading past the office/dining room to the living room at the back, Albert listened again. If Daisy and Marsh were here, there would be some sign of them. Did he call out? Was Marsh comforting Daisy with a hug and that was why he couldn't hear them?

Doubting he would find anything of the sort, Albert started moving again only to stop a pace later when a shadow moved.

It fell across the patch of carpet just inside the living room, it's movement fluid and obviously human. It wasn't inside the house though, the shadow being cast was coming through a window.

Albert reached Daisy's living space and what this afternoon had been neat and tidy was now a scene of confusion. An upturned table and a broken lamp grim evidence of a struggle. Of Detective Constable Marsh there was no sign. Cursing yet again, Albert looked about for a phone.

Maybe Marsh had walked in on whatever was happening and was currently in pursuit of the person behind it, and maybe she was dead. Albert had no way of knowing whether she might have called it in, but his search for a phone drew a blank and he knew why: young people don't have land lines. Everything is mobile now.

Raging at himself for not insisting he accompany Marsh into Daisy's house, he ran from the living room to the kitchen. Guessing the layout he found a back door and ran through it.

Albert crashed to the ground unconscious before he even saw the person waiting in the shadow to his left.

Greg Garside looked down at the old man sprawled across the garden path, his left arm stretched out awkwardly where he landed half in and half out of a barren vegetable patch.

Dropping the rock, he asked the air, "Now, who the heck are you?"

Listen to the Dog

The dogs had started jumping into the load bed of the professor's blue pickup truck before he got the chance to invite them. It was as if they understood what was happening and knew where he was going.

At the hospital Albert joked that his dog would be out trying to solve the crime. The professor had taken it for a joke, but now he questioned if there might be a hint of truth behind it. Some of the smaller dogs had to be lifted and placed in the back of the truck, the old Basset Hound in particular wasn't going to climb in by himself, but he looked keen, his tail spinning in a circle.

Rex didn't bother with the load bed; he followed Cooper into the front where he claimed prime position in the middle of the front bench seat.

"Come on!" Cooper demanded, desperate to get going. "We need to get there!" He was calling Daisy, something he'd avoided doing for nearly twenty-four hours, and she wasn't answering. He had dozens of missed calls and messages from her, each of which he'd ignored because telling her anything meant telling her everything. He hadn't been able to face it or her and now his cowardice might have cost her life. His whole body twitched with adrenalin.

Slamming the tailgate shut, the professor asked, "Can't you just message or call her?"

"I tried! She's not answering! I might believe she was ignoring my calls because she's mad I didn't come home last night, but she would have responded to the text. Something's wrong. I know it is."

The professor turned the key, his V8 engine roaring to life like a dragon rudely wakened from a deep sleep.

Twisting to look over his shoulder, he shoved the gearstick into reverse and was about to gun the accelerator when he remembered the dogs. There were maybe twenty assorted pooches in the back, any or all of which might fall out if he drove too fast.

Just as he started to coax his truck back past the storeroom door, two cats leapt up and in among the dogs. That the crazy one had escaped his metal cage demanded some investigation – the professor, having seen the size and muscle definition on the cat – worried it might have bench pressed the wire basket and ammonite used to pin it in place. Or perhaps headbutted them until they exploded.

The dogs were giving the cat a wide berth.

Once out in the street and with directions from Cooper, the professor drove as fast as he could with his canine load hanging on in the back.

"Up here," Cooper pointed down a dark passage lined on both sides by garages. "Park by the one with the red door. We'll go in the back."

"Still worried about the police, huh?"

"Damn right I am. I got out of jail twelve days ago. I am not going back."

Thinking the son took after the father and that he needed to watch his back, the professor stopped the truck where Cooper indicated and killed the engine.

Rex was already on his feet. He'd been sniffing the air all the way. The car's air conditioning unit filtered out too much of the outside smell for him to be able to detect anything worthwhile and now they were here, he wanted to see what was what.

The second the professor cracked his door, Rex bolted.

The scent of his human was here, and it was fresh.

Behind him, those dogs who could jump down from the back of the professor's truck were doing so. The cats too, inquisitive nature not something they ever chose to hide.

Cooper ran around from his side, bursting through the garden gate Rex had already leapt.

The scent of the man who almost ran him down was here. He was Cooper's father; Rex now knew his first assumption about their connection was correct. He knew who the killer was and unless Cooper was lying, the kid, even though he still needed to answer for hurting Albert, was innocent of the murders.

There were two other scents beside the killer's and his human's: two women, both young, neither in season though very much breeding age. The scent of one was everywhere, suggesting to Rex this was her house and his nose, when he pushed it for answers, found a subtle connection between her smell and that of the two Fielding brothers.

Rex lifted his head – this was the home of the daughter his human had talked about last night. The knowledge brought him no closer to stopping the killer.

Cooper had torn past Rex to charge into the house. His scent was here too though not as fresh as the others. It had to be a day old or more, which corroborated his story. He was inside now, shouting for his mate.

No one else had got to the house before Cooper ran back out, his face deeply etched with panic.

"She's not here! There's been a fight."

Rex barked to get the humans' attention. "She was taken by his father," Rex explained. "My human was here too, but I cannot tell if he went with them, or went after them. The scents are all jumbled."

The professor frowned. "Did that look like he was trying to tell us something? That wasn't just me, was it?"

Cooper flared his eyes. "What? What are you talking about? It's a dog! Didn't you hear me? Daisy isn't here! There's a lamp knocked over inside and the doors are both open, front and back. Daisy always keeps them locked!"

"Kid, we need to call the police." The professor wasn't asking a question and already had his phone in his hand. He was also walking back to the car. "Where would he take her, Cooper? If your dad plans to hurt her, where would he go?"

Cooper's head swam with confusing emotions that threatened to rob him of consciousness. He couldn't think straight. His throat was tight with the terror of losing the one good thing in his life and he wanted to rage at the skies.

Rex barked again. "Can you two dummies listen for once. He'll have gone to the cliffs! Isn't that what he did with the first two victims? He keeps staging suicides. I don't know if my human is in trouble or not, but I'm not hanging around to find out. Let's get this thing moving!" he growled out a command and jumped back into the cab of the truck.

The professor had the emergency dispatcher in his ear, but Rex's odd behaviour and sudden interest in going for another ride had planted a seed of thought in his head.

"Hello, sir? Which service do you require, please?"

"Um, police," he mumbled, fishing his keys from a pocket. The noise in his ear changed when he was connected to the local police dispatch office and in the gap between speaking to one person and the next, the professor said, "I think we should head to the cliffs."

Rex rolled his eyes.

Time to Die

Albert came to with a start. His head felt like it was splitting in half. He hadn't seen his assailant, but had a pretty good idea who he was. Greg Garside had seen him moving inside the house just as Albert saw Greg's shadow outside. The big difference was Greg moved faster.

Trying to sit up, Albert found his hands were secured behind his back. It felt like one of those plastic zip tie things he knew law enforcement and other agencies favoured these days.

His ankles were secured too, but that was all. Lying on his front, he pulled his knees up to his chest and used his forehead to lever himself upright.

He was in the back of a van, and it was in motion. That much was easy to discern. How long he'd been out and where they might now be were more pertinent questions. Unfortunately, they were also ones to which he had no answers.

A bump rocked the back of the van, sending Albert airborne for a second. He landed with a crash that sent spikes of pain through his knees and ankles. It got worse from there and Albert knew why: they had left the road.

The van slowed to allow for the undulating ground. Not that it made much difference to the ride in the back. Unable to stay on his knees, Albert rolled onto his back once more.

In so doing, he bumped into something soft on his left. Finding another person, he shuffled until he faced away from them and used his hands to feel their clothing and body. It was Marsh, he felt certain.

"Marsh! Marsh!" Albert didn't bother to keep his voice down; he couldn't see the point.

Marsh didn't answer, but making his heart just about stop, a scream of terror burst from a different set of lungs right in front of his face.

That he was listening to Daisy Fielding was never in doubt.

The van lurched to a stop just as Daisy ran out of air.

The scream seemed to continue inside the tortured bruise that was Albert's skull, the high-pitched sound bouncing around like it was trying to find an exit and being constantly denied.

"Where am I?" Daisy blurted, "It was ... it was Cooper's dad! He hit me!" The memories of her evening came back in a wash of horror. Sitting alone in her house, miserable and frightened, she'd leapt from her sofa the moment her doorbell rang.

She prayed it would be Cooper, returning safe and sound from wherever he had been for the last day, but halfway there she remembered he had his own key and would have just let himself in. Thinking maybe he lost it, she nevertheless called out to the person outside.

"Who is it?"

"Daisy, it's Greg. Cooper's dad. Can I come in? I need

to talk to you about Cooper. And about your dad and the bakery."

Daisy knew Greg Garside. She knew what kind of man he was. She'd seen the bruises on Cooper and believed the stories he told her about his dad and how he blamed him for his mother leaving. He'd tortured the poor boy his entire life, always reminding him that it was his fault there was no mother in the house. How could a toddler be held responsible in such a way? It was the basest cruelty.

Regardless, she wanted to hear what he had to tell her about Cooper and never once thought to worry he might turn his violent streak against her.

And he didn't. Not to start with. He apologised for turning up unannounced and asked if she'd seen his son. Greg claimed to have been unable to get hold of him since the previous evening.

She didn't know where he was of course and said she couldn't get hold of him either.

That was when Cooper's dad started to show his usual self.

"Are you sure, Daisy?" he challenged, his voice dripping with the suggestion she was lying. "Are you sure the little twerp isn't just cowering out of sight in your living room?"

"Quite certain, thank you?" she snapped, a frown on her brow.

"I think maybe I'll just check for myself."

She tried to stop him by closing the door, but the ninety-eight-pound woman proved no match for Greg Garside's bulk and muscle. He barged into her house, roughly shoving her to one side. Thinking better of it, he kicked the door shut behind him and grabbed her wrist. Dragging her along the hallway, he shouted for Cooper to show himself.

Slapping and clawing at Greg's wrist, Daisy screamed, "He's not here! Let go of me! You're hurting me."

Greg did let go, timing it so he released her hand just when she was pulling away. She fell backward, knocking over a table and breaking a lamp before landing awkwardly against the sofa.

Looming over her, Cooper's dad produced a sheaf of paper, something official looking which he brandished in front of her face.

"I've got a contract for you to sign. You have a career of your own and no use for your family's bakery." He looked her up and down. "If you'd like to take your clothes off right now, I might let you have free scones once a month," he laughed as if it were funny. "I must say," he stared lecherously at her chest, "I see why Cooper's been dating you all this time."

Feeling defiled, Daisy pushed herself to her feet.

"I'm not signing that. I'm not signing over my dad's bakery. Not to you. Not to anyone. His legacy will live on." She didn't know where the fire in her belly came from, but she was livid. How dare he enter her house and make her feel like something he might scrape off his shoe? How dare he presume that he could buy her father's bakery?

That was when he hit her.

The first blow knocked her down though she remained conscious. Tasting blood she looked about for her phone. It was on the sideboard under the television in its charging cradle. She tried to move toward it though she knew Cooper's dad was lining up to hit her again. She got halfway.

Snapped back to the present when the van's rear door opened, Daisy looked out as moonlight flooded in around the broad shoulders of Greg Garside.

She burst from the bed of the van, screeching with

outrage and fear when she launched herself for the thin gap on his left.

She never stood a chance.

Greg Garside swatted her to one side with a club-sized hand that sent her head into the sidewall of the van. She bounced off and was caught again, Greg gripping the back of her neck to drag her out.

Marsh was yet to move, and Albert could do little but stare.

"You probably should have signed the contract, don't you think?" Greg smirked. "You could be relaxing in a nice warm bath now, lavender and camomile scented bubbles against your skin and a hefty wedge of money on its way to your bank account. Instead, you're going to find yourself so terribly overcome with grief you decided to take your own life."

Albert couldn't see a way out of his predicament or a way to save Daisy, but that didn't mean he wasn't going to try. First off, he tried some stalling tactics.

"A third suicide in the same manner in the same family for the third day straight?" he spat. "No one is going to buy that."

"Really?" Greg smiled. "They bought the first two hook, line, and sinker. Daisy taking her own life now she has no one left to live for is perfectly believable."

"What about her boyfriend?" Albert challenged. "Your son? Shouldn't she live for him?"

"Well, she could have, but she chose to be stupid instead. I would have given her the money, but you know what? I think I've about had it with that useless fool of a boy. Maybe he should commit suicide too."

"He's not part of this then?" Albert probed. He had the man talking, and Greg's confidence was clearly such that he felt no need to speed through the deed and get it done. He didn't think they were going to catch him ever, let alone tonight in the act.

"My son?" Greg laughed. "That idiot? I sent him on a simple errand last night and I haven't seen him since. Honestly, I was worried for a while that the police might have found the previous contract and come asking a few uncomfortable questions. Oh, I've got alibis, but always best to not need them I say."

With a flourish, he produced a knife from his jacket. It was a standard nine inch kitchen knife one could buy anywhere and completely fit for purpose. He shoved the tip into Daisy's neck, drawing a drop of blood and a squeal of pain.

Albert sat up again, crunching his abs and proud that he'd been able to perform the sit up unaided. Keeping his eyes locked on Greg's he said, "You mean the contract Daniel signed three days ago? The one that shows you were trying to buy their bakery and had every reason to kill Karl Fielding when he returned?"

Doubt showed in Greg Garside's eye for the first time.

"You're bluffing."

"How could I possibly know anything about it if I'm bluffing?"

Getting angry now, a state he was rarely far from, Greg demanded, "Just who are you, old man?"

Albert leered at his captor. "I'm Albert Smith."

A beat of silence passed.

"Who?"

Albert felt like filing a complaint. It seemed everyone everywhere knew who he was except the one person he needed to now quake in fear.

"Come on, man. The Gastrothief. Surely you must have heard of him."

Mystified, Greg asked, "Is that the fella on Channel 4? Does that food show?"

Daisy said, "No. That's the Gourmet Chef."

Giving up, Albert said, "Look, the point is, the police know about the contract and that," Albert indicated Marsh's inert form with his head, "is a police officer. You kill her and they will never stop looking for you."

Greg gave a one shoulder shrug, utterly unbothered. "They'll be looking. They won't be looking for me though. In many ways, being forced to wait for the Fieldings' estate to be settled to then buy the bakery, works in my favour. There's less of a connection leading back to me and it will cost me less. So maybe you're telling the truth about the contract; it wouldn't surprise me, my son is a useless streak of nothing. Maybe you're not though. Either way. I can't let you go. I think I'll do you here too. If I'm lucky, they won't even find the bodies. That's the joy of the cliffs, you see. By the time they find the remains, they are so beaten about and bedraggled, they can't tell what happened. It's not like they'll find a stab wound, is it?"

Albert was going to say something, but Greg brought his knife hand down in a vicious sweep that cut through the tie around Albert's ankles. Not given time to react, Albert found himself pulled from the van when Greg grabbed one ankle and gave it a vicious yank.

He landed on his backside on the grass, dampness seeping instantly into his trousers.

"Get up!"

Narrowly avoiding a kick intended to encourage him into moving, Albert rolled onto his knees and struggled to his feet.

Greg pointed the knife and swung Daisy around, his strength and grip on her neck sufficient to ensure she went where he wanted her to go.

The cliff was fifty yards ahead. The land just ended. There was a barrier in the way, but not one that would stop a person from getting to the drop off. Rather, it was a low fence with warning signs every few yards.

Albert figured he had a minute to come up with a plan. He could run, but how far could he get. Exiting the van, it was clear there was no one around. He could see the lights of Lyme Regis far below and could make out Sunny Days Caravan Park to his left. It was two hundred yards to the east and might as well have been on the moon.

"The mistake I made with your dad," Greg felt like talking again, "Was I killed him before I put him over the cliff. That was a mistake because it left behind evidence. I'm clever though, see, so I made sure to get it right the next time. I told your uncle I had news about what happened to his brother and said I needed to meet with him. I wasn't sure the fool would turn up, but he did. The idiot. I took his key and went to his house so I could write a nice little suicide note. He confessed to killing his brother and I left the rock I used to kill your dad in your uncle's garden. As I understand it the police found it already. How clever is that? I'll make sure I write a nice note from you too, Daisy. Is there anything you would like me to include?"

Daisy spat a torrent of filth and flailed her arms, trying to break Greg's grip on her neck.

He laughed. "I'll take that as a 'no', shall I?"

Albert chose that moment to charge. He might not be able to get away, but he was willing to bet Daisy could outrun the overweight baker. She was young and light and clearly athletic if her nimble friends at the gentleman's club were anything to go by.

Greg's head was tipped back in mirth, and coming back to level when Albert swung his tied hands upward to connect under his chin. It didn't have all that much power to it in Albert's opinion, not like it would have done in his prime, but both fists smacked into Greg Garside's jaw with all the energy he could muster.

Greg's head snapped back, and his hand lost it's grip on Daisy's neck.

"Run!"

The breeze blowing along the shore whipped Albert's shout from his lips, but not before it spurred Daisy into motion. Not that Albert was watching. His focus was on the man with the knife. His two-handed uppercut took him off balance, costing Albert a precious second he needed to capitalise on the first blow. All he could do was follow through with a shoulder barge that shunted Greg backward and over.

The baker's feet tangled, toppling him to the ground. It was all the opportunity Albert was going to get, but the question was one of fight or flight? If he ran, could he outrun him? If he stood and fought, could he beat him?

Since the answer to both was almost certainly a resounding 'no'. Albert did what he knew he ought, he bought Daisy more time.

Greg Garside was getting up already. He'd fallen, but rolled with it to get his feet back under his body. Albert aimed a kick at his face, hoping he might do enough damage to make the killer run away. He wasn't quick enough. The kick, well-aimed and with plenty of force, was parried by Greg's forearm which he flung instinctively in front of his face.

With his foot knocked away, and his hands still tied, Albert fought his own balance to stay on his feet and that was the end of the fight. All Greg needed was a second to regain his feet and all the advantage swung back his way.

Albert sucked in a deep breath, his lungs demanding oxygen the way they always do in a fight. Squaring off against his opponent, they were two yards apart, the wicked knife in Greg's hand held upwards and ready to thrust.

Greg spat blood, his tongue missing the tip after Albert's first blow. Beyond reason now, his hope for verdicts of suicide ruined and Daisy to chase down and kill, he was going to kill the old man quickly.

Taken by the Waves

Rex couldn't run faster than the dalmatian, but he led the way regardless. Bruno heard Rex claim his right to defend his human and no one was going to challenge him. Arriving in the caravan park with a fervent prayer they would find Daisy there, it was Albert's voice on the wind that drew Rex's head around to look farther to the west.

He could see nothing, but then he didn't need to, the wind carried all the information he needed.

The professor and Cooper were still trying to pinpoint the shout they heard when the dogs set off. Even the Basset Hound was lumbering after the pack at his best speed. Bizarrely, they both noted the two cats were riding on the back of the bull mastiff and chose not to comment for fear they were imagining it.

Just when the humans were getting their feet moving, a second shout caught their attention and this time they could see where it came from.

A tiny human form wearing a pink sweatsuit was

running toward them. Forty feet higher and more than a hundred yards away, to Cooper's ears the screaming female voice was like a choir of angels singing.

"Daisy!" he squealed, trebling his pace as he ran to meet her.

The professor, about as bewildered by events as he could get, kept pace with the teenage kid as best he could.

Ahead of them, the dogs reached Daisy, but they didn't stop. The female human had the smell of fear and a trace of blood about her, but she looked unharmed. Rex's human was farther yet and he wasn't going to stop until he got to him.

There was blood on the breeze. That alone ensured Rex ran as fast as his body could carry him. However, the wind had more information to deliver – the killer was up there with his human. There could be no doubt, and the combination of both men and blood had Rex about as fired up as he could get.

There was nothing in his head except the need to get to Albert. The old man with his odd habits and need to constantly get himself into trouble was the entire world to Rex. He would die before he let anything happen to his human.

Cool air filled his lungs, which seared from the effort of running at maximum speed up a steep incline. His fur coat flowed with each bound, his legs powering him closer and closer to the source of the scent.

The pack made no noise save for the sound of their laboured breathing and the almost imperceptible drum of their paws on the grass. Another bound, another yard, another bound.

Two indistinct figures emerged from the dark. At the

head of the pack, Rex could see who they were: his human and the man who almost ran him over.

A glint of moonlight caught on something – a knife, Rex grimaced with the recognition of the threat it represented.

His human was being backed toward the cliff edge, the larger man holding the knife seconds away from pushing him over, Rex seconds away from reaching them.

His legs ached, his lungs burned, but rage pushed him to go even faster.

"You don't stand a chance, you know," Rex heard his human's voice carried on the wind. "Greedy men always lose in the end."

"You'll lose first," Greg lifted his knife. "Time to go for a swim, old man."

"I don't think so. I think I'll make you stab me first. That way there will be no question I committed suicide." Albert stole a quick glance over his shoulder; he was two feet from the sheer drop into the sea below. It was too high to be survivable.

Turning his head back, he caught movement from the corner of his eye and had to fight not to stare.

Licking his lips, his nerves making his legs feel weak, Albert knew Garside wasn't going to use the knife, he was going to shove him over the edge. He was easily strong enough to pick Albert up if he wanted to.

"There's one important thing you don't know, Greg."

Throwing the knife so it buried itself in the ground by his feet. Greg said, "Oh, yeah, what's that?"

"I've got a dog."

A laugh formed on Greg's lips, but the mirth never made it to his eyes. Something about the knowing look on the old man's face sent a flutter of worry through his core.

That was all he got. Rex hit him teeth first before Greg

got the first sense that he was there. Albert got to watch it all, unable to breathe.

Rex bowled the killer over, the pair of them falling toward the drop not away from it. Rex had his teeth clamped on his target's left forearm, but landing hard on his side, the breath burst from his lungs and his mouth opened.

He rolled to get up, one leg sailing into free air. Rex heard his human cry out in alarm, and distracted, failed to dodge the killer's boots as he kicked out to push Rex over the cliff.

Rex felt his back legs swing into nothingness. He was going over. Scrambling for purchase with his front paws, Rex yelped in fear. He couldn't find anything to grip! His back legs flailed in the air and when he looked to see where the killer was, Rex saw the man lining up a kick that would send him to his death.

"Death to all humans!"

Greg never saw the cat coming for him. There were dogs all around which struck him as bizarre, but he was a little too preoccupied with everything else to give it much thought.

He was going to dump the dog over the side followed by the old man, but a rabid cat came out of nowhere, climbing his leg like he was a tree.

He swatted at it, but what seemed like a thousand pins being jabbed into his skin ran up his chest to latch onto his face where it raked his skin.

He took a step back, wanted to get away from the terrible devil clawing at his eyes.

Albert lunged for Rex. His hands were still tied together but that worked in his favour. Hooking his arms around Rex's shoulders like a lasso, his body acted as an anchor.

Rex's backend floated in space, but his front was securely held in place.

Man and dog got to watch as the killer's back foot stumbled on the loose grass near the edge. A piece of soil gave way, and Greg Garside overbalanced.

Penelope screamed, "Arthur!" her voice matching the wail of fear the human voiced until the waves below took him.

Albert's nose was an inch from Rex's. Rex licked it.

"Good boy," said Rex, wagging his tail.

The professor, out of breath and wheezing from the effort of chasing the dogs up the hill, arrived at the top moments after Greg went over the edge. He missed the whole thing but needed a nanosecond to assess that Albert needed his help.

"I've got Rex!" Albert shouted. "Save him first! I'm not going to fall."

With Rex's paws safely back on solid ground, Albert pushed himself away from the edge. He already knew he was going to have nightmares about the cliff crumbling and wasn't going to spend another moment looking out into the abyss.

Between ragged breaths, Albert begged for information, "Daisy?"

"She's fine," the professor promised. "I left her with Cooper. It was really his dad behind it?"

Albert nodded. "Yup."

"Was that scream I heard him going over the edge?"

Albert nodded again, unsure how he was supposed to feel about the killer meeting such a poetic end.

Having to fight Rex who wanted to shower his human with affection, Albert wanted to get to the knife Greg left behind so he could cut through the tie pinning his wrists together. It had to wait until Rex was calmer.

Finally able to release his hands, Albert collapsed to the grass where he hugged his dog and said nothing.

It wasn't Albert who broke the hug, it was Rex for once, fighting to get free for some reason that only became apparent to Albert when he shouted in panic. Rex was heading for the cliff again and running to get there which sent an icy spear through Albert's heart.

Rex wasn't endangering himself needlessly though, he was rescuing a cat.

"Arthur, how the heck did you survive?" Rex barked in the alley cat's face.

He was joined at the cliff edge by all the other dogs and Penelope the cat who was mewling tearfully to see Arthur still among the living.

"I jumped off, didn't I," Arthur explained as if talking to someone particularly dense. "Didn't time it all that well though. I was supposed to land on the ground, not find myself clinging to a root and having to climb back up."

Penelope rubbed her face against his, nuzzling him like an old friend.

Albert sat on the grass and watched, shaking his head at yet another unexplainable sight.

The professor came to kneel by his side.

"I've, um ... I've owned a couple of pets in my life. I grew up with dachshunds, actually. None of them ever acted like this."

"Yeah," Albert grinned. "Life with Rex is often unexpected." For the first time since finding Karl Fielding's body on the beach less than an hour after arriving in Lyme Regis, Albert Smith felt himself relax.

That lasted about as long as it took for him to remember Marsh.

With a burst of expletives, he jumped to his feet. Now upright again, and moving inland, a pack of excited dogs trailing behind and around him, he could see flashing lights tearing out of town. They were heading up the hill and coming his way.

"Oh, yeah I called the police." the professor explained.

"Albert!"

Albert turned to face the direction of the voice calling his name to find Marsh standing with one hand holding her head. She was bent at the waist using her other hand to press against her thigh. It looked to be the only thing keeping her upright. She was no longer bound and had clearly come looking for him despite being barely conscious.

By the time Albert and the dogs got to her she was sitting on the grass.

The professor went ahead to flag down the police, talking to the dispatcher to guide them in.

"You're okay?" Albert enquired, checking Marsh for injury. She had a lump on her head and blood matted into her hair, but she was otherwise unharmed. She asked about Garside and got an honest answer though Albert chose to be skimpy with the details; he knew he was going to have to go over it a dozen times yet.

Sitting on the grass, with Rex tucked under his left arm, Albert felt at peace with the world. He also accepted that it was time to go home. He'd known already, of course, stopping off in Lyme Regis had just been a way to delay it for a day or so. He never expected his layover would turn out to be quite so filled with murder and mayhem.

To avoid further brushes with death, he would go back to his quiet corner of the country and do what he imagined gentlemen his age were supposed to do: read the Times while listening to the cricket on the radio and perhaps take a stroll to the village pub once in a while. It sounded heavenly.

A huffing and puffing noise made Albert twist around to see what was there.

"I missed it all, didn't I?" asked Tailspin, flopping his whole body to the ground with a sigh. "Oh, to have been born a greyhound."

Heading Home

Albert's breakfast was everything a person could want. The landlady was particularly generous on account of her husband having lost Albert's dog the previous day; something she apologised for numerous times at a volume she knew Tony would hear.

She made one for Rex too upon Albert's request. He could have given Rex his usual dry dog food for breakfast, and questioned if the assortment of eggs, toast, mushroom, bacon, and more would be good for his dog. Somehow, though, the full English breakfast seemed like a just reward for Rex's heroic actions.

Refusing to go to hospital the previous evening because they wouldn't let Rex go with him and he wasn't going to risk being separated again, Albert was given a tentative all-clear by the paramedics at the scene.

Marsh *was* taken away for treatment; she needed stitches in her scalp, but would make a full recovery. The assortment of cats and dogs were rounded up by animal control who already had a list of pet owners in the town reporting their animal missing. They even recognised a few, including Tailspin, because they were regulars in his pub.

Alverez arrived at the scene later than most, DS Rogers a little after her. They were off duty but called in to be a part of the investigation since she had already closed the case that afternoon. Albert said nothing to demean or reduce her efforts or conclusions; he had nothing to gain by doing so, and every cop has a right to get it wrong once in a while. Just so long as they don't do it deliberately.

A launch was sent to look for Garside's body which was found quickly enough and brought to shore. His son, Cooper, was arrested on sight for his assault on Albert, but released when Albert insisted he'd got it wrong. The person who attacked him was taller and had a moustache. He knew they could tell he was lying, but without his statement they had no case to prosecute.

Daisy thanked Albert with a kiss to his cheek and apologised for throwing him out earlier. How much strife she could have saved if she'd just been willing to listen. Her parting words were about her father's legacy and how she planned to make sure the bakery was open as soon as the police would allow. She was the only person alive who knew the recipe for Dorset Knobs and that was a tradition she couldn't allow to slip.

Cooper was the heir to the Greg's bakery empire whether he wanted to be or not. It changed the couple's situation quite dramatically. Albert didn't say so, but he was glad the young lady wasn't returning to her old job and hoped Cooper's change of fortune would keep the young man away from the scrutiny of local law enforcement.

The police took an initial statement, but when Albert begged to be allowed to get some sleep and a bath, plus maybe something to eat and a drink or two, Alverez had

Constables Pearson and Massie take him back to his lodgings via an Indian takeaway and an off licence.

Polishing off the last of his breakfast, Albert thought back to waking up this morning and just how refreshed he had felt. It had been the best sleep in weeks and Rex had occupied the other side of his bed; a first for them both.

Mrs Beeler came back to collect the dirty plates, not that Rex's had so much as a smudge of egg yolk on it, and to enquire if he wanted anything else.

When he said that he was quite full, she hovered.

"There're some people from the press outside, Mr Smith. I didn't let them in. Should I? I was hoping they might film you on your way out of the guesthouse if that would be possible …"

"Is there a back way out?" Albert enquired.

"I think we can help you with that, Albert," offered the professor, followed swiftly by an apology for eavesdropping.

The professor and his wife were sitting at one of the other tables, enjoying their breakfast and planning their day.

Claudia had been most impressed by her husband's actions and his part in helping to stop a murderer. So much so that she released him from her (mostly joking) demand he name his recent dinosaur find after her.

To Albert's great surprise the great leviathan was to be called Albertus Rex. Rex popped his head up at the mention of his name and got a pat and a cuddle while his human tried to explain something about a new dinosaur Rex couldn't follow.

He'd had enough of dinosaurs anyway, stupid dead things with their stupid rock bones.

True to his word, and much to Mrs Beeler's disappointment, the professor helped Albert avoid the press. Loading both Albert and Rex into his blue pickup truck after sneaking out the back of the guesthouse, he dropped him outside the police station in the town centre.

With his backpack on and small, blue suitcase at his side, Albert leaned in to shake the professor's hand.

"You know, I never did get your name."

The professor's face crinkled, lines showing around his eyes when he smiled.

"It's Hunter. Professor Hunter Hemsworth Higgs."

In the passenger seat, Claudia rolled her eyes. "Do you know how many people introduce themselves using their middle name, Hunter? None. That's how many."

The professor grinned. "That's because no one else has got a name as cool as mine."

Hours later, having given the press the slip and provided a detailed statement to the police, Albert boarded a train bound for London's Waterloo station. From there he would walk across to Waterloo East, stopping perhaps to collect a coffee and sticky bun to sustain him for the final leg of his journey.

His trip around the country had been more ... epic, than he intended, and what had he learned? He was supposed to return with his head full of recipes and clever techniques so he could reproduce some of his favourite dishes at home. There had been a few lessons, most notably in Melton Mowbray and Bakewell before the mayhem really settled in, but he doubted his skills extended beyond a borderline acceptable cheese and pickle sandwich.

Secure in the knowledge that the train terminated in London, and someone would wake him, Albert scratched at the fur around Rex's neck, closed his eyes, and allowed himself a little doze.

Rex lay with his jaw on his human's left thigh, his eyes open, and he watched the countryside rush by outside.

They were going home, so his human said. Rex had to stretch his memory to remember where they lived. He knew it would all look and smell familiar when they got there, but so many months on the road had dimmed his recollection, the details fading.

None of it mattered to him. Rex didn't much care where he was. The only constant he craved was the company of the human on whose leg his head now rested. Presently, when he heard his human begin to softly snore, Rex closed his eyes and let slumber take him too.

The End

Next in the Albert Smith Culinary Capers Series

vinci-books.com/majestic-mystery

Step aside, humans, it's time for the real hero to get involved.

Albert and Rex are going to the palace to get their knighthoods, but, as always, there's trouble. With his family in tow, Albert is embarrassed by the affair. Yet all of that is forgotten when he spots a man guilty of murder. A man who can only be at the palace for one thing. But Albert is about to be presented to the king; now is not the time to chase criminals. That's why he's Rex's sidekick.

Turn the page for a free preview…

Majestic Mystery: Chapter One

GETTING READY

"Rex, I feel like a right wally in this get up."

Rex tilted his head to one side, trying to decipher his human's words.

Unable to make sense of the old man's latest dilemma, he opted to remark, "If you want my opinion on your choice of removable pelt for today, then I would have to say that it looks a tad impractical."

Albert twitched his eyes down and left, catching sight of his dog as Rex sauntered from the room.

Over his shoulder Rex said, "It also makes you look like a bit of a wally."

Albert stared at his reflection in the mirror, grumpily fiddling with his bow tie which was perfect fifteen minutes ago when he first tied it and was still perfect now. Bedecked in a full morning suit with tails, a grey waistcoat, and a top hat, he was due to be collected in less than half an hour and was giving serious consideration to feigning that his hip had gone out and he couldn't walk. Or possibly just throwing himself down the stairs for real.

That would get him out of it.

Out of a trip to the palace to be knighted by the king.

Knight Commander of the British Empire. He'd never even heard of it until he got the letter from the palace. How could it be that Albert Smith, a former copper and son of a greengrocer was about to be granted the title of Lord and be recognised in the King's birthday honours list?

It was a rhetorical question, obviously. Albert knew precisely why he was being honoured. He saved a bunch of people and then gave away millions of pounds he'd unwittingly won. Gave it away before he even saw it. That was probably for the best, but how was he to know the attention his charitable act would attract?

There were times when he wished he'd kept it. Then he could have funded his disappearance. Not that he was short of money. His pension from a senior position in the police provided more money each month than he needed, and he'd been prudent over the years, investing and saving so Albert suspected he would run out of life before he ran out of cash.

"Are you ready, Dad?" his daughter, Selina, called up the stairs.

Left by her brothers to make sure he was ready on time, Randall and Gary were at the pub just along the road. Selina cursed them, but she'd lost the game of rock, paper, scissors used to determine who dealt with their father.

Grumbling, Albert pulled a face at his reflection and left his bedroom.

"I'm coming," he called down the stairs, using the banister for support as he descended. Going up wasn't so hard, but at nearly eighty, his legs were less inclined to descend.

Rex trotted past him, the stairs offering no such obstacle

for his young body. At the bottom, Rex turned, wagging his tail slowly as he watched the old man and waited for him to catch up.

Selina called for her daughter, Apple-Blossom, to come. The seven-year-old was lost in a world only a person her age could understand, her eyes glued to the tablet fixed between her hands.

"Apple-Blossom!" Selina raised her voice when she got no response the first time.

Jolted into action, the small voice of a girl who knew better than to sound annoyed when she said, "Coming, mummy. Sorry, I didn't hear you."

Selina ground her teeth and let it pass. Her youngest was becoming a little too precocious in recent weeks, testing her boundaries as all children do.

Selina smiled at the sight of her father. "Dad, you look wonderful. Very statesmanlike." Like her brothers, and everyone else in the family, she could not be more proud to be related to the old man about to be honoured by the king. Her father had single-handedly tracked down and brought to justice a lunatic distant relative of the reigning monarch. Earl Hubert Bacon kidnapped dozens of people and had them stashed inside an inescapable underground lair in Wales.

Selina's father, with the police after him because they believed Albert was the one behind many of the crimes that occurred during his unsanctioned investigation, tracked the Earl's agents – a team of hired mercenaries responsible for dozens of deaths – and was able to overcome them through an incredible network of friends he attracted along the way.

The tale was simply too fanciful to be true and yet it was. Then her father discovered he'd won millions on a longshot bet he'd placed almost by accident while trying to solve a murder in Melton Mowbray. Most people would take the money and look forward to a well-funded retirement, but Albert Smith gave it all away by publicly creating a charity to support those persons affected by Earl Bacon's crimes.

In the wake of the news coverage, those people and their food industry businesses were enjoying a boom in sales. There's nothing like free publicity they say, and there was a lot of it going around.

Every last one of them had sent Albert a care package of food or drink, but the term package fails to describe the magnitude of gratitude the rescued persons chose to show in gastronomic form. Trucks and vans started arriving at Albert's little semi-detached house the day after he got home. Initially he'd tried to turn the food away, but that proved futile.

Next, Albert distributed it among his friends and family, but when the gifts just kept coming, he contacted a few local homeless shelters and soup kitchens. To the best of Selina's knowledge, they were still working their way through it three months later.

"I look like a penguin," Albert grumbled at his daughter, omitting the mild expletive before it left his mouth in deference to his granddaughter's presence. Focusing on her, he said, "Apple-Blossom, you have to be the most beautiful granddaughter ever to walk the face of the earth."

"Granddad you're so silly," she giggled. Her smile ended when she remembered a question she wanted to ask. "What is Rex going to wear?"

Rex's eyebrows tried to shoot off the top of his head. "Wear? I'm a dog. I come fully clothed with a coat that stays on me. It's you weird, bald humans who need the removable ones."

Albert spotted the look on his dog's face and with a devilish grin, whipped a bow tie from a trouser pocket.

"I thought he might look good in this," Albert pumped his eyebrows at Rex.

Rex uttered something rude and made a break for it.

Selina frowned. "Wait, did he just understand what was being said?"

Albert shook his head. "Of course not, he's a dog. He must have picked up on the cues from what we were doing and because I looked his way."

The truth of the matter was that Albert knew his dog understood a great deal more than any other dog he'd ever met or heard about. Rex had an uncanny way of knowing what to do. It was how they managed to survive their journey around the British Isles. Rex came to Albert's rescue more times than he cared to mention and over the course of the months they were on the road, Albert found he could not avoid one rather worrying conclusion: that Rex was also trying to solve the cases they came across.

Watching his dog scramble around the corner and vanish from sight, Albert chuckled to himself and called out, "The back door is locked, Rex."

When he arrived in the kitchen with his granddaughter leading the way and Selina just behind, Albert found Rex staring dejectedly at the back door. Rex had figured out how to operate the handle and for that reason Albert had taken to locking it.

Five minutes later, the party arrived at the pub down the road where Albert's eldest, Gary, and his youngest, Randall, had a pint waiting for their father. There was also a gin and tonic for Selina, a fruit drink and some crisps for Apple-Blossom, and a half pint of Guinness for Rex.

Rex finished first.

Lyme Regis Layover

"Can't dawdle, the car will be here soon," remarked Gary, checking his watch.

Albert wanted to complain that he didn't have enough time to finish his drink, but he knew that was down to how long he spent arguing with himself about his outfit.

It was expected, you see. The people from the palace were very specific about it. Quite why the king couldn't have got it over with during Albert's previous visit he had no idea. Of course, the first visit to the palace had been all business. The king wanted to thank Albert in person and discuss with him the charity he set up to help Earl Bacon's victims get back on their feet.

The palace offered to not only take on running the charity, which Albert had no desire to manage himself, but also to double the pot of money Albert pledged when the bookies handed him the cheque.

Albert was still grumbling about all the unnecessary pomp and ceremony eighteen minutes later when they loaded him into the sleek, black limousine outside the pub.

It was time to head to London and Albert's children, at least, were full of smiles. Had they known then what was going to happen that day, they might have chosen to stay in the pub.

Majestic Mystery: Chapter Two

FAMILIAR SCENT

For most people, a visit to Buckingham Palace is a big deal. That was certainly the case for Albert's three children and his granddaughter, Apple-Blossom, who could not wait to get to school on Monday to tell all her friends and show them the pictures.

Albert had other grandchildren, of course, and his two eldest children both had spouses, but the invitation was limited to four guests, so the rest were going to have to hear about it second-hand.

The limousine, hired by the palace, waltzed through the security checkpoint at the end of The Mall and pulled up to a drop off point behind another car that looked to be the twin of the one they were in.

It was a slick operation, each car deploying its passengers before gliding forward again to make room for the next. Opening the car doors were palace staff, dressed in red tunics with gold brocade that made them look like something from Downton Abbey or Cinderella, and a few steps beyond them, police with automatic weapons loitered, eyes open and alert.

Albert accepted a hand from Gary in sliding out of the car and stepping away, he straightened his jacket. He was done moaning. His kids were excited, and he recognised this was an honour. Also, he'd played what he thought would be a trump card in insisting that Rex had to be honoured too and they agreed. They were supposed to say no and that would be the end of it, but apparently the king or someone in the palace's PR department more likely, thought it was a great idea.

Whatever the case, Albert accepted there was no getting out of it. He was about to be knighted and Rex was going to be at his side when it happened.

Rex, unhappy about the bowtie around his neck and hoping there wouldn't be any other dogs around to see it was most disappointed to find two German Shepherds with the human police officer handlers looking his way.

One nudged the other and said something Rex wasn't able to hear.

Annoyed, Rex turned his head away and sniffed.

Albert, holding Rex's lead, was just starting to move forward, but found his left arm jerked backward when Rex chose not to follow.

"Rex, come on, boy," Albert encouraged.

Rex's eyes were closed. He found it helped to focus his most powerful sense if he could shut out the messages coming from the rest of them. There was a scent on the air, he'd caught it the moment he drew air into his nose. Now he needed a moment to be certain he wasn't being misled.

"Rex!" Albert hissed. Turning to Gary, he said, "I might need a hand here."

Rex tried again, but the elusive smell was gone. Opening his eyes, Rex looked at his human.

"I think he's here," Rex attempted to explain.

Albert couldn't understand and was too busy attempting to obey the request to 'move along, please, sir,' as there was a long line of cars, and his party was holding things up.

Rex trotted forward, determined to find the source of the scent if he could. It was coming from somewhere, that much he knew for sure. All he needed was a decent whiff and he would be able to track it.

Following the procession of people ahead, Albert's family found themselves entering a glamorous room. It was filled with excited babble, as the guests milling around inside were plied with glasses of champagne and offered tiny morsels of food from silver trays being carried by more of the immaculate palace staff. They were barely in the room when Randall whipped a glass of champagne from a tray that came by.

The server stopped so Gary and Selina could take one each and crouched so Apple-Blossom could have one of the 'safe-for-children' non-alcoholic drinks. Her eyes sparkled at the fizzy concoction served in an elegant champagne glass.

"Be careful with that, sweetie," warned her mother, spoiling the moment.

"I'm not going to drop it, mummy," the little girl all but growled.

Albert didn't want a drink. What he wanted was to drain off the pint of beer he regrettably chose to swiftly down before they left the pub. His bladder control still worked just fine, but that was no good reason to challenge himself. It was an hour before they would begin to be called down to meet the king and he wanted to be comfortable for the big event.

Handing Rex to Randall, he should have noticed how distracted his dog was acting, but didn't; his eyes were too busy scoping the area for a sign that might tell him which way to go for restrooms. There wasn't one, but a tell-tale line of men and women coming back and forth from one corner of the room suggested he might find what he wanted over there.

Sure enough the corner hid a narrow corridor – narrow for the palace that is – that led to what could only be described as the nicest toilets Albert had ever visited.

Coming back out two minutes later, he was heading back to the reception room when one of the palace service staff went by ahead of him. The man passed through a door and vanished from sight, but just like Rex when he caught a scent he knew, Albert was now rooted to the spot.

"Can't be," he mumbled, unable to believe his eyes.

Grab your copy...
vinci-books.com/majestic-mystery

Author's Note

Hello, Dear Reader,

Thank you for selecting this book, I hope you enjoyed it. That being the case, I would encourage you to pop on over to Amazon and leave a review.

If you picked this book up on a whim and have just finished your first Rex and Albert story, you might be pleased to know there are fourteen that precede this one. There are some short stories too and my man and dog crime-solving duo even appear in some other stories outside of this series.

This is the last book in their tour of Great Britain which was a tale about an old man trying to find purpose in his life after the passing of his wife. They will be back though, so do not despair, I have much planned for these characters. You can find the cover for the first book in the new series on the next page.

There are a few matters to explain now.

I decided the last book in the series would be set in Lyme Regis when I visited the coastal town with my family

Author's Note

last summer (2022). There to hunt for fossils with my dinosaur mad son, I noted the scenery and dramatic landscape, visited a fossil museum, and revelled in the very Britishness of it all.

It would not be true to claim I came away with a story, but walking around the town, it was easy to imagine Albert and Rex hurrying by.

People who know the town may have frowned at my slightly tortured version of the landscape. One cannot exit the town heading west and climb a hill to the cliffs above the beach. There are, however, many places along the same piece of coast where this is quite accurate. I merely fudged the details to achieve what I wanted and hope those who know better will forgive me.

Mary Anning, if you have not heard of her was a prime example of how the world has changed. She could not be called a palaeontologist at the time because she was a woman. Identifying untold fossils, finding the first and best examples of the prehistoric marine reptiles Ichthyosaur and Plesiosaur, she was a leading authority on the subject yet was barred from inclusion in the royal society for her gender.

There is a well-known tongue-twister rhyme here that starts, 'She sells seashells on the seashore'. It was referring to Mary Anning who I hope would be proud to see how the town still treasures her memory.

With the nature of the geography, I wanted to include a dinosaur expert as Albert's sidekick for this book. He doesn't always get one, sometimes it's Rex who finds a friend to give the book some added depth and a bit of fun. However, having decided to use a palaeontologist, there really was only one name I could give him. It's terribly clichéd to put one's children in a book, but on this occasion, with roughly

Author's Note

eighty books under my belt, I thought perhaps it might be okay.

My seven-year-old son, Hunter, has been dinosaur crazy since he could say the word and his bedtime story most nights, this evening included, was several pages from one of his text books on the subject. At seven he is determined to be a palaeontologist and has already drawn a plan for the changes I will need to make to his playroom when we convert it into a laboratory and workspace for his specimens and fossils.

He has gone so far as to pick out the car he would need: a tricked out utility vehicle with a wide load bed in case he finds a sauropod skeleton. He likes the colour blue.

This book and indeed this series was an absolute pleasure to write, and I look forward to crafting more tales about Albert and Rex in the not too distant future. They will be off to Europe where they will get into more scrapes exploring some of the wonderfully exotic destinations the countries there have to offer.

Along the way I am fairly certain they might run into Patricia Fisher. In Napoli perhaps. Or they may stumble across Felicity with Amber and Buster in Prague if she were to find herself managing a celebrity wedding in the Czech capital. There could even be a spooky adventure with the Blue Moon team at a castle in Lichtenstein. Who knows.

Until next time.
Take care.
Steve Higgs

Recipe and History of the Dish

A Dorset knob is a hard, dry savoury biscuit, now made by just one producer for only a short period each year. Once common across the county, these crunchy curiosities have become a seasonal rarity.

The knobs are made from a bread dough enriched with extra sugar and butter. Each one is rolled and shaped by hand before being baked not once, not twice, but three times, which gives them their famously brittle, rusk-like texture. They've been likened both to old Dorset knob buttons and, less romantically, to miniature doorknobs.

Traditionally, Dorset knobs are eaten with cheese. A good choice would be the local Dorset Blue Vinney. Thomas Hardy himself was said to be fond of them, according to his parlour maid. Given their jaw-testing hardness, many prefer to soften them first by dunking them in sweet tea.

Although several bakeries once produced Dorset knobs, today only Moores of Bridport carries on the tradition. The Moores family have baked biscuits in Dorset since before

1860, establishing their main bakery in 1880. While the company now produces a wide range of traditional biscuits, Dorset knobs remain their most iconic product. They are baked only in January and February and are usually sold in distinctive decorative tins.

The Dorset knob has also inspired its own sporting tradition. The first knob-throwing contest took place in 2008 at a festival in the village of Cattistock, after organisers spotted a Yorkshire pudding throwing game on television. Competitors hurl knobs as far as possible, with the record standing at an impressive 31.9 metres or 105 ft, set in 2019. Alongside the main event, the festival has included knob-and-spoon races, knob darts, knob painting, and even 'guess the weight of the knob'.

The festival moved from Cattistock to Kingston Maurward House in 2017, but after several cancellations the tradition has become unpredictable. Still, the Dorset knob's place in local culture, whether on a cheese board or flying through the air, remains secure.

Recipe

Ingredients

- 2 cups strong white bread flour
- ½ cup unsalted butter, cold and diced
- ½ cup whole milk, lukewarm
- ¼ cup water, lukewarm
- 1½ tsp active dry yeast
- 1 tbsp granulated sugar
- 1 tsp fine sea salt
- ½ tsp freshly ground black pepper
- ½ tsp ground nutmeg
- 1 large egg, beaten (for glazing)

Recipe and History of the Dish

- 1 tbsp unsalted butter, melted (for brushing)

Method

1. Preheat the oven to 350°F (180°C) and line a baking sheet with parchment paper.
2. Mix the dry base. In a large bowl, combine the flour, salt, black pepper, and nutmeg. Give it a good stir.
3. Add the butter. Rub the cold diced butter into the flour mixture with your fingertips until it looks like fine breadcrumbs.
4. Activate the yeast. In a small bowl, mix the yeast and sugar into the lukewarm water. Let it sit for about 5 minutes until it turns frothy.
5. Bring the dough together. Pour the yeast mixture and lukewarm milk into the flour and butter mixture. Stir with a wooden spoon until a rough dough forms.
6. Tip the dough onto a lightly floured surface and knead for 8–10 minutes until it becomes smooth and elastic.
7. First proof. Place the dough into a lightly greased bowl, cover with a clean towel, and let it rise in a warm spot for 1 hour, or until doubled in size.
8. Shape the knobs. Punch down the dough, divide into 12 equal pieces, and roll each into a neat ball. Place them on the prepared baking sheet with a little space between each. Cover loosely and leave to proof again for 30 minutes until slightly puffed.

Recipe and History of the Dish

9. Glaze and bake. Brush the tops with the beaten egg, then bake for 20–25 minutes, or until golden brown and sounding hollow when tapped underneath.
10. As soon as they're out of the oven, brush the tops with melted butter. Transfer to a wire rack to cool completely.

About the Author

When Steve Higgs wrote his debut novel, *Paranormal Nonsense*, he was a captain in the British Army. He would like to pretend that he had one of those careers that must be blacked out and generally denied by the government, and that he has to change his name and move constantly because he is still on the watch list in several countries. In truth, though, he started out as a mechanic - not like Jason Statham in the film by that name, sneaking around as a hitman, but more like one of those sleazy guys who charges a fortune and keeps your car for a week even though the only thing you went in for was a squeaky door hinge.

At school, he was largely disinterested in all subjects except creative writing, for which he won his first prize at the age of ten. However, calling it the first prize he won suggests that there were other prizes, which is not the case. Awards may yet come, but in the meantime, he enjoys writing mystery and thriller novels and claims to have more than a hundred books forming a restless queue in his mind because they are desperate to be written.

Now retired from the military, he lives in southeast England with a duo of lazy sausage dogs. Surrounded by rolling hills, brooding castles, and vineyards, he doubts he'll ever leave, the beer is just too good.

www.ingramcontent.com/pod-product-compliance
Ingram Content Group UK Ltd.
Pitfield, Milton Keynes, MK11 3LW, UK
UKHW040803100426
469759UK00005B/55